THE SURVIVAL OF TOM

Life in a Post-Apocalypctic Virus Ravaged World

M. J Brierley

CONTENTS

Title Page	1
Chapter One	5
Chapter Two	29
Chapter Three	43
Chapter Four	66
Chapter Five	82
Chapter Six	97
Chapter Seven	106
Chapter Eight	120
Chapter Nine	133
Chapter Ten	148
Chapter Eleven	161
Chapter Twelve	172
Chapter Thirteen	185
Chapter Fourteen	202
Chapter Fifteen	218
Chapter Sixteen	236

Chapter Seventeen	253
Chapter Eighteen	266
Chapter Nineteen	279
Chapter Twenty	299
Chapter Twenty-One	314
Chapter Twenty-Two	331
Chapter Twenty-Three	341
Acknowledgement	359

CHAPTER ONE

Tom awoke to the glow of the rising sun. It was still early, looking up at the sky showed him that, the temperature steadily increasing, making it impossible to get back to sleep.

Another restless night, he knew that would be the best he got. The crows loudly cawed in the distance; the flies buzzed around already. Jesus, he thought, I'm not dead yet, swatting at them idly with the back of his hand.

He pulled himself up from the sand where he'd laid his head just a few precious hours ago. Sat on the beach, he could hear the waves breaking in the distance. The woodland, just meters away, casting a growing shadow down the golden sand as the sun continued its ascent in the sky behind him.

This would be paradise; if there was anyone left to enjoy it. To Tom, it was hell. It was the best he could find, secluded and with slight protection if conditions worsened. It wasn't as good as his previous shelter, the small cave nestled into the cliff around the cove. He'd had to leave after the tides had cracked the cliff face. Rock fell about his head as he slept, it was no longer safe to stay there, he'd had to come out into the open.

This was life now. Ever since the globe had been consumed by the virus spreading like wildfire, things went to shit. Quickly.

They claimed it was just a new strain of flu, a virus from some far-flung region of some far-flung place. It would never disrupt the modern world, the globalised metropolis that humankind had come to know. At first, this could perhaps have been true. There were isolated cases, people got sick, people died. The authorities claimed they had it under control, that the peak had been reached, the curve was flattening. Then one day, they didn't. One day, the televised announcements stopped, the news stopped reporting, people stopped venting their feelings on social media. And then it was all gone. There was no more television. No more social media. No more civilisation.

Tom couldn't recall the exact time all things ceased. It happened suddenly, but it felt so gradual. No one took notice until it was far too late.

He sat upright on the beach, watching the tide slowly recede. He stretched and grimaced as he caught the aroma of his putrid smell.

I really need to wash more, he thought solemnly. Tom had roamed the coast ever since he was forced from his home, he had no desire to enter the water. The smell didn't bother him too much, there was no one left to complain or guilt him into changing the new habits he had become accustomed to.

Tom wasn't always like this. Before, he had a job, a family, a life. And then he didn't.

He tried to ignore his past. He was never a big fan of it, a life he lived, but never felt like his own. The life he'd left felt to him like watching a movie, walking through life in someone else's shoes, going through the motions he was told he should.

When the world ended, he was pleased at first, he was sure it would be a new start, a chance to make the life he craved and become the person he so wished to be. A fresh opportunity to leave the horror of the past behind. He had been wrong about that, too.

In the early days of the outbreak, when the second wave wreaked havoc on humanity, Tom barely ventured out. His large house and shiny car, now just shimmering memories of a distant past, like his family. He'd been moved on, forced from his large home, to follow the wallowing masses to the government sanctioned accommodation further towards the centre of town. Somewhere they would be safe, somewhere they could be protected, at least that's what they were told. The accommodation in town was small and dreary. The smell of mildew hung in the air, the bugs bit at him as he slept. He rarely saw anyone from authority after he moved. Their promises remained unfulfilled.

He only left the small cramped flat for provisions when he finally ran out, despite his strict rationing. He had stretched every bit of food and water he could, it didn't last. Leaving hadn't really helped. The supermarkets were empty, the corner shops trashed, the markets long gone. There was no money left to buy things. Money became a thing of the past when unemployment escalated, millions lost their income in a few short weeks. The economic packages announced by the governments of the world weren't enough to stem the flow, there simply wasn't enough to go around.

Those braver than he, the ones who went out in the first days, had already smashed the windows, overturned the tills and took what they pleased. Tom noticed first the absence of alcohol, which was the first thing to be pulled out of the overturned shelves.

I guess whoever lived through the horror, didn't want to see this new life through sober eyes, looking for any excuse to escape the new reality of this new world, he thought bitterly to himself.

The first time Tom ventured outside the dingy flat, it was as successful as he could have hoped. He found small things he could bring back from the nearby houses he'd carefully entered after he could be sure they were empty. A tin of soup left discarded in the back of a cupboard, a half-empty bottle of water resting in the road.

He felt fortunate to live alone, he didn't know how he could have supported dependants with the meagre offerings littering the broken town.

He had survived on his own with what he could

find for a few weeks, the boredom and loneliness wasn't a problem, not for him. He'd found he quite liked the solitude, once it had been forced on him.

When the second wave hit, his wife and child had become sick. His baby girl first, then his wife. It happened so quickly. It started with a cough, his daughter had cried through the night, her mother tried in vain to comfort her. By morning, she was still. The virus acted quickly, most succumbed in hours, she had lasted well to survive until the sunrise. By early afternoon the following day, Tom's wife was still too. She died in a few short hours of her first cough. This was the last day he would spend in his home in the suburbs.

I wish I could remember them, he thought, *I wish I could remember their names, their faces.* He had blocked large parts of his life from before out of his mind, and now he struggled to remember. He'd never have imagined that he could forget those most important to him, the people he loved. He could still recall snippets, like dreams. Playing in a park, pushing a baby in a pram, dining with a beautiful woman on a restaurant balcony. He knew these people were his family, but he could never remember their faces, never remember their names. It was blank, like old black and white movies, their features grainy and indistinguishable. Tom felt the sorrow threatening to overtake him. Was he a monster? How could he forget these people that meant so much to him so quickly, so easily, all to protect his fragile mind?

He shook himself out of his rising despair, it wouldn't help to start the morning in such a dark place. The day was sure to provide that itself, it didn't need his help.

He walked awkwardly to the line of trees that overlooked the beach. His limbs ached from the night spent sleeping in the sand. He recovered the filthy plastic bottle he'd been using to store the small amounts of water he could find and took a long swig. It tasted unpleasant, like stagnant water siphoned from the only puddle he could locate in a drying landscape. It tasted like this, because it was. He knew soon he would have to leave, to move in search of water. Spring was arriving quickly, and the temperature was rising sharply. Just weeks ago, Tom had dug into the sand, wrapping his hands around him as he tried to find every bit of warmth he could. He couldn't start a fire, the risk of being discovered was too high.

He'd thought he would appreciate the warmer weather, but after such a bitter winter the sudden onslaught of heat had made him feel sick. He hadn't expected it, the glare from the sun was unbearable, the sun's rays felt as though it was scarring his skin.

In reality, it wasn't even that unseasonable, perhaps hotter than average for the time of year, it was nothing more than a warm spring day. The kind of day where families might have packed a picnic and spent the day on the beach.

He looked around. No one would be doing that today, or ever again. The only picnic taking place on the beach was the crows as they noisily attempted to rip flesh from the bodies that had been washed in overnight and left to fester in the heat. Tom wondered where they came from. Had they floated in the sea, crossed countries, continents?

No, he knew better than that. The corpses were still intact, their flesh still clung to the bone. He doubted they had spent more than a day in the sea, perhaps less. It was likely they had been pulled in by the current from the docks at the nearby town. The waves lapping over the flooding car parks and pulling the bodies of the dead back with them, depositing them on the beach just a few hours later. To taunt him, to show him what he would become, to prove there was no happy ending for him.

Back to the despair, he thought, as he forced himself to walk further into the cover of the trees, shaking his head to clear the images burnt into his mind of the bodies on the beach.

His stomach rumbled, the stagnant water hadn't helped, but it was better than nothing.

Tom could usually find something to eat in the smaller coastal settlements surrounding the beaches if he looked hard enough. He was amazed where people left a tin of dried fruit in their cupboards, forgot about. The lifeline that kept him going.

He didn't know how much longer this would

last, he had already searched quite a distance, having to travel further inland every time. He often thought about spending the night in one of the newly abandoned houses, their beds perfectly made up and the curtains drawn, the doors firmly closed. He could never bring himself to stay any longer than he needed to, though. Every empty house had a history, a scream he could hear when he closed his eyes. Even the guest houses and hotels dotted on the clifftops overlooking the sea, he tried to settle in these, back when he first left town for good. They felt somehow worse. The ghosts of the travellers, who would never again visit, still roamed the halls.

Tom began the slow walk towards a nearby village. He knew there should be a few houses on the outskirts untouched, by him at least. The journey was arduous, his shoes were past their best, the sole detaching from the body and a distinct hole where his big toe could now be seen poking through, water seeped in as he walked through the long grass.

The rest of his few possessions were not much better. He wore the same clothes he had on when he abandoned the flat, the t-shirt now a filthy shade of blacks and browns, the hem around the neck unravelling. His jeans were faring better, their dark colour helped hide the filth. They still provided a level of modesty and protection from the insects, intent on eating him alive.

He carried a satchel with him, this was in the best condition of everything he owned, ironic as its purpose was to carry those things he treasured. Now, it held his coat, he wouldn't need that for a while, his bottle of water that he refilled at any opportunity, things he felt essential. Matches to light the gas fires where he could find them, those that still had a small amount of gas in their pipes, or the camping stoves he picked up from the back of cupboards, a disposable respirator he had found discarded in the street. Not that he thought it would help him. In the bottom of the bag, the last link to his past, a necklace he had given his wife many years prior. An anniversary gift, he'd kept that to remind him of who he had been, before the world had burned.

As Tom stumbled up the winding, uneven road, he noticed the birds seemed to be out in larger numbers today, maybe that was just the world moving on as the spring approached. Or perhaps they were following him, waiting for their next easy meal.

"Fuck off," he shouted at them, surprised by the venom in his raspy voice. The birds took no notice, they had reclaimed the world since the people died. It hadn't taken long, wildlife had already shown signs of remarkable recovery during the lockdown, the time when people were prohibited from leaving their homes. The army had been drafted in to ensure compliance, patrolling the streets day and night, loaded weapons to deter anyone who thought about venturing out into the failing world. Tom was not alone back then, his family were still alive, they lived in their house in the suburbs of the nearby town. They had a garden, a new car parked on the driveway, a fridge stocked with food. Water ran from the taps, the television turned on, the internet connected to updated websites, the world was still alive, back then.

He frowned, it wasn't helpful to think about the past, his life before the outbreak and everything he had lost. Especially as the crucial details remained a haze. He rounded the corner of the country lane; high hedgerows blocked the sun and hid him from any prying eyes that might be tracking him. He saw the old cottage that sat abandoned on the outskirts of the village. The first time he tried to scavenge, he'd knocked, actually knocked, on the front door before entering. Just in case the previous occupant might still be home.

The decor was dated and there was a notable absence of technology, he assumed this was once home to an older woman, maybe a couple who lived here happily, once upon a time. The cottage had been left in an immaculate state. The bed was still made and the cupboards full. He was sure that whoever had lived here must have died early in the outbreak.

The old were vulnerable, that's what they had been told. It was only the old that were at risk of the quick and ruthless death that had come to be a part of daily life just several short months later. Maybe they were right, when the virus first emerged. The first outbreak had been deadly, but it could perhaps be beaten, had the planning and implementation measures been adequately carried out. The virus took the old, the injured, the infirm. The healthy generally recovered and went to continue their daily lives as if they had picked up a mild dose of flu. It was these recovered people, the experts later cried on the daily news updates, who caused the second wave.

The first had killed in its thousands, but the second had taken the world by surprise. The healthy and the cured were starting to feel unwell, the symptoms returned. Only this time, they did not recover, this time they died within hours.

Health authorities were quick to identify that the virus had mutated, it overwhelmed the immune system. It extinguished the life from its host with terrifying speed.

This didn't make sense, they had cried at national briefings, a virus that kills its host so quick was counterproductive, it had to be an anomaly.

They were wrong about that too. They hadn't understood just how contagious the mutated strain was. They hadn't considered the lengthy incubation period where the infected were contagious, despite showing no symptoms, allowing weeks for the new strain to spread unseen across the country.

The first wave was declared over, hundreds of thousands cured. It would be confined to the history books, a blip in the great history of mankind. The second wave destroyed the books and took the history with it.

Tom walked past the cottage, he'd searched every inch of the place on a previous trip, it was empty. Wondering up to the main street through the village, he stopped to look around. Everything looked the same, weeds claiming back previously manicured gardens, doors swinging open, hanging off their hinges, gently blowing in the wind. Other people had been here, he knew that, he'd seen the bottles they had left behind. He'd seen the damage left by those with no future, no hope and nothing left.

Windows were smashed, shop displays pulled over, houses and cars burnt. Tom wanted desperately to believe there was still good left in the world. Deep down, he knew this was just proof of the human psyche reverting to its basic instincts, the desire to destroy.

Tom had made it his priority to avoid other survivors, the few he had come across so far were unhinged, often dangerous. The new world changed people. People with no hope, people with nothing to live for, they were the new threat.

Not everyone had died in the second wave. However potent the virus had become, some avoided infection, by luck, or like Tom, by avoiding others. Plenty were still alive when the spread of the virus started to slow.

When the news reports stopped coming, the

authorities had estimated half the population had perished. Bodies had been stored in refrigerated trucks, repurposed ice rinks and by the end, wherever they fell. Watching from the window, Tom had seen infected stumbling down the street. They must have known their remaining hours were numbered, looking for the miracle that didn't exist.

Most were quiet, they didn't scream or cry. Maybe it was shock or delirium at the eventual outcome that was barrelling down on them.

Some dropped to their final resting place on the street outside the window he watched from, they would be a problem, when he finally did work up the courage to venture out. The stench was what overpowered him first.

The first time Tom left the small flat the government had allocated him, after he'd been told services could no longer be provided to his previous home - after he'd lost everything in a single day, he'd returned inside, unable to take the smell of death from the street or accept the sight in front of his eyes.

When he was ready to try again, he wrapped a scarf around his mouth and nose, preparing himself for the terror rotting on the pavement. He took a deep breath before opening the door once more and gingerly headed into the city. He quietly walked down the street, trying to look as indistinguishable and small as possible. There were others out, mostly trying to avoid each other. Looking for a slim glimmer of hope in a burning world, looking for something to help them make it through just one more day. The water still flowed then, and the toilets still flushed. Tom had been forced out by the gnawing pain in his stomach, he'd eaten everything he had in the small flat, although it wasn't particularly well-stocked before everything ended. When the authorities rehoused him, he'd been given a basic box of provisions, canned soup, a bag of pasta, some instant potato. He'd been told a box would be delivered outside his home once a week and that he must live on what it contained as there would be no more until the following delivery. No further box came, the world fell apart so quickly.

His first trip had been successful enough, he'd found a few packets of biscuits, a rare luxury, and a small bag of pasta in one of the surrounding flats. The smell from the bedroom warned him the previous occupant was still there, he left the door closed. He had no desire to see what the virus had done to them.

Tom had given himself a few more days of precious life. He'd watched the diminishing number of people passing on the street below, until he no longer saw anyone, he no longer saw anything.

Without warning, the sounds of the city ended abruptly. The sight of other people vanished, and all that remained was the sounds of nature reclaiming a ruined world.

He cried that night, he thought this was what he wanted - the quiet - but he now knew he was wrong. As he stared into the small bathroom mirror, resenting himself, he wished he could have died with his family. He would have avoided having to live in the horror and terror of what the world had become.

Tom left the small flat for the final time, leaving the memory and failures of the past to die in that dark, morbid place.

The lack of change in the small village unsettled him. He knew no one had been here since his last visit several days ago, but they should have been. Some other desperate person should have ripped doors from the hinge that held them on. Sunken eyes darting over every possible hiding place for anything that might have been missed by those before, searching for that thing that could keep them alive for just a short while longer.

Maybe the others are all gone, he thought to himself, *maybe it's finally won, and I'll be next. A cough, that's how it'll start, then I'll sit by a tree and wait to die.* It wouldn't take long, then the planet could be rid of the scourge mankind had made itself.

He knew this wasn't true, he couldn't be the last, that would be too easy. Like a virus, mankind would never truly die out. They would come back from this, to wreak their own second wave of destruction on the world through another age of globalisation, industrialisation, greed.

Tom knew soon he would need to move again, there hadn't been much fresh water available anywhere he'd stayed. The winter weather had provided plenty of rain which he'd been able to collect, the changing season would take that from him. He was terrified he would have to move inland, closer to where the others might remain. Assuming there were others still left.

How long had it been? He struggled to tell. Months, years, longer? No, it couldn't have been. It was cold when he first left the flat, he hadn't been there too long since leaving his house and life in the suburbs. *Shit,* he thought, *it can't have been more than six months since the first case was announced.* Six months, and everything ended. It must be April now. He suddenly felt cold, He stood still as it dawned on him, it would have been his wife's birthday, had she still been alive. He wasn't sure of the exact day, but it would have been close. He felt like crying, but what was the point, he'd shed enough tears back in the early days, they hadn't helped.

He had to look on the bright side, he'd remembered something. He might not be able to picture her face, but he remembered her birthday. He was going to take that as a positive, one small step at a time.

He walked to the final row of dilapidated houses in the far edge of the village. He hadn't been here before, they looked like old miners' houses, built hundreds of years ago when the village bustled with activity. The road was littered with debris, blown in over the winter or left when the occupants first fled in the final panic. Several doors remained ajar, the elements had already started to strip the paint and the decorated paper from the walls visible inside.

Tom skipped these, those that hadn't had everything of use ruined by the weather, were almost certainly sure to have been ransacked by animals, or worse, people. The animals had adapted to life well since the end. They had taken what they could, what humanity left behind, and moved on.

Tom occasionally found a family of foxes or dear using the abandoned building as a shelter through the winter. *Why not?* He'd thought, something might as well make use of humanities accomplishments, now they would no longer need them.

Walking to the first house on the street, he studied its exterior. The door was faded red, paint flaking around the frosted window, curtains drawn, garden gate firmly closed.

Whoever had lived here had long gone, probably when they first created the refuges in the countryside.

The surviving government had announced that virus-free areas were being created throughout the country, in the form of secure, and secluded, encampments far from the infected cities. Everyone entering was to be checked for fever and allowed to settle in the hastily assembled container housing. These camps were meant to be a haven, only one way in, only one way out. No one could enter or leave without being assessed at the military checkpoint, stood by the giant gates where the barb wire chain-linked fence met. They were designed to house 5000 people. With beds and recreation facilities, uninfected people were to report to their allocated camp where it was promised they would be cared for, protected.

The camps weren't ready, they weren't liveable, and they didn't work. Of the very few who were reported to have escaped, they were compared to concentration camps and the many makeshift camps used around the globe to house the diaspora of migrants forced from their homes long before the outbreak.

It was impossible to keep all infected out, the chain-link fence was a joke. The virus spread quicker in these camps than outside; the entire population was slaughtered. They had hastily built thousands of these camps across the country. Someone must have thought it had a chance to succeed. Someone was very wrong.

Tom had been instructed to report to the closest of these camps just weeks after he'd moved to the dingy flat. He had instead drawn the curtains to avoid the patrols and kept as silent as he could. He knew these were destined to fail; it was the second time they had tried to move him to the camps, the second time he'd resisted. Humanity needed hope and so many wandered blindly to their death.

He tried the door. Locked. He'd come to expect

that. Most who voluntarily left had locked their homes, trying to preserve their previous life. They dreamed about one day returning, as if nothing had happened. Like their neighbours hadn't gotten sick around them, like they hadn't heard their quiet cries through the walls as they waited to die.

The frosted window was old, it didn't look very secure. Tom picked up a nearby rock the size of his hand and as respectfully as he could, smashed the glass, watching it fall in shards around his feet. The break in the glass revealed a long dark hallway, the smell of mildew and damp hit him instantly. Reaching his arm through the broken remnants of the glass, he turned the latch and heard it click open. He pushed the door in to rest against the wall and peered into the gloom. The doors of the hallway were closed. Tom had been through enough houses in this part of the world to know the layout remained the same. He walked to the first door on the left and depressed the handle, opening the creaking white door to reveal the sitting room. A small chair sat next to a stuffed bookcase; an old television sat unused hung on the middle of the far wall. A layer of dust settled over the surfaces, undisturbed before his intervention, scattered as he softly walked across the carpeted floor. He didn't expect to find much here. People who needed hope were often desperate, and desperate people had little left.

The room contained nothing of use, an old lighter sat on the fireplace. Tom picked it up and flicked the spark wheel, it no longer worked. He tried it a few times, then carelessly tossed it aside.

He studied the walls of the small room; it was sparsely decorated. Pictures of a young woman on a beach sat on side tables in the corner of the room, a copy of an old newspaper lay folded on the arm of the chair. He quietly retreated out of the room and closed the door. He didn't know why he did this; he knew the owner would never return, yet he didn't want to leave evidence of his presence, he didn't want them to feel the violation of having had someone in their home, just in case. Heading further down the dank hallway, he opened the second door. The kitchen was brighter than the other rooms, no curtains were blocking the natural light, the window opened onto the back garden, overgrown and unloved. He searched the cupboards, looking for anything he could take, he knew by now to avoid the fridge. Anything remaining in there was sure to be putrefied, that wouldn't help the gnawing hunger he could feel growing inside himself.

He looked for the bathroom, in the hope that there might be a medicine cabinet containing aspirin, paracetamol, morphine, anything.

It was the headaches that were the worst thing about the hunger and thirst. He hadn't expected that. The blinding pain while his body screamed for sustenance was much worse than he'd ever expected. The pills, when he could find them, helped dull the pain. They helped to make life that little bit more manageable in the worst moments.

No such luck. He found the bathroom, its basin and bath a garish shade of green, a cabinet with a mirror sat above the sink, empty. The mirror had forced Tom to gaze upon himself as he opened it. He hated his reflection. He no longer recognised the person in the mirror, the gaunt, unshaven and unkempt man staring back at him through strangers' eyes.

Tom had been almost handsome once, blue eyes and neat blond hair. He had watched his weight and worked out most evenings. The man he saw in the mirror was the opposite. His hair, now a dirty brown, plastered thick to the side of his face. His beard tangled and matted around his chin. His eyes frightened him the most, the eyes of a stranger. His face was sunken and shallow from the months of neglect, pain and despair.

He watched the man in the mirror as he raised his arms, his thin wrists and bony hands, long fingernails caked in dirt, taking hold of the edge of the cabinet. He watched as the man mirroring his actions put every bit of effort he could muster from his weak frame into ripping the cabinet and mirror from the wall and throwing it to the floor. He heard it shatter under the impact and closed his eyes, panting. Then he heard a different noise.

His eyes grew wider, what was that? He looked down, the tap on the sink had been struck by the falling cabinet, water poured from the open faucet. Coming to his senses, he quickly turned the tap off, letting the remnants of the red-brown water drain down the waste pipe.

He looked around for something he could fill. Remembering his filthy bottle, he retrieved it from the bag. It would be nice to have fresh water again, even if it had been sitting for months in a water tank located in the attic of the house.

He wondered if he could bring himself to stay here a few nights, the running water would be a luxurious change. He couldn't do it. No matter how much he wanted to feel normality again, even temporarily. Every time he closed his eyes, the walls screamed in agony. He settled instead on using the rest of the water to finally bathe, and maybe try to sort his scraggly hair. After all, he couldn't carry it with him.

He started to fill the bath with the cold water. It spluttered several times and his heart dropped, worried the water flow would suddenly cease. Each time the dirt and sediment blocking the pipes came shooting out the tap. The pressure returned, forcing sparkling water into the now discoloured bath being run below.

He turned the tap off with the bath half full, undressed and lay himself in. The icy water sent shivers through his body as he slowly submerged. Gasping, he rubbed his shoulders to warm through, determined not to give in and leave before he could bear to look at himself again.

Slowly, he felt the warmth returning to his body, he stopped uncontrollably shivering. Lowering himself further and pushing his head underwater, he relished the sensation of the water surrounding him.

Once he'd cleaned the best he could, he dried himself on one of the moulding towels resting on the radiator. He took a small pair of nail scissors from the windowsill, and using a shard from the broken mirror, began to cut at strands of straggling hair. He didn't know what he was doing, he'd had never cut his own hair, but anything had to be better than what he'd let himself become.

Small piles of still matted hair and beard lay on the floor. Tom looked at himself, his face now visible. Somehow his eyes seemed to have filled. He glanced at his hands, the water had washed away the filth, he trimmed his overgrown nails and admired the transformation. He still didn't recognise himself, but at least there was now a passable person staring back at him from the broken shards of mirror littering the floor.

He glanced at his clothes in a pile in the corner. They were filthy, he couldn't remember when he last changed. Searching through the final room of the house, a small bedroom containing just a double bed and a wardrobe pushed against the unfurnished wall, he selected a new black t-shirt and a pair of clean jeans hanging on the door. They were slightly too large and smelled like they had been sat for a long time. They were better than he had, though. The feeling of finally being clean lifted Tom's spirits, he felt a world away from the stranger he woke as that morning.

He stood still, enjoying the feeling for several long moments, before a bang from outside the window brought him crashing back to earth. He quickly ducked back into the hallway and raced out into the road, taking care to stay to the overgrown hedgerow between houses to keep him out of sight. He stared in disbelief. In the middle of the road, doors slammed shut and the engine still running, was a large black truck, red writing for some long-forgotten landscaping contractor down the side. A chrome bull-bar extending from the front, giving a sinister appearance of a wild animal, tusks poised, sharp and ready to skewer.

Tom looked around, fear filled his veins, then he ran.

CHAPTER TWO

Tom didn't stop running until long after he'd left the village. He'd followed the road leading inland and kept going. He'd left his bag and shoes in a pile in a bathroom. He couldn't believe he'd been so stupid, for a simple wash, he'd now lost everything.

Worse, he dared not return to the village to collect it or scavenge anything new. Feeling his bare feet scratched by the road, he put his hands in the empty pockets of his new jeans and slowed his pace to a walk, listing for the distinct sound of a running engine. He walked for the rest of the day, he heard only the birds call from the nearby trees and the sound of his laboured breath, as he pushed himself to keep going.

He had a lot of time to think, maybe whoever had driven to that street wouldn't have done him any harm or tried to take anything from him. Or perhaps they were looking for him, maybe they had seen him and had followed him there. The paranoia of living through the apocalypse made logic redundant. Tom had long decided people were not to be trusted, he had no plans to change that philosophy now.

The sight of a running vehicle had taken him by surprise. He hadn't seen anything mechanical like that for months, not since the last green army truck had rolled down the road leading out of town.

This wasn't the first time he had seen others in the days since the world ended, as he thought of it, although becoming more infrequent, he'd found himself hiding from people more often than he would have liked. The first time he encountered another person was a few days after he first left the flat. A lone man walking on the opposite side of the road, head down, hands firmly in his pockets.

The man didn't speak, he didn't even raise his gaze. Tom passed him, he hadn't heard the man stop and turn, nor did he hear the man strike him on the back of the head, he still has no idea what with. All Tom knew was when he woke several hours later, everything he had packed from his flat was gone. His head was throbbing in pain, a streak of dried blood stained his shirt collar. Never again would he trust another person, never again would he let someone take him by surprise.

Tom had done the right thing, he didn't know why there was someone in that sleepy village near the coast, and he didn't want to. He was heading inland now. He knew he'd have to eventually; he'd have to leave the safety of the beach at some point.

He hadn't seen any indication he was near anywhere he could salvage from in some time, he was desperate to replace the lost shoes. His feet were soft, not made for the hours of walking without protection. He could feel the blisters that had formed many miles before, each step was becoming agony.

Forcing himself on, eventually he saw a sign pointing down the road. A village, three miles, just three more miles and he could finally rest.

Tom continued, step by step, the pain in his feet now becoming unbearable. He saw the steeple of a church in the distance, the centre of all villages in this area. Struggling through each step, eventually he came to the doorstep of a thatched cottage at the edge of the village, red window frames and a green door resting against a whitewashed cob wall. He ambled up the path, glancing at the garden which was remarkably well kept considering the length of time since they must last have been tended to. An apple tree stood tall in the centre of the garden, no help now. He hadn't thought about fruit trees blooming later in the year, a small smile crept to his cracked lips, maybe there was a future after all. Trees would fruit, crops would likely grow where they were planted years before. He could perhaps try and cultivate some in the future, storing their bounty to get through the barren winters. He mustn't think of that just now. If he was still alive, he could consider this another time, consider a new life.

The cottage door was unlocked, he walked into

an old country kitchen. The room had been undisturbed for some time, it remained eerily preserved.

Tom headed for what he hoped was a utility room attached to the kitchen and breathed a sigh of relief as the row of wellington boots and outdoor footwear came into view. He selected a worn pair of hiking boots. They were slightly too large, he didn't care, he slid his feet in and laced them up.

He searched the rest of the cottage and found a bounty to replace his lost gear. He picked up a red and black rucksack from the hook in the utility room, a coat from the inside of the kitchen door, a box of matches and several stubs of candles, stashed forgotten in the back of an overflowing kitchen draw.

The kitchen cupboards were not entirely bare. He found half a bag of dried pasta and a few tins of preserved peaches sat gathering dust stashed in the back of the cupboard, he shoved them into the bag. As he searched further through the old cottage, he found more and more. He wished he could take it all with him. A boxed gas camping stove in the hallway cupboard, a folded tent, wrapped with pegs inside. Various coats for all seasons hung to the back of doors, tools, both gardening and power, he tried some of these out, wondering if they might make a useful weapon, should it come to it.

He decided to take only the gas stove. The tent would offer some much-needed protection from the elements, but would take too long to put up and away. The sign of a tent pitched along a rural road was sure to make him a target for those who may wish to take it from him. Stashing his new possessions into the rucksack, he filled a clean, plastic bottle with water from the small storage tank connected to the cottage guttering by the front door. He walked back out into the street, surprised at how quickly the day had vanished. The sun was setting, the temperature rapidly cooling and the light fading. Shivering, he pulled the coat from his rucksack and wrapped it around himself. The weather was quickly becoming worse, he could feel the hair on his arms standing on end as the swirling wind started to lash into him. *That's the problem with spring*, he thought, the elements change quicker than he can.

Walking onto the unfamiliar street now quickly being bathed in darkness, Tom glanced around. He hadn't been this far inland since he arrived at the coast all those months ago. He knew he couldn't be more than ten miles from where he'd started that morning. The change in the landscape had thrown him off balance, he didn't recognise any of the landmarks, he didn't know where he was or where he would sleep this night. As he walked further into the unknown, he could feel the panic starting to rise inside of him. He had used the beach as a feeling of familiarity, the sound of the crashing waves to help him sleep. Now he heard only the whistling of the ever-increasing swirling wind for company.

He settled against the far end of the dilapidated wall surrounding the churchyard in the centre of the village, it provided some protection from the weather. He could hug into himself and pray for morning, while being away from the road where any passing visitors may have spotted him. He should be safe here for one night, while he decided his next step.

Sleep eluded Tom for most of the night in his temporary resting place, his mind raced. Should he have stayed by the coast, should he have seen who was driving the truck? More pressingly, should he have nicked it? He supposed not, no use to make enemies when he had nowhere to go in a vehicle, anyway.

He couldn't help but wonder who this person had been, he had vowed to avoid people at all costs, but part of him, he realised now, was missing the companionship. Huddled against the crumbling wall, he felt himself start to drift off into sleep.

As morning arrived, the weather had calmed, the wind had stopped, and the sky was clear. Tom blinked his eyes open, he felt rough, this had not been his best night sleep. He'd spent most of the night wrestling in his mind how he was going to survive the coming months, years if he was lucky enough. He knew that his past life of isolation wasn't sustainable, he'd die out here, alone and scared. He had realised his desire for solitude wasn't as strong as he'd believed, he missed company.

The events of the past day had proven he wasn't alone. He was not willing to confront those who were confident enough to drive brazenly around the countryside, he didn't trust that type. But maybe, throughout the country there were others. People like him, hiding in abandoned houses, warehouses perhaps, maybe there were actual settlements. Camps, not like the ones the government had hastily created. Real communities, people that had come together to make a new life. He decided that he needed to search. He needed to know if there were others, maybe he needed to join them. He needed companionship.

Knowing he was now further inland than he'd ever been and not being entirely sure of his location, he decided to continue to follow the road. The country lane he had the previous day run up, snaked through the village and continued out the other side. It was as good a route as any until he could gain his bearing and come up with a destination.

Maybe he should have nicked the truck, after all.

Tom folded the coat he'd wrapped around himself last night into the bag, took a large swig of water and slipped out of the church grounds.

He headed back to the main road and continued to walk towards the far end of the village. He walked past the multicoloured houses and thatched roofed cottages dotted throughout, their gardens were overgrown, the air of abandonment surrounded each one. This village didn't look like it had been ravaged by any marauding travellers, it looked undisturbed, abandoned. Dead.

He was eager to leave, he wasn't sure why, but this seemed much worse than the places he'd been where visible signs of people had existed. In the light of day, Tom could see this village representing only a past life, a prior existence, a relic of a time gone by, which was very unlikely to return.

Tom increased his pace, heading out of the village. He didn't want to spend any longer being reminded of the past than he had to. As he walked, he realised he didn't know where he was headed, how long it would take, or what he would find when he got there. He ambled aimlessly forwards.

The day dragged on as he walked further and further up the same road. The sun had passed overhead, he supposed it must now be early afternoon. He'd seen several signs for other nearby villages, names from olden times. More relics of the past, preserved as they were left when they were abandoned all those months ago. The thought made his heart race, he kept on the road.

He noticed the haze in the distance, the concrete jungle rising from the mist like a mirage. He wasn't sure what he was seeing was real at first. It looked wrong, like an oil painting just too far away to make out the detail. Skyscrapers spiralled from the mist on one side, silent chimneys the other. *Financial and industrial*, he thought, admiring the contrast of the skyline from his vantage point several miles out. There was no visible sign of damage from this distance, no fallen buildings, no raging fires.

Tom had to remind himself how little time had passed since the pandemic had first begun. It felt like another lifetime. He was sure that by now, nature should have reclaimed mankind's monstrosities. The concrete pavements should be cracked and broken. Giant, unnatural vines snaking from the earth. Climbing lampposts and buildings, smothering rusting cars, crushing them like a snake.

As Tom arrived at the edge of the city, he saw just how wrong his vision had been. The apocalyptic scene he built up in his mind, the scene he expected to confront him, it didn't exist here. He wasn't sure where he was, but it had undoubtedly fared better than the town he had come from. No bodies littered the floor, no rotting flesh suffocating the air. The streets looked clean, cars sat parked at the side of the road, houses stood empty, but intact.

Something wasn't right. He knew he couldn't be too far from where he started, unless he'd wandered the coast further than he thought... How was this place so clean, so untouched, compared to the concrete hell he'd left all those months earlier? Even the beach he sat on a few days ago, with the bodies washing up on the shore.

He glanced nervously around, looking for any small sign of life, any sign of recent movement, from anything. There was nothing. The bird song floated on the wind. The slight breeze shook the grass as it passed through it, somewhere in the distance a dog barked. Tom continued further into the city, pausing every few steps to watch and listen for anything to indicate he was in danger. Nothing happened, he walked several streets before he felt himself calm. The sound of his footsteps bounced off the brick with every step he took. The houses were all the same, curtains drawn, gates securely closed. None of them looked as if they had been scavenged or plundered. There was no sign that anyone had stepped foot here for weeks, perhaps months.

He wondered where to go next. He was hungry. He stopped and opened his pack, the pasta was useless, he'd have to start up the stove to boil it, too much time and a waste of gas. He hadn't eaten all day, and his body was letting him know. His stomach was starting to cramp, he knew the spasms would be next. He settled on the tin of preserved peaches, pulling the ring on top of the tin to release the sugar-filled fruit within. He took a slice of peach from the tin with his hands, feeling the sticky liquid drip down his fingers. Savouring the taste, he ravenously ate the rest of the tin. He couldn't store them; they would only stick to the inside of the bag if he tried. He drained the fluid from the tin, he wasn't sure what was in it, it had to contain something nutritious. No use in wasting anything these days. He felt bad about discarding the tin on the floor in front of him, it was the only litter he could see, the only evidence of people in this sleepy street.

He continued further into the city, he still couldn't figure out where he was, he hadn't seen anything obvious to tell him. Come to think of it, he couldn't recall passing a sign on the way in, or anywhere on the road during his approach. *This is odd*, he thought, his senses heightening with each step. Something was off, he just couldn't put his finger on it. After what felt like hours, he passed a small, boarded-up corner shop. It didn't look like anyone had been inside since the previous owner had secured the window. He walked over to one of the large ply-wood sheets covering the door and tugged at the corner. Months of neglect and the winter weather had rotted the wood, he pulled it away with ease, it split down the middle as he tugged at it. He discarded the piece of board that had come loose in his hands and stared at the locked door beyond. He looked around for something to smash the glass window with. Locating a small rock and in one now experienced swing, he shattered the window. Unlike the homes he had previously entered, this glass did not fall to the ground with the distinct sound he'd become accustomed to. It simply stayed in place; spiderweb-like cracks revealed on its surface.

Security glass, he thought, *typical*.

He removed the coat from his bag and wrapped it the best he could around his hands. Grabbing the glass where the stone had created a small hole, he tugged it towards him. Nothing happened the first few times, he found himself putting more and more effort into trying to pry the broken glass out of its frame. Eventually it gave, with one massive crash it slid sideways down onto the floor. He glanced through the hole left in the door, carefully glancing side to side. There was no movement. He examined the street behind him, the noise from his break-in was loud, amplified by the unnatural silence surrounding this place. If there was anyone nearby, they would have been sure to have heard him. It was quiet, only the birdsong audible. Tom grabbed the frame of the door and hoisted himself inside. Landing with a bang on the floor he lost his balance and spilt forwards, he felt his chin connect to the cheap lino flooring and cursed to himself as blood seeped from his lip. He sat upright on the cold shop floor, rubbing his sore chin and took stock of his new surroundings. There wasn't much visible on the shelves. As rationing began to take place, the small family-owned shops sold out quickly and were unable to restock. He wondered if that's why this one was professionally boarded up. Maybe they ran out of things to sell early on and joined the masses to the havens, intending to return later and resume life where they left it.

He walked the bare aisles, surveying anything left on them. There wasn't much, a few packs of wet wipes wrapped in blue plastic lay in an untidy pile next to a ripped box of washing machine detergent, the once bright colours of the box now faded and dull. He noticed the shutters had been pulled down behind the counter, he hopped over the flimsy wooden table between him and it and tried the latch. Locked. He retrieved the rock he had used to enter the store and with several precise blows, broke the lock holding the steel shutter down and noisily pulled it open. It was full, cigarettes of every brand, liquor, pain killers. Precious pills.

He immediately started emptying the strongest into his bag, shoving them in with his arms, he didn't know how much longer he'd be able to find these. Feeling elated at the find, he turned to survey the cigarettes.

He hadn't smoked since they lived in their family home in the suburbs, he hadn't been able to afford to, after he lost his job. He took a pack from the shelf, he didn't know the brand, he didn't care. Removing the plastic sleeve, he pulled a single cigarette from the box and brought it up to his nose, inhaling its smell in one deep breath. He reached for one of the green disposable lighters from the bottom shelf, leant back against the counter and lit the cigarette. He inhaled deeply, savouring the taste, the feeling of ecstasy flooding over him. Then he coughed uncontrollably. He doubled over, unable to stop the cigarette initiated coughing fit. He reached for his bag, the water inside seeming like the only relief. It wasn't there, he grabbed only air. Tears streaming from his eyes, he tried to stand to look at the floor where he'd dropped the bag. He heard something rolling down the wooden counter. A small glass bottle bumped against his right hand, glancing down he saw the bottle of cough syrup through his watery eyes. The silhouette of a person stood the other end of the counter, arms folded, overcoat concealing their features.

"For the cough," came a woman's voice.

CHAPTER THREE

The woman stood still. She was shorter than Tom, the overcoat hiding her build, her bright blue eyes squinted as she watched him over the collar of her coat, blond hair tightly tied at the back of her head.

He jumped back, slamming against the cigarette stand, packs fell around him. He was in a panic; he threw several boxes at the woman stood the other end of the counter. A dull thud forced him back to his senses. The woman had let a sharp red axe fall onto the counter, sitting between the two of them, the catalyst for Tom to stop and think. He'd been cornered and whoever this was had the upper hand. And the sharper weapon.

The woman's name was Kate, as she explained once Tom had finally calmed down.

She'd heard his entrance to the shop from several streets over and had come to investigate. It was clear Kate wasn't going to trust him, she kept her distance and her axe handy, but she hadn't tried to kill him yet. That was a positive.

She told Tom that she lived nearby, several of them did. There was no real structure or order, no security or defence, no idyllic summer camp, but there were survivors. There were other people, and Tom had found some of them in just a few short days, he knew there must be more, maybe lots more.

Kate told him they had been here since the beginning. There had been issues with others, people had tried to take from them. She told Tom that people had wanted to take *them*, the women at least. They had done what they needed to stay alive in the first weeks. Law and order fell apart rapidly in the early days, people were left to fend for themselves.

A group of students from the nearby university had banded together in the student halls to ride it out. To wait for safety rather than evacuate to the camps. The safety had not come. Like Tom, over time, they adapted to their new life and did what they had to in order to survive.

Eventually, the inhabitants of the city had left. Many of them perished, either due to the virus, or at the hands of each other. Kate and the others had stayed locked inside a floor of the halls. They had enough dried food to last them a few weeks. With the curtains drawn, they remained silent for as long as they could, trying not to draw the attention of anyone who might want the security and what little food they had. The others left, one by one, Kate was then alone.

The food had run out, Kate had been forced to

leave the relative security and scavenge the dead city. The city had also been home to the central government after the capital fell. To slow the spread of the virus, they had kept the rubbish collection going, the streets were disinfected nightly. Bodies had been removed from the ground for cremation, soldiers patrolled for longer than they had in the town Tom had left, this was one of the last places to fall to the virus. Of course, this had all eventually stopped. Like everything else, it slowly succumbed to the virus. Kate told of how they threw their own out of the administration building as soon as they showed signs of infection. How they discarded anyone in the government hierarchy as soon as they were a threat, it hadn't been enough.

The buildings eventually went quiet, all signs of life here also soon stopped.

After hours of questions back-and-forth, using the counter of the small corner shop for security for them both, Kate had agreed to take him back to where she and the others were staying. She didn't tell him much about the others.

Tom was anxious as he walked down the street with her, he could feel the fear threatening to overwhelm him. The prospect of other people, being inside again, it filled him with dread. He took several deep breaths as he tried to settle himself.

"So, tell me," Tom said after a long period of silence. "How many of you are there?"

Kate gave him a sideways glance; it was clear she still didn't fully trust him.

"There's a few," came her curt reply.

Tom walked in silence for the next few streets, feeling deflated as his attempts at further conversation were met with increasingly colder replies.

Once they were outside of the dimly lit shop, Tom had time to thoroughly study Kate. She was beautiful, her blond hair somehow silky and clean, not matted like his own had been. Her silky-smooth skin looked as if she still lived in the past world. There were no scratches from sleeping on the floor, no sores from the sun or the lack of hygiene.

Thank fuck I washed, he thought to himself, he smiled as he did so.

"Something funny?" Kate asked sharply. They had come to a stop, she'd been watching him, immersed in his own little world.

"Sorry, no, I was just thinking to myself," he replied. "Is it much further?"

"We're here."

Tom looked around. They were in the industrial area of the city, chain-link fences around old redbrick factories, stumpy chimneys rising from the slate roofs. They stood at the entrance to a car park of what, according to the sign taking pride of place on the wall, was previously a textile factory.

"Come on," said Kate impatiently, beckoning Tom to a steel fire exit door on the side of the building.

She rapped the head of the red axe three times

to the door, the metal-on-metal echoing around the empty buildings. The door clicked and swung open; a young man stood in its place. He was taller than Tom, his beard patchy and not fully grown, curly brown hair resting on his forehead. He wore a white loose-fitting t-shirt and corduroy trousers, sport trainers laced on his feet, a single earphone dangled from his ear, with nothing to plug the cord into.

"Kate... Who's this?" the young man asked, his voice cracking. Tom studied him; he couldn't have been out of his teenage years.

"Matt, this is Tom."

Tom nodded in acknowledgement. Matt's face had turned pale, he stood there, holding the push bar on the back of the fire door, not moving to allow them inside, transfixed on Tom's face.

"Matt?" Kate asked impatiently. "Move."

"Sorry, sorry," he replied as he stepped back, allowing enough room for the two of them to enter the warehouse floor.

Tom took a step inside, steadied himself and looked around. The building was empty, what he could see at least. There were none of the giant machines he'd expected to see, no rows of sewing machines he'd seen in reports of sweat shops in distant countries. Nothing, just a large, empty space. The red brick wall continued inside, windows the length of the building, set just above head height, allowing light in, but not granting a view to those inside. A black steel mezzanine ran the length of the far side wall, leading to what Tom assumed was the back offices, the break room, the toilets and whatever facilities this building once housed.

"Welcome to our home," Kate announced, her arms stretched as if inviting a guest to view a new house. "It's not much, but it's better than nothing."

Her admission of a few other people was about as accurate as she could have been. Tom met just one other person, aside from Kate and Matt. Living in the factory with them was Rose, an older woman with white hair. She wore a colourful shawl around her shoulders and an ankle-length summer dress, she walked with a distinctive limp, previously a professor at the university where the others were studying. Rose had taught physiology. Although she and the others hadn't met before the virus took hold, she had sheltered in the student housing when her townhouse had been broken into and ransacked by the last of the desperate masses abandoning their homes.

At the back of the factory was a long corridor with several doors heading off to previously unused dormitories. They had been built to house the migrant workers, before manufacturing went overseas. Kate told him others had stayed with them throughout the months. But it never worked out, she had to ask them to leave. She glanced in Tom's direction as she said this, her eyes narrow and focused directly on him.

Recalling what Kate had shared on the walk back, he wanted to find out more. Still, sensing he would do best to stay quiet and learn what he could, he silently nodded to show he understood and allowed himself to be given the tour of the rest of the factory. It didn't take long; the building wasn't large and most it gave over to the space where they had entered. There was a canteen with steel tables bolted to the floor, a separate door led to a kitchen area with a gas stove connected to a large tank outside the building.

"Any questions?" Kate asked with a smile.

"Why did you invite me here?" he replied. "Why were you out miles from here today and who else was here, why did they leave?"

"Okay, okay, one at a time," she retorted. "I invited you here because I need help. You've met the others, Matt is a nervous wreck, Rose is in her twilight, I can't do this alone. They still need to be fed, they still need water, they still need to be safe." She looked to the floor. "I can't do that alone. At some point, we have to start trusting other people. I wasn't sure about you at first. I heard you breaking the glass. I wasn't sure if I should introduce myself, but after that drag on that cigarette, you didn't seem too threatening, even if you do look like shit." She looked him up and down.

Tom was suddenly very conscious of his ill-fitting clothes, his jagged haircut and sunken appearance. He felt slightly ashamed, the smell of weeks of his unwashed body came flooding back to him. He hoped the reek from his body had gone with the bath, not that he'd just got used to it. Although considering how far he'd run after that, he doubted it. His concerns were confounded with Kate's next remark.

"We have running water here, you know. It's cold and from the outdoor storage tanks, but I don't think a shower would go amiss."

Tom felt himself redden. "Sorry," he stumbled out. "It's been a while since I've seen anyone else, I've been living on the beach mostly, since I left my home." Tom shocked himself with that last statement, had he come to remember that dingy flat as 'home'?

"It's okay," Kate replied sweetly. "I get it. Go clean up, we'll talk when you're done." She beckoned him to the large shower room at the end of the corridor. Several showers rested in the tiled wall, the entrance to each had a pulled back blue plastic sheet tied to a bar on the ceiling.

"There's spare clothes over there," she motioned to a row of metal lockers, like those which could once be seen in gyms and sports halls around the country. With that, she turned and left. Tom heard the door close, the silence returned.

He walked to the shower and turned the water on, it spluttered, and water shot out in a single, heavy stream. He removed his clothes and plunged his body under icy water, washing the best he could with his hands. After several minutes he couldn't stand the cold water beating against his skin any longer. He turned the tap off and walked out of the cubicle, shivering as the water dripped off him. He picked up the clean white towel that had been left hanging over the side of the tiled, chest-high wall that separated the showers and dried himself.

Searching the lockers for clean clothes, he found a simple array of shirts, t-shirts, jeans and shorts. He chose the best fitting he could, a dull red t-shirt and a tight-fitting pair of jeans. There were socks and underwear, a treat in this world. He dressed, the new clothes fitted him much better than the last set had, he felt better for it too. A small dust-covered mirror sat on the far wall above a row of porcelain sinks. He walked over to it and studied himself, he could see his colour had returned slightly. His eyes still sunk into his face from months of malnutrition and lack of basic care, but right now, he felt happier than he had in months. He would not have believed that something as simple as a few hours company would have lifted his spirits as much as it did. Maybe he did miss people more than he admitted.

He walked out of the locker room and back into the long corridor. He was immediately hit with the most delicious smell he could remember, the aroma of spice floated in the air. His mouth started to water. He'd eaten nothing more than a tin of peaches in the last few days, this was not out of the ordinary. Food was a luxury he could ill afford countless times over these last months.

Tom followed the smell down the corridor, he noticed the space becoming darker, the sun must be setting. He glanced at the ceiling; industrial strip lights covered it. They weren't on, there was no indication of power here, not that he had suppose there would be working power.

He reached the door on the left of the corridor where the inviting smell was coming from and pushed it carefully open. He was at the kitchen entrance of the canteen, he saw a figure bent over a stove, gas flame emanating out of the lit hob. It was Kate, she was busy over a pan of something sizzling away, Tom felt his stomach scream.

He walked over to her.

"Hey," he mumbled as he neared.

"Hey yourself," she replied. "Just making something to eat, you look like you could do with it. It's not much - just potatoes and whatever herbs we could find, but it'll get some energy back into you."

"It smells delicious," he replied truthfully. "I've lived off tinned food for months now, I had pasta, but could never bring myself to cook it."

"Pasta?" her brow lifted as she looked at him. "That was the first thing to disappear from the shelves here. I guess there's probably quite a lot in the houses around here, but I try not to venture too far, unless there's a good reason to do so." She studied Tom again. "You look better, the clothes are a good fit. I can't smell you from here, that's either a good sign, or there's more spice in this pan than I thought. It's the same most days, potatoes and whatever can be thrown with them. Rose managed to grow a large number in those daft grow bag things you can get from the garden centres. They've really saved us."

Tom patiently waited in the kitchen with her. He made what small talk he could, learning further small snippets about the lives of the three people living here until the meal was ready. Kate had called Rose and Matt, the four of them sat at one of the long metal tables with full bowls of the spiced potatoes and vegetable mix. It didn't take him long to finish his portion off, accepting seconds when offered. He sat at the table, watching the other three eat. He was full, it was the best feeling he could recall in a long time.

He found out much more about the three people he was sharing his meal with. Matt was a first-year student of engineering. He had only been away from home for a few weeks when the first cases were reported. He had tried to go back when the situation began to worsen, but the lockdown meant he'd been forced to shelter in his accommodation. He loved music, he had those damned headphones wrapped around his neck long after his phone was useless, wearing them like jewellery.

Rose had taught at the university for over 20 years, she lived in one of the professor's townhouses just outside the campus, they were elegant three-storey properties. This had made them a target for people assuming they would be well-stocked. Rose had left when the first houses were looted, she hadn't known where to go, so headed towards the university. Kate had saved her life soon after, they didn't elaborate further.

Kate was older than Matt, she was nearing 30 and starting the second year of her course, she had studied English. She wanted to change her life and become a teacher after a misspent youth of working in supermarkets and fast-food outlets.

"That won't be happening now," she joked.

When everyone had finished, they sat in silence, the room now eerily dark as the sun had nearly fully set.

"What do you do at nights?" Tom asked. "When it gets dark?"

"Candles, mostly," Rose replied before the others could speak. "It's nice, it gives a good ambience."

"You expected electricity? Hot water, maybe. Everything you were used to before the virus?" asked Kate, Tom hoped she was joking.

"No, no, not at all," he replied, hoping he didn't seem ungrateful for the hospitality and meal. "So, tell me," he added, folding his arms and leaning into the table, eager to move the conversation on. "Why here, why only you three?"

"This seemed as good a place as any at the time, we had to leave the student halls. The food had run out, more and more people were arriving, looking for... I don't know what they were looking for, nor why they thought they'd find it there." Kate's expression changed at the memory, he sensed there was more to the story, but not for tonight.

He barely slept the first night, he struggled with the bed. After months of sleeping on the ground, the softness of the mattress was unsettling, it felt unnatural. His fear of sleeping indoors crept upon him, he struggled to keep it under control. He tossed and turned, running over in his head the events that led him there. The last 24 hours had raced by, his life had changed so much in such a short time. He shouldn't be surprised, just last year he was drinking cocktails at some late-night bar, pop music blaring in his ears.

He tried to get into the routine of living with the others. He woke, washed and joined them for breakfast, offering to help where he could with cooking or cleaning. He found it strange how quickly he fell back into a routine, back into the closest that could be described as a normal life.

After a few days, he had gotten to know the others much better. Matt missed home and still believed his family would be alive. He also believed the government hadn't fallen and they were fighting back right now. Any day soon there would be rescue, men in green suits would scoop them up, put them on a bus and get them all home. Matt's family had lived the other side of the country, he'd been so excited when he was accepted into this university, the independence and the distance appealed to him. Now he vowed never to leave them again.

Tom felt sorry for Matt, he was naive. He was sure Matt's family were dead, just like his own, just like Kate's and just like Rose's would be, probably.

Rose never really spoke about herself; she shared very little about her private life and the people in it. She loved to talk, she told stories long into the nights, but she never spoke about the people she had loved. He was still no closer to knowing what had happened in the past that had the other three so on edge, they were unwilling to talk about it. He'd asked Matt the following morning, but he'd made excuses to leave and scurried off. He was waiting for an opportunity to go outside with Kate alone, he hoped she might tell him more when they were on their own.

It was several days later before the opportunity finally came up. Supplies were starting to run low, and Kate had to see what she could find locally, Tom immediately volunteered.

"It's the least I can do," he chirped before Kate could object. "You've been feeding me for days now, you've given me a place to stay."

She frowned. "Alright then, just keep up."

Tom smiled to himself, deep down he was sure she wanted the company. He suspected that was the reason she first invited him back, she lived with the others, but they were not alike.

Rose and Matt talked like old family, a grandmother and grandson almost, Kate didn't fit in with that. Tom had seen enough to know she was the carer in this group, providing for them, cooking for them, even sending them to bed at the end of the day.

They walked through the tall gate of the chain-link fence, out onto the deserted road, empty rucksacks draped across their shoulders.

"There's a few houses not too far from here that I haven't checked," she said, pointing down a side street. "We should start there and see what we find."

Tom nodded, that was fine with him. As they walked, he noticed Kate was always on alert. He'd been careful when travelling on his own, but she was vigilant, studying every side street, glancing at every car they passed, her eyes trained on everything.

She'd brought the red fire axe with her, to make getting in places easier, she'd told him. Recalling the way she displayed it in front of his face when they first met, he wasn't so sure that was the real reason.

"Kate?" Tom asked carefully, she glanced over to him. "What happened to you?"

Her gaze dropped to the floor, he saw her shoulders visibly slump, she sighed and closed her eyes.

"It wasn't good, Tom," she said tearfully, gazing back up to his face, her wide blue eyes glistening in the sunlight. "I was in the halls, a few weeks after the official lockdown, there wasn't anyone else staying there then, most of the others had bolted. Tried to return to their families when the rumours first started about the second wave, when the food started running low. I didn't believe it, so I just stayed put. Not that I had anywhere to go. I mean, I'd only been back a few months at this point. Things got bad, people took to the streets, they rioted, Tom. The army shot people, live bullets, they just shot them dead on the street. I saw them fall from my window. I heard the screams, people started running, trampling each other and they just kept shooting. I could see people, dying on the street, I tried to help them. Rose had been shot. Her leg was bleeding pretty bad, I managed to get her back inside and we wrapped her up, I think she's fine now, but she needed a doctor, proper medical care. She still can't walk right."

"Why do you care for them?" he asked, after a small pause. "I've seen you, playing mother, carer to both of them."

"I owe them," Kate replied simply.

"But you saved them," he retorted.

"In the beginning, maybe, but they both saved me too." Kate's gaze fell to the floor again. "It wasn't long after I pulled them from the street that the real shit started to go down.

A few days later the army disappeared, I don't know, maybe they deserted. Maybe they got sick and died, maybe they couldn't live with what they'd done. Whatever the reason, they just... vanished, the soldiers." She paused; Tom heard her take an audible breath.

"Then the worst people came. Those with nothing to lose. They attacked people at random, they beat kids to death on the street, raped women

THE SURVIVAL OF TOM

in public, took anything they wanted. The way you could hear them laugh about it from the window, Tom, it made me sick. I don't know how they knew, maybe they had been following me, maybe it was just luck." She pointed up the road. "They were up there, followed me back and burst through the front door, I just stood there and asked what they wanted. I actually asked if I could help them! They made it pretty clear that they wanted me, they had an axe," she tapped her axe in her hand lightly on the floor. "This axe, they threatened to kill me if I didn't let them, not that killing me would have stopped them, fucking animals," she spat on the ground.

"Kate..." Tom started.

"No," she replied firmly. "It wasn't like that, they tried, they had me pushed against the wall before Rose sunk the axe they had dropped into the back of one of their heads."

Silence filled the air, for several long moments, neither Kate nor Tom spoke. He was shocked, he suspected something had happened, but to hear Rose had killed a man, that he had not expected.

"Of course," Kate continued. "That was only one of them, and it's a lot harder to get an axe out of a man's skull than you might think. Especially if your nearing 70 and have recently been shot in the leg. The other two backed off at first. I guess the surprise of their pal being butchered by an old lady took them by surprise. I thought they were going to kill us both, it was only down to Matt that they didn't. Shaking like a leaf, he'd had the sense to grab a knife from the kitchen. He threatened them, nothing more, they turned tail and ran. I guess we weren't worth the risk anymore.

"I kept the axe, figured it could be useful. Someone thought it'd made a good weapon. I have to say, I agree."

Silence again.

"Come on," Kate finally said. "Let's get on with it."

The next few days were a blur to Tom, he learned more about the people he was living with, more about their past. This clean, untouched city held more secrets and horrors than Tom could comprehend. At least in the town he'd come from, everything was laid bare on the pavements, the sight of the dead and the sound of the screams had wiped any pretext of normality or safety. He had known where he stood.

The riots had hit his hometown hard, hordes of people descended to the streets, they attacked the police. The troops sent to quell the violence had fired live rounds, people fled, screamed, fell.

Tom was sure this had accelerated the spread of the second wave and the demise of humanity. Thousands of people were gathered together. Their blood had stained the ground when the shooting started, millions of spores would have been released into the air that day, blanketing the crowd below. He supposed the spread had eventually been more deadly than bullets, but they would never know

now. There was no one left to keep track. It was clear the city had been abandoned to its fate, left to die.

He couldn't imagine spending the last few weeks before humanity fell in this place. A government trying in vain to maintain a semblance of power, an ever-increasing portion of the population turning on each other. The cat-and-mouse game of kill and clean, maintain order by any means necessary, then hide the evidence to prevent further revolt. It had failed.

Kate told him of mass graves, of bodies being burnt in piles in the city's furnaces, of the length they went to hide what was happening. She couldn't recall exactly when everything stopped, when the patrols retreated across the entire city. She'd already fled her home, she fled after the attack. They had abandoned that part of the city by then. Kate and the others headed to the industrial area of the city, hoping it would be less populated, that less people would be stalking the streets here.

It hadn't taken long for them to reach this spot, armed with the red axe, people left them alone, even those out looking for trouble only wanted battles they could easily win. They had stayed in the shadows, using side streets where they could as they snaked their way through the darkening alleyways, heading further away from the chaos with every step.

They had selected the textile factory as it was

at the far end of an industrial estate. Only one road leading to it and continuing out of the city, they would see anyone approaching from either direction. The fence running across the perimeter was not perfect, a tall chain-link fence with a roll of razor wire to stop it being climbed. Not that it wouldn't be hard to cut through, but Kate hoped it would make the place look like more trouble than it was worth.

The only entrance to the car park was the sliding gate that connected the two sides of the fence that could be pulled closed. Kate had decided that this might draw more attention and left it open, reasoning that at least a single entry point could be monitored.

The main door to the factory had long since been boarded up. She had managed to force the fire escape open with the head of the axe, and since then they had used this as their only entrance. It could be opened from the inside only and was strong enough to withstand anyone trying to break it down. Kate hoped no one would try to force it in the way she had, this was the obvious weak point.

She told Tom about the others still living in the city, for the most part, anyone who might still be trying to live a civilised life hadn't lasted long. Those not taken by the virus had found themselves at the mercy of an increasingly large band of survivors, intent on causing nothing but misery. She wasn't sure why people had reverted into soulless beasts, these people must have had

THE SURVIVAL OF TOM

jobs, friends, families, before all of this. Now they stalked the streets, taking what they wanted, killing who they wanted.

Tom felt pity at learning the current state of the world. He knew others had survived, they had to have done, and he knew he probably wanted to stay away from them. He never imagined things would turn this bad so fast. He thought back to that black truck by the coast, he was glad he'd run. He'd wanted to believe so badly that people were still good. That life had continued, that there was still a sanctuary to be found. Now every trip outside the protection offered by the brick and metal of the textile factory was akin to running with wolves. Every corner they turned, every home they entered might reveal the face of their killers.

He looked towards Kate, her sparkling eyes glancing off into the distance, strands of her perfect golden hair blowing lightly in the breeze. He had found her, not everyone left alive here was evil. They didn't all want to spread this destruction, this terror. There were people left with good in their hearts, she was proof of this. She was one of the kindest people he'd ever met, the end of the world hadn't changed this.

He smiled as she turned to catch him staring at her.

"Come on," she said softly. "Let's find something for Matt to eat before he gets cranky." The smile on her face warmed Tom's heart, maybe the world wasn't so bad after all.

Tom had initially found sleeping inside to be unsettling. He soon reverted to old habits, the walls and door were starting to provide an extra level of security to him, a sense of safety.

Sleeping in a bed now even felt normal again, suddenly he couldn't imagine sleeping on the hard, cold floor. He'd been in this factory with Kate, Matt and Rose for nearly two weeks. He was happier than he could remember being in many months, but they still had to search for food every few days.

Every time the pair of them left the relative safety of this new home, Kate would harden, her vigilance increased, she seemed more on edge. Tom still wasn't sure he was being told the whole story, but sensing he had all he would get, gave up on pushing. There were other people left in this city, Kate had assured him of that. They would hear a noise in the distance, a scream, a cackle, unnatural banging. Tom could see the smoke rising into the night sky as the sun disappeared behind the mountains in the distance. Kate always ensured they stayed as far away from the source of the commotion. She had no desire to investigate any further.

The noise and smoke emanated from the centre of the city. Each night Kate would watch from the glass windows, ensuring it wasn't moving closer to them. She didn't tell Tom who was behind the smoke, he had a reasonably good idea from the fear and anger etched on her face.

CHAPTER FOUR

Kate watched the rain fall outside her window, steaming cup of coffee in her favourite white mug clasped in her hands. The term had been suspended, she was the only one left in the student halls she was supposed to have called home for the next nine months. Most of the others had made their way back before the lockdown was announced. The rest had recently left when the food started to run low.

Kate didn't have any family to speak of, her parents lived far away, and she hadn't seen them in years. She had no real family of her own. She had nowhere else to go. She'd decided to stay put, hoping this would burn out and she could continue with her life, finish her studies and look forward to the future.

She didn't mind at first, it was nice not to have to wash up after the others. She was older than the rest of the students staying here, they were all first or second years. Kate had a good few years on them all and never truly felt like she fit in. They would go out partying, mingling, sleeping with each other. Kate was only there to learn, to gain her degree and move on with her new life.

THE SURVIVAL OF TOM

At first the quiet was calming, she couldn't go anywhere now, thanks to the lockdown, the novelty of quiet had run out. She still had a small amount of food stashed away she'd selfishly kept quiet and hidden from the others, and she still had coffee, although the milk had run out a week ago and the rations were not getting through. Maybe they didn't know she was there. She couldn't complain too much, at least she had a place to stay.

She'd watched people walking up the street outside the square block of brick buildings that the university had converted to housing, they were heading somewhere, she wasn't sure where. Watching some of them walk, she wasn't entirely sure they really knew either.

There had been an announcement recently, the second wave had come quick, they had only just got over the measures to calm the first wave, and the second was much worse. People were dying in vast numbers; Kate had seen the ambulances racing up and down the road for days. The university hospital connected off the main campus, anyone taken for treatment had to drive this road to the emergency entrance. At first, she'd thought it'd blow over, like the first wave had, but as the weeks rolled by, the numbers just kept rising. She'd figured by now that this was here for the long haul, but at no point did she realise just how bad it would yet become.

The government had announced they would start to empty the crowded cities where the virus was spreading from host to host with terrifying speed. People would be moved to temporary camps around the country, where they could be separated and segregated more effectively. Everyone being moved would be thoroughly tested for signs of the virus, to ensure contagion didn't get in.

Kate laughed at this announcement, what would they do? Check for a fever? A cough? A running nose?

It was well known by now that the mutated virus did not display symptoms, sometimes for weeks. At the same time, the host remained infectious the entire time. She knew there was no way to keep the infected out. The idea was there; at least they were trying, she thought, but she couldn't help wondering if people staying in their homes would have been more effective.

Kate had holed up in her temporary accommodation, the relocation was being broadcast as mandatory. She knew they had no way to enforce it, so long as she stayed put and quiet, she should be fine.

She watched the first exodus happen from her window, a small slit in the curtains providing her vantage point. It was funny, she remembered thinking, what people tried to take with them. She watched families stumble down the road, loaded high with heavy bags, prams dragged behind them. People had pillows tucked under their arms, rugs poking out the open rucksacks, keepsakes they couldn't bear to part with.

Many possessions were discarded on the way. She noticed the volume of bags piling at the side of the road was increasing. They must have realised soon into their journey they wouldn't be able to carry these things with them the entire way. The closest camp was five miles outside the city. With the fuel commandeered for emergency vehicles and the military, they couldn't use their cars, they had to walk.

She wondered how far some of them would have to travel. She'd heard that each camp would house a maximum of 5000 people; she'd seen many more than that walking the road from just the parts of the city that funnelled past the university complex.

She didn't know if it was an official announcement, or if everyone had just passed on their way to the promised salvation. After a few days, the crowds diminished to a trickle and eventually stopped altogether. She saw soldiers on the street still then, they were checking the discarded bags, no doubt looking for anything they might want to call their own.

A few days later she heard the rumbling of an engine. Carefully peering through the small gap in the centre of the curtains, she saw the strangest sight. There was a rubbish truck rolling down the road. Men in high visibility jackets were collecting the items discarded on the road, throwing them carelessly into the back of the truck, where they were crushed by the enormous mechanical jaws. She was sure she glimpsed a body being thrown in out of the corner of her eye, but she didn't recall seeing any deaths at that time, maybe the light was playing tricks on her.

She couldn't work out why they had gone to the trouble of cleaning the streets. She heard the rumble of engines all day, it sounded like the entire city was being cleaned.

She walked to her kitchen and placed the cold coffee onto the counter. How long had she been watching through the window, letting her mind wander, remembering the events of the last few days?

She opened the kitchen cupboards, the oak painted doors sticking slightly as she pulled them free. There wasn't much left, a few tins of various reconditioned meat, a bag of rice, a box of strawberry flavoured tea bags. She shut them again, a few days, that's about as long as she could go now.

Kate flicked the light switch, the bulb illuminated. *At least the powers still on*, she thought to herself. She walked to the small bathroom, it was usually shared by four of them and was never really clean. A shower cubical stood in one corner, black mildew growing between the tiles. Kate turned the handle and watched the water fall from the showerhead, waiting patiently for the steam to show it had warmed through. She was going to enjoy hot showers for as long as she could, even with the black spores watching her every move from the white, cracked tiles.

She let her knee-length skirt drop to the floor, removed the woollen jumper that was fighting back the autumn cold and threw it to the ground. She stepped into the steaming shower and let the warm water soothe her skin and mind. Kate tried to scrub the day away, it was only early afternoon, but the loneliness was starting to take its toll, she missed having things to do, people to talk to. She missed having a purpose, however small.

As she washed the last of the suds from her wet hair, she heard a woman's scream from somewhere below the window overlooking the street. Even with the warm water falling over her, her body suddenly felt cold.

She scrambled for the handle to turn the water off, pulled the shower door back and grabbed a towel drying from the rack attached to the wall. Wrapping herself in the towel as best she could, she ran to the living room, making her way to the vantage point by the window. There it was again, a blood-curdling scream, begging for help.

Kate's heart was racing, she knelt on the floor and peered through the small gap in the curtains. She saw nothing down below. Slowly separating the curtains as much as she dared, she glanced up the road, towards the main university campus, the majestic glass buildings still shimmering on the skyline.

Towards the top of the road, at the far end of the accommodation block, she saw a sight that made her stomach turn. A young woman, from this distance she looked like she might have been a student, taking refuge in another of the nearby blocks, was being dragged by the hair by a large man wearing a blue hooded top, black tracksuit bottoms and white trainers. They were too far away, she couldn't make their faces out, but she could see the other two men, following the commotion from behind, laughing and clapping in glee. She had taken too long to get here, the young woman was dragged around the corner into a side street, out of view, the men followed, whooping in joy.

Kate still saw this image when she closed her eyes. She'd seen worse since, but this was the first sign of humanity eroding, this is when she lost faith. She wished she'd done something, she wished she'd helped. Chased the group, maybe freed the girl, fought them off, made everything better. But she'd been frozen with fear. Sick at the sight of what was playing out in front of her. If she was honest with herself, she wouldn't have had the courage to do anything, she would have walked on by. She wasn't brave then; she hadn't been hardened by the months since.

Tears flooded from her eyes, she collapsed to the floor, the towel falling around her. Everything was changing, and there was nothing she could do about it. She was pathetic, crying alone on the floor. It was a long time before she moved again, the cold making the hairs on her arms stand on end. She peeled herself off the cold floor, looked around and saw the towel that had fallen from her naked body in a heap next to her.

Dried tears streaked her face, she walked to her small bedroom, opened the closet and dressed. She wasn't sure what she grabbed, throwing on whatever she came across first.

She spent the rest of the day in silence, sat against the wall in the corner of the communal living room, her head resting at a slight angle, hair obscuring her blank eyes. She was pulled back to reality by the sudden burning in her throat and her dry, cracked lips. Steadily rising to her feet, she made her way to the kitchen, removed a glass from the cupboard and filled it with tepid water. She gulped greedily and downed the glass, moving towards the tap to refill it. With the immediate thirst satisfied, she examined the glass in her hand. The water was no longer clear, it was slightly cloudy. She looked closer, she could see the tiny sediment floating in the glass. She emptied the rest of the water into the sink. Glancing around, she noticed the morning glow emitting from the gap in the curtains. She'd sat in that corner all night, consumed by her thoughts and the image that she would never be able to release.

Kate went through the routines, she forced herself to eat, to drink. However meagre the portions, she knew she had to keep her strength up.

She didn't go back near the window, she heard nothing sailing in with the wind from the street below. That night, she lay on her bed, and she slept, she didn't dream, she didn't stir, she just slept deeply.

The following day, just as she was returning her bowl to the kitchen that had contained the last remnants of stale cereal, moistened with the ever-clouding water which was losing pressure every time she turned the tap, her ears pricked at a sound she hadn't heard for a few days. A sound she wasn't sure she ever wanted to hear again. A voice. It wasn't screaming, it wasn't shouting, it was a calm whisper carried into her ears on the breeze, an indistinguishable, nondescript noise.

She crept back to the window, she only ever seemed to creep there now. Resting on her knees in what had become her now usual position, allowing her to peer from the gap in the curtain. On the street below, she observed a small group of soldiers, three of them, riles strung by their sides, distinctive green uniforms draped over their dishevelled figures. Behind them, being directed by the soldier at the front was a larger group of people, dressed in various attire. They appeared to be in the early stages of malnutrition. These people looked filthy, she couldn't make any of them out, but the gait with which they walked, and their evident broken demeanour clear as they shambled along, told her all she needed to know. These were the people who had stayed at home, like her.

They must have run out of food much earlier, praying for salvation until they saw signs of authority outside. Kate watched as people walked out of nearby doors to join the huddle. She was in awe, there wasn't just one or two, but a steady trickle of people slowly exited from the surrounding buildings.

They must also have seen the soldiers walking up the road, seen the people following close behind and recognised that the government, or at least some authority, still existed here. They must have seen this as salvation, protection from worst of society that had made themselves known in the absence of objection, they must have seen them as a way out. Kate watched as more and more people appeared, from doorways, out of side streets or running up the road from behind to avoid being left behind. By the time the soldiers passed under the window where she watched, the group of people following closely behind had swelled to dozens, huddled together. The only audible voice from the soldier at the in front, instructing newcomers to follow the others at a safe distance.

How many of these people had heard, had watched the young woman being dragged by her hair? And not one had tried to help.

"Keep apart," the soldier barked. His voice cracked, he was young, likely a recent recruit, maybe he started training before all of this, maybe not.

Kate watched as the group came to a stop, she

couldn't hear what the young soldier at the front was saying, he appeared to be talking to someone in front of him. Her view was obscured by the line of green trees that ran parallel to the road. He appeared to be getting agitated, his movement becoming erratic as he gesticulated to the ground, she couldn't see why.

Suddenly, without warning, Kate heard a crack. It rang through the air, breaking the relative calm. He had his rifle pointed in front of him, the muzzle smoked in the cooling air. She couldn't see what had happened, but she saw the motionless soldier standing in the middle of the road. She saw the group of people who had been following him blindly run in all direction, screams and shrieks began to fill the air.

People ran, diving into doorways, behind bushes, trying to find any form of safety they could. Kate saw the soldier, still motionless in the road, rifle outstretched, his face too far away for his expression to be read. She watched him hit the ground. She never saw the shooter. She saw the figure of a man, the paving slab raised high above his head, as he walked to stand above the soldier and forced it to the ground with both of his hands in a single, jarring, violent motion, to crush the fallen man's head. Kate imagined the life extinguishing from his eyes as she watched his skull break.

The other soldiers had scattered with the rest of the people, she hadn't seen where they had run to, she hadn't noticed them in the chaos. The man stood above the dead soldier, reached down and tried to tug the rifle from his hands, he was struggling, the strap must have become stuck behind his shoulder. The man continued to pull, not wanting to dig through the viscous and bone that she imagined scarred the floor like abstract art.

There was another sharp crack in the air. Kate had been so fixated on the man wresting with the lifeless body, she hadn't seen one of the soldiers running up the road, taking aim and shooting at the assailant, but she saw him fall. The shot must have connected, the scene played out in front of her eyes as if in slow motion, she watched him fall as he jerked backwards, red mist clouding the air behind him. He slumped to the ground without a sound, the soldier had already run off.

The street was suddenly clear, just the two dead bodies the only sign of anything that had taken place, red blood pooling around them. She felt her heart sink, she knew there were so many desperate people, hiding on the street below, but she didn't know how to help them, she didn't know what she could do.

The silence that filled the air was eerie, as if the city was mourning the dead lay to rest on its streets. It didn't last long, Kate soon heard the distant hum of an engine, growing steadily louder. Concealed by the curtain, she watched as a military truck rolled up the street, it came to a stop in front of her window. Two men dressed in the same green uniforms jumped to the road from the green canvas back. They walked over to the dead soldier lay just feet in front of them, his arms splayed to the side as if in greeting. One of the men walked to the shot attacker and kicked his hand, checking for life. Nothing. The two men stood either side of the dead soldier, grabbing his outstretched arms, they hoisted him off the barren concrete and carried him to the back of the truck.

A black plastic body bag lay on the floor, they manoeuvred the dead soldier into position, and zipped it around his head, unceremoniously throwing it into the back of the truck. Kate watched as they spoke softly to each other, she couldn't make out what they said. A man appeared from behind a near bush a few meters from them, his arm outstretched, his ripped shirt clearly showing his dishevelled figure, prominent ribs protruding out of his chest. He started to talk, but the words never came, they shot him before he could exhale.

People emerged from their hiding places and once again ran; shots rang after them. She watched as several of them fell, running for salvation, they made it just steps before they were cut down. Her eyes were stinging with the tears she tried to hold back, the lump in her throat choking her. She couldn't watch, the screams had returned, people ran in all directions, shots rang out, blood stained the streets.

THE SURVIVAL OF TOM

Kate pulled away from the window, her heart racing, the emotion inside of her threatening to burst out. She knew what she had to do this time. She ran for the door, grasped for the lock, pulled the door towards her and ran down the stairs to the street. The main entrance had been locked from the inside. She pulled the latch and swung it in, kicking the worn makeshift doorstop into place to prevent it slamming shut and locking her out.

She quickly surveyed the carnage outside, people lay dead on the road, some still screamed and tried in vain to drag themselves to safety. The soldiers walked through the street, pausing above the dying to administer the final shot.

She saw a young boy on the other side of the road, he looked like he might have been a student. He was pressed against the wall on the opposite side of the street, his face contorted in fear. He wasn't moving, but she could see he was alive, uninjured for now.

Checking to ensure the soldiers were not looking in her direction, Kate darted across the street, coming to a halt next to the boy. Resting next to him, her eyes darted around. Parked at the top of the road was a black truck, Kate couldn't make out what the red writing down the side said, the chrome bar on the front reflecting the sunlight into her eyes.

"Are you hurt?" she asked forcefully, returning her attention to the boy. He glanced at her, his lip quivering, he shook his head no.

"Come on then, we need to move, they'll kill you if you stay here." The boy just looked at her blankly, she hoped he understood as she took his arm and pulled him from the wall.

She ran, her head down, heading directly for the propped open door of her dorm building, she dragged the boy behind her.

She pushed him through the open door, his momentum carried him to the wall on the far side. He slumped down it and came to rest in a heap on the floor, breathing heavily, his messy brown hair matted to his head with sweat.

Kate glanced back outside, the sounds of shots still thundered through the air. They sounded further away, the soldiers must be at the other end of the street now, wiping out the injured and the stragglers.

She saw movement out the corner of her eye. Swirling around, she gazed at the older lady staggering towards her, using the side of the building for stability as she hobbled slowly forwards. Kate ran to her; she was much older than the rest of the group. For a moment, she wondered where this old lady had come from, how she ended up with the group following the soldiers. She gasped at Kate, her face was gaunt, pain twisted her features. Kate took her arm, then noticed her hand red with blood. The woman grabbed for her leg, holding tightly to her thigh as Kate watched thick red blood oozing around her fingers.

Kate couldn't talk, she could smell the blood in

the air, the death all around her blocking her senses, choking her every instinct and clouding her mind. She grabbed at the woman's arm and started half leading, half dragging her back towards the door leading to the relative safety of the housing within.

As they approached the entrance, the old woman winced with every straggled step. Kate noted the gunfire was becoming more distant, the big green army truck was still parked just meters from the entrance, she knew they would be back. The boy she'd left slumped against the wall remained where he'd fallen, his eyes open but unfocused.

"You," Kate commanded, pointing at him. He looked up, she saw clarity return to his glassy eyes. "Help me, we need to get her inside. Upstairs, quickly," the boy again nodded, but didn't say a word. He hoisted himself off the ground and moved over to Kate, helping to support the older lady from the other side. Kate kicked the door closed, and together they navigated the flights of stairs back to the floor she'd been staying on. She pushed through the door, the other two came crashing behind her, she heard a moan then a whimper as the older lady hit the floor with a sickening thud.

CHAPTER FIVE

Days had turned into weeks, playing house in the textile factory on the edge of the city. The daily routine continued. Tom woke, showered, dressed, then headed to the canteen for breakfast. Kate was always there first, preparing a meagre meal of whatever they had managed to return with the days before.

He sat at the closest long steel table bolted to the floor, Kate walked over and handed him a steaming cup of weak coffee. A large plastic jar of the stuff had been found nestled on one of the near-empty storage racks, it wasn't great, but it was better than nothing.

"Thanks," Tom smiled.

"Sleep well?" she asked kindly.

"Yeah, great thanks." The mattress on the dormitory beds were not the thickest, but he genuinely meant it. Now he was with other people, people who seemed to like him, he slept as well as he had back in the house in the suburbs.

"Listen, Tom," began Kate, she faltered and looked to the ground. "I don't know how long we can stay here; it's getting harder to find anything to eat,

Matt and Rose aren't going to like it, but we need to think about moving on soon."

Tom sighed; she was right. He knew that, and although he was starting to settle comfortably into the routine, he'd always known this could only be temporary.

"Yeah," he replied slowly. "You're right."

A short time later, Rose joined them from her room, she wore a long flowing summer dress, flower patterns running its length, a strip of fabric tied in her hair to hold it back. She always seemed happy, she'd told Tom one night she was just glad to be alive. If Kate hadn't dragged her off the street, her body would have been burnt along with all the others, once they had scraped them off the floor.

Rose still walked with a distinct limp, but her wound had healed, and she was mobile. Tom watched her slowly amble to the kitchen to refill her cup and wondered how they were going to do this. Rose could walk, but she'd never be able to keep it up for long. Their only option would be to slowly head deeper into the city, towards the noises they tried to ignore at night, towards the place they knew there were others holed up. They needed a better plan, Kate was right, they had to leave, but they had to do it right, and they had to do it safely.

Tom had lost one family; he was starting to feel like he'd found another, and he wasn't prepared to let them go. He sat in silence for the rest of the morning, deep in thought, trying to figure out where they should go, how they should get there, and how to keep them all alive. Kate had sat with him for a short time, she tried to engage with him on her ideas, she wanted to head out of the city, find an old farmhouse in the country, maybe even raise cattle. A dream, Tom had scolded her. The countryside was where those godforsaken camps had been built, the dead likely littered the ground like a plague. None of the camps had been created by the coast, there was little to protect them there. Other than the bodies washed ashore with the morning tide, Tom had few glimpses of other human life during his stay traversing the coastline. There were several times he had to dart into the trees, hide behind rocks when he thought he saw or heard another living person. After months of hiding from everyone including himself, he'd gotten quite good at it.

Tom wondered to himself if heading back to the coast was the safest option, but the lack of security and shelter for the four of them made him worry. He had thoughts of fishing off the quay, coming to camp in the morning with a bounty of fish, which would be prepared by Kate over the open fire she would tenderly care for whilst awaiting his return. *Who was dreaming now?* He thought to himself scornfully.

Early that afternoon, Kate came and sat next to him, he hadn't moved much all day, his mind racing at the possibilities and options, finding fault with all of them.

"Okay," he started, without waiting for her to talk. "So, we know we need to move, but we don't know where. We can't go deeper into the city, and there's likely not much left there anyway. We know there are others there and from what you've seen of them, we stay as far clear of that as we can. The country is out, the closest camp is a few miles from here, I don't know if the virus is still active around the world, but that's a sure fire way to find out." He paused to mull over what he'd said.

"We don't know that," Kate protested. "If the virus was still killing, how come we're alive? How come we can hear others in the distance? No, I think it's over, I think it's died out."

"You could be right, I guess. Come to think of it, I haven't seen anyone sick in months, but is the virus really our biggest problem now?"

Tom was thinking not just of anyone left alive, but of what the countless dead and what they must have done to the earth. Their fluids seeping into the soil, contaminating the water, poisoning the land. The flesh slowly rotting from the bones, being picked off by the wildlife, stripped clean and consumed. He pushed the glass of water sat in front of him away.

"How will we get Rose to wherever we go?" he continued. "She wouldn't make the journey, we'll need transport." His mind flashed back to the black truck idling on the road in the village.

"I know," Kate replied. "I tried to take a few cars in the past, but mostly their tanks are empty, people ran them until they dried up. With the fuel rations, it was hard to get any more, I doubt there are many still running. I don't know if the fuel would be any good if they were anyway."

He thought silently to himself.

"You said the university you stayed at had a hospital nearby?"

"That's right," she eyed him suspiciously.

"The fuel was reserved for emergency vehicles, I guess it had an ambulance bay. Plus, with the army on your road, the barracks must have been nearby, maybe there's something there we could use?"

"I don't know," she countered. "Even if there were, that part of town was pretty messed up when we left. The army pulled out, disappeared, whatever. There were some awful people left, I don't know that's a great idea, Tom."

He looked at his hands resting on the table, she was probably right, but what else could they do? They needed to leave, and they needed to go far. The only way to do that was with fuel, and the more he thought it through, the more he thought that was the only place they would find it, assuming there was any left.

The four of them had sat around a single table that night as they talked through the plans. Rose had objected, she was happy and comfortable - why should they leave, they were safe here. Matt had stayed quiet, he didn't talk much. He never left the factory, but he did what was asked of him. Tom was sure he'd help if he was needed.

THE SURVIVAL OF TOM

Eventually, they all agreed begrudgingly that Tom and Kate would head out towards the hospital and survey the situation. They would be careful, it wasn't too far, they should be able to get there and back in a day. They would leave at first light the following morning, carefully snake through the city, using as many back roads as they could to reach the hospital. They would only search around if they were sure it was safe, and they were alone. If nothing was left, they'd try to locate the temporary barracks the army must have set up nearby.

Kate made extra food that night. She put two portions of fried potatoes and onions into plastic containers, placing them at the bottom of a rucksack she was filling with provisions. She emptied the rest into a larger bowl, wrapped the lid with cling film that had been left on the kitchen workbenches and placed it on the metal serving rack the kitchen would once have used before they sent food into the canteen.

They ate quietly in the communal kitchen, no one said much. Kate and Tom were going to leave early the following morning. Hoping that anyone living further in the city would spend the night partying, committing their debauchery and be sleeping through the day. It seemed like the safest option.

Sleep eluded Tom that night, he was terrified of what the following day would bring, he'd only met these three other people in months, was he ready to face more? He wasn't a fighter, he'd never been in a real fight in his life, he'd made it this far by hiding in the shadows, moving silently and staying invisible. He'd also never intentionally walked into the middle of what was likely to be a lawless war zone. A first time for everything though.

He pulled the scratchy covers back as soon as he first noticed the light creeping through the window. His heart raced in his chest, he took several long breaths to try and calm himself. Walking into the long corridor connecting the rooms, he saw the glow of candlelight from the kitchen, the door ajar. Walking into the room, he saw Kate sat at one of the tables, a cold cup of coffee rested in front of her.

"Couldn't sleep?" he asked.

"Not really," she replied. "I don't like this, I know we've got to go, but I really don't want to go back there."

Tom gazed at her; face illuminated by the flickering flame of the candle resting on the table. She looked in thought, memories and emotion trying to burst through. She hadn't told him everything that had happened back at the university. Still, he knew enough to understand how difficult this was going to be for her.

They packed last night's food and a bottle of water each into rucksacks. He watched as Kate took a large knife from the kitchen, wrapped the blade in a cloth and carefully placed it at the top of her bag. She zipped the bag and swung it over her shoulder, picked up the axe and looked to him.

"Ready?"

They left the main gate of the factory car park, the sun was now fully making its ascent over the horizon. The glow of dusk evaporating, giving way to the bright light of the late spring morning. As they walked up the road leading to the centre of the city, Tom noticed how quickly the once manicured grass and flowing bushes, bordering the large houses on this side of town, had become overgrown, weeds growing tall out of the knee-high scrub. The spring had allowed them to prosper, more evidence of nature reclaiming from mankind.

They didn't see anyone else moving on their walk towards the university. Tom was sure he'd seen curtains twitch from one of the townhouses they passed on the short journey, when they had to use the main road to enter the complex. It was mid-morning, the sun burning high in the sky when they stood at the end of the road where Kate had started her journey months before. There were no bodies on the ground, they had been removed. The street appeared abandoned. Fences broken, pulled down or pushed over by the might of the past winter. Doors swung creakily from the entrances to the homes scattered throughout the streets, the glass double doors of the student blocks broken, dragged from their hinges, the elements transforming the building within.

Tom saw watermarks where the rain had lashed against the once pristine decorated walls, the paper slowly unravelling down the wall. Black mould had grown in the corners, broken branches strewn across the floor, carried in on the wind.

They kept walking, Kate came to a stop and glanced to her left, her gaze stopping on the window with the drawn curtains on the second floor, a small crack still visible between them.

"This was home," she said coldly. She glanced around her. Nothing. "This is where we stayed first," she motioned to the ground in front of her. "This is where I first saw one man kill another."

Tom said nothing. He'd seen some sobering sights, but he'd left when the virus was still the worst thing out there, before people became the primary concern. He couldn't imagine being in the middle of this, watching the world end first-hand.

Keeping to the shadow on the building still cast in the shade, they made their way up the road, heading towards the curve in the road Tom could see in front of them. The hospital was half a mile further up, there was no way other than this route to get there. They walked in silence as they listened to their every step resonate from the empty pavement.

They approached the curve in the road. There was nothing around the corner, either. Tom had expected the city to be littered with broken, burnt-out cars, discarded bodies rotting on the ground, like the town he had initially left. They continued their walk, the hospital came into view in the distance, the glass towers dominating the sky the closer they got.

"Okay," Kate started. "There's the hospital. The emergency entrance is off the road, it goes into an underground car park. Hopefully there's something still to be found there."

Tom nodded to show he understood, they were about to enter one of the most dangerous places they could be. The large building provided protection, and Tom was also sure they would be seen long before they saw anyone there. It had also occurred to him that they couldn't be the only ones with this idea, if there was anything left, others were sure to have wanted it too.

They stayed close to the perimeter fence as they slowly made their way to the entrance to the underground car park reserved for staff and ambulances. The red and white barrier was broken. All that was left was a stub of the arm connected to a metal box. The rest of the barrier had been discarded several meters away, the jagged edge where it had broken pointing out the ground menacingly.

Every step they took as they descended into the car park echoed, bouncing around the empty concrete structure with alarming volume. Tom slowed his walk and tried to step as lightly as he could. He could see that this level was empty, there was no cars, no ambulances, and no sign of fuel.

Kate tapped him on the shoulder and pointed towards the ramp descending further into the structure. He nodded as they headed deeper into the dark. The second level was not empty, he could see dust-covered cars sat neatly parked in the bays, a large van parked in the distance. Even here, a layer of sediment and vegetation coated the floor. He heard the small branches cracking under his foot, every noise made his heart beat faster in this chest. Tom walked to one of the parked cars and peered inside. He tried the door, it was locked.

"Over here," Kate called quietly, she was pointing to another ramp leaving this level. The red and white sign above it read, 'EMERGENCY VEHICLE ENTRANCE ONLY', the floor and walls illuminated by the yellow and black zigzags painted to reinforce the message.

"I've been here before," Kate whispered. "But I've never seen what's down here."

He nodded in acknowledgement.

They ducked through the car park and made their way to the ramp, it was getting darker the deeper they travelled, the lights no longer worked, sunlight didn't penetrate this deep. They stopped at the end of the ramp, just before it levelled out to the darkest tier of the complex. Kate peered around the concrete corner, she nodded at Tom, indicating it was clear. They slowly crept into the dark open space; their eyes blinked as they adjusted to the ever-increasing darkness. Tom could see shapes, vehicles, but he couldn't tell what they were. They sat like shadows on a foggy moor, concealed by the dark.

Silently, they approached the closest shape. As they drew closer, they could see it was an ambulance, although clearly not moved in a while. Both tyres on the front of the vehicle were flat, the chrome door handle dull where the dust had settled. Tom peered through the window, no keys, he hadn't expected there to be. He squinted his eyes, looking at the four walls for any sign of an office, a locker where the keys might be stashed away. He caught sight of the glint of clear glass the other side of the concrete box, an eerie shadow extended around what he hoped was a square building hid away in the corner. He indicated to Kate, and they both started to head towards it.

As they got closer, he could see that he'd been right, this was an office in the corner of the car park. The top half filled with glass, the bottom the same soulless concrete that had created the rest of the structure. Tom stopped; the wooden door hung open, it had been forced. Splintered wood protruded from the frame around the lock, a clear indentation where something heavy had been used to force it. He held his hand up to Kate, she glanced at the door and raised her axe to her body, holding it with both hands just in front of her face. She nodded and slowly stepped through the open door.

It was empty, whoever had broken the door had been there a long time ago. The same layer of dust coated the surfaces, metal lockers on the walls had been forced open, their locks bent, doors ripped from their hinges.

Larger equipment lockers stood against the left side of the office, Kate forced one open with the head of the axe, hung inside was a green paramedic uniform. Connected to the chest of the uniforms was a small handheld light, the type where the head could be angled to the user's requirement. Kate removed it from its cotton strap and pushed the switch. A yellow light illuminated the desk in front of her, casting spiralling shadows down the wall where the light hit the items left there months before.

"One positive," she announced as she shone the light around the room, the darkness had been making her anxious. "But I don't think we're going to find anything here, the keys are gone, I guess whoever beat us to it already took them. Or maybe the drivers never returned, maybe they just kept going when they knew it wasn't going to get any better."

Deflated, they looked at each other, the torchlight illuminating their faces, Tom could see disappointment etched on Kate's.

"What about where they fuelled the ambulances from?" Tom offered brightly. "There are still plenty of cars left, I bet we could find one with keys and fuel in the tank if we looked hard enough."

"That was probably the first place whoever else has been here checked. Besides, I don't know what the chances of finding a working car are now, these don't look like they have moved since the country first went into lockdown," Kate said sadly.

She was probably right, they needed something that had been in recent use, he thought back to the black truck from the coastal village. Now he knew the answer to his question, of course he should have nicked it.

They had heard the rumbling of engines in the distance deep in the city some nights, they knew there were still people around, and some of them had what they needed. How would they get it though? He didn't think they would be able to just walk in and take it; he certainly wasn't the type of person who could just walk in and steal from others. Although he wished right now that he was.

He had flashing images of sneaking up behind a faceless figure, sat in a garden chair placed inside a large garage. A broad-shouldered man wearing a black vest, tattoo visible on his arm, sitting with his back to the door. His massive head shaved clean. Striking a metal bar at the back of this head and watching him slump to the floor, taking the ring of keys from his pockets and walking to the black truck sat waiting like his prize in front of the garage door.

Tom was pulled from his thoughts by the sound of glass shattering, a laugh in the distance. A figure stood in the dark, halfway between the office and the ramp leading to the lighter sections of the car park, the silhouette barely visible in the dim glow. The shadow of a baseball bat in their hands resting on the shattered window of the car partially concealing them. Tom couldn't see their face, but he knew the eyes on that face were fixed on them.

CHAPTER SIX

Tom walked through the pale blue front door of his large family home on the outskirts of town. His car engine still hot from his commute home from work. He worked in the city. He spent his days in an office, signing papers, dictating emails, trying to pay attention to the abundance of internet conferences he was obliged to attend. The sun was setting. It was early September, and the days were drawing in. Placing his laptop bag on the oak table positioned against the wall in the hallway, he heard a voice float from the kitchen.

"Hey honey," his beautiful wife called. "I'm just making dinner, it won't be long. I hope you're hungry."

He smiled, at least not all of his life made him miserable. He had a beautiful wife and a newborn baby. A little girl, they had been back from the maternity ward for just a little over six weeks. She'd had to stay in the intensive care unit longer than usual, her lungs hadn't developed properly. They had to be sure she could breathe on her own before being allowed home. As soon as his wife had given birth to their child, doctors and nurses in blue scrubs, masks covering their face had taken her away.

She'd spent the first few weeks of her life in the small plastic box, tubes extending from her nose and mouth. They hadn't been able to touch her, to hold their new daughter, they could only stand and watch her lovingly from the other side of the large plastic window.

A man being pushed past in a hospital bed by porters in a hurry took Tom's attention. The man was lay on the bed, a mask covering his face, oxygen being forced into his lungs. Tom didn't see any sign of movement from him, but the porters were in a hurry, they were clad in masks and long black gloves, plastic visors pulled over their heads. They pushed through the door marked, 'No Entry I.C.U', and were gone.

The doctors had told them their baby would be okay, they just had to be patient. Soon, she would be strong enough to return home with them, and then they could put all of this behind them. He felt anxious as he stood there watching her. She didn't move much, she didn't cry. He knew she was in the best care. The hospital was staffed with the most dedicated and experienced people he'd ever known. He couldn't help feeling helpless as he watched her vulnerable arms move around her head, her eyes still firmly shut. The machines beeped away, giving their little miracle life. Tom and his wife had tried for a child for many years, they were never successful. Eventually they decided to try IVF, the first few rounds were useless, nothing took. After the fourth try, the doctor gave them the news they had been waiting for. It had worked, they were pregnant, after years of trying and failing, they were going to have a child.

He still remembered the feeling of elation inside of himself at this news. They had returned home, unable to wipe the smiles from their faces. That feeling had kept Tom going through the long days, the job he hated, the colleagues he couldn't stand. He was paid well, that's the only reason he stayed, he would have a family to provide for soon. His wife would give up work. Tom had to give up his dreams of leaving his job, starting a new life to do something he didn't find soul-destroying.

He kept a framed picture of his wife and new baby girl on his desk. It was his inspiration to pull through each day, to end the monotony of his working life. He'd find himself looking at it, wishing he was with them both as the voices on the other end of the phone droned on, numbers and figures being banded around, warning of poor performance, targets not being met. He ignored most of this, he was good at his job, if called upon he could usually make something up to show he'd been listening and understood the situation.

He kicked his shoes off and let himself stretch, walking into the large drawing room situated at the front of the house, overlooking the manicured grass of the lush gardens. He meandered to the beaten armchair in the corner of the room and sat down. The room was decorated with floral wallpaper, his wife's request. The colourful red and blue flowers tapering down the walls, the cream plush carpet cushioning every step, the flat-screen television taking pride of place in front of the window.

Tom let out a relaxed sigh as he folded into the chair. He reached for the remote control and pressed the button to power the television. The news was on, it was always on these days.

The reporter was announcing the latest figures of infection of the not yet named virus ravaging the other side of the world. The cases were ever-increasing, but the deaths were seeing daily reductions. This was good, it must be coming to an end.

This is all he'd heard for weeks, this mysterious virus, first mistaken for pneumonia. It had taken hold before local officials knew what it was. Once it had been identified, they had implemented a strict lockdown. They restricted the movement of all their people, confining them to their homes until it could be brought under control.

The news had shown videos of people protesting over the rules. They didn't have any food, or running water, how were they to survive confined to their homes, those that still had homes? Businesses had been forced to close, stock lay unsold on shelves, food rotted in warehouses.

There had been rioting on the streets, police lined up against people dressed in filthy clothing, their faces covered, holding whatever they could find in their hands for protection. People had been killed, the report continued, police had opened fire, killing hundreds in just one protest. There was international outcry, the governments were condemned, nations banded together in their condemnation over the actions taken, and then it went quiet. Things continued as if this had never happened, the reports continued to show the daily figures as they were released, the pictures showed people watching from the apartment windows. Families stood together, their eyes empty as they stared into the lens of the camera.

There had been a few cases reported in neighbouring countries. It wasn't a concern, it was a problem for that part of the world. Tom had full trust this would be over soon. It's what he was being told on the nightly bulletins, and he had no reason to doubt them, yet.

.

A few of his contacts at work had recently gone quiet, those based in countries close to the epicentre. He supposed they had been forced into isolation. There had been plenty of debate on the extreme measure being taken to force people to stay in their homes. Tom suspected they had just fallen foul of the new laws in their home countries. A breaking news banner flashed on the screen; a new case had been reported, the first in the western world, a man had returned from travelling and had fallen ill once he'd arrived home. He'd been quarantined, he was fine, and there was no significant risk to the public, the report had continued. Tom took notice at this, it was quite a progression, he'd been told there was no risk, and yet now there was a confirmed case, here at home.

Thoughts ran through his head. He'd always been quite an anxious person. He'd seen the economic damage the virus had caused abroad. He'd seen the dire consequences to the inhabitants who suddenly found themselves out of work, no way to feed their families. He watched the masses slowly starving through the eye of the camera.

Government intervention had been limited. They had protected their assets, the industrial centres, the big cities and the tourist attractions. Tom couldn't help thinking that the people he saw on the news reports were those forgotten, the poor, the people with no value.

He decided not to allow himself to be too concerned by it. After all, the man had been to an affected country, he'd been found and isolated, the risk of spread here was so small, the hygiene was better, people didn't live in slums, the medical care was superior, it would be fine.

Tom had full trust in this government, why wouldn't he? They lived in a democracy, the government was employed for the people, to decide the best interest of the public. They wouldn't risk a large-scale infection here. If it did happen, they would be able to sort it, he was sure. He had trust that plans laid out to prevent the situation replicating at home would be perfect. He didn't know what they were, he didn't need to – as long as they worked.

Tom let himself believe that the scientists, working hard in their laboratories around the globe, would have this wrapped up long before it could spread further around the world. They would announce a vaccine, a magic bullet to protect the nations that could afford it. They would keep their populations safe while the rest of the world slowly perished, their unseen suffering going unnoticed.

It already happened every day, they had announced that 80,000 had now died, but how many had died in the wars in the Middle East, how many had died in the refugee camps, hastily constructed on boarders, sanitation lacking, disease rife and deadly? How many had died seeking a better life, crossing treacherous seas in the slim hope of salvation promised in the land they could see in the distance.

How many died much closer to home, cold and hungry in their small hostel rooms, frozen by the elements sleeping on park benches or in tents hid in the wasteland. How many died every day on roads? How many were murdered - shot, beaten, stabbed? How many perished around the globe, their bodies slowly shutting down as it ate itself from starvation. Malaria, Ebola, how many succumbed to disease and virus every day of every year? Tens of thousands, maybe many more.

Tom leant back in his chair, letting his mind wander. The thoughts of the suffering around the world played heavily on him. Why should this be any different, why should this take the spotlight away from the other issues that had been prevalent for years, exposing the inequality running through every corner of the globe?

The report ended, the news moved on to other stories closer to home, a farmer being interviewed about low crop yields this year, nothing that interested Tom. He reached for the remote and turned the television off. He looked around the darkening room. The pictures hung on the wall of memories, a skiing trip in central Europe, a long weekend in cities steeped in cultural history, a pyramid in Egypt. Tom holding the leg of a crocodile at some farm in Africa. Tom and his wife had travelled extensively before their marriage. They spent a month in India, a commune for those looking for enlightenment. It wasn't his thing, it was hers. Always trying to please, he went along with it. India had been hot and crowded. He remembered the sweltering days, the never-ending bustle of the overpopulated and cramped cities. He remembered the poverty he'd seen too, the people begging on the streets, limbs missing, unwashed and dressed in donated clothing.

It was his past experiences that made him worry for the current situation; he knew how the poor would be treated, how they would be ignored and left to die. Only the wealthy would be protected. At least here he was sure that support would be equal, no one would be cast aside like trash. Not here.

"Dinner's ready," came the sweet calming voice from the kitchen. "But I'm afraid the bread is store-brought, there was no flour left in the shop, the eggs were gone too."

Tom frowned, shops didn't run out of anything, not here. That was strange.

CHAPTER SEVEN

Kate fumbled for the switch on the torch to extinguish the light that had given their location away. As the darkness returned, Tom saw her dive for the floor, he quickly followed.

"Oh, come on!" came the rasping shout from the middle of the car park. "I'm not gonna hurt you, I just wanna play!" The cackle that followed would haunt Tom's nightmares for a long time to come.

Kate felt around for the axe she'd lent against the wooden table, retrieved it and drew it close to her chest. Tom could hear the man noisily walking towards them, banging the bat off cars as he passed.

"So," The man stopped as he called out. "What can I do for you folk? We don't get many visitin' around these parts no more."

They kept silent.

"I know you're there," he snarled. "Come out, don't make me come in after you." He'd stopped halfway between them and the ramp leading to safety, their only escape.

Kate prodded Tom on the shoulder and pointed to the open door. On her hands and knees, she crawled towards the exit. As soon as she was through the gap where the door had once been, she turned and continued to crawl towards the solid wall on the car park floor. Tom guessed she was trying to flank around the man before he saw them again. The darkness should give them some cover, the only light coming from the ramp entrance above.

Glancing around, he could make out the shadow of the man, still stationary where he'd stopped. His gaze appeared to be on the room they had just left. Tom wondered if the man was alone. He didn't seem confident enough to enter the little office himself. He was waiting for them to come out, that was a good sign, maybe they could sneak away unseen.

"Oi," the man called out again, rapping his bat off the car he'd stopped in front of. "I told you, get out here!"

They were now crawling against the wall adjacent to him. Silently moving, they had nearly passed when he turned. Tom froze, he still couldn't make the man out. He hoped he and Kate couldn't be seen where they were. The man walked back to the ramp, the light reflecting around him. Tom could now see the features of the man who had been screaming at them. This wasn't the picture from his daydreams, the large tattoo-covered muscle-bound man, but rather a wiry man. He was tall and skinny; his greasy hair straggled down from the top of his head. A scraggly beard shrouded his face. His clothes were filthy, Tom could see from where he crouched the many stains that had incorporated into the once grey top the man wore. He briefly thought of himself, back by the beach, he wondered if he'd looked as deranged as this. The man wasn't traditionally menacing, but his neglected appearance, and the wild glint in his eye, made him appear dangerous, Tom didn't want to find out for sure, but this man stood between them and the only escape.

Kate changed her direction and came to rest behind the wheel of a small family saloon car. Resting her back against it, she motioned to Tom to join her. As carefully and slowly as he could, he crawled the distance from the wall to the car, glancing up he saw the man still stood on the ramp, surveying the area in front of him in anticipation.

"We need to get passed him," Kate whispered. "He needs to move."

Tom nodded and motioned for her to stay where she was. He turned and crawled to the next car, keeping low to the shadows. He kept crawling past three more cars. There was now a reasonable distance between himself and Kate, he needed to make the man move, but he had to make sure Kate was safely out of the way first.

He felt around the floor, looking for anything he could use to create a diversion, a rock, a bottle, anything. His hands came up against nothing, there was nothing here he could pick up, nothing he could throw, he'd need to think harder. Continuing his crawl, he was now in the middle of the open space of the concrete building, the cars were sparse here. He prayed he couldn't be seen as he scrambled between them. Kate was still over against the wall, the man still stood in the middle of the ramp, now directly in front of him. He came to rest behind the ambulance with the flat tyres. He held his breath and inhaled deeply, with all the force he could muster, he brought his fist crashing into the bumper of the ambulance, the resounding smash resonating through the echoing acoustics of the car park.

He glanced over the bonnet of the ambulance, looking towards the man blocking their way. The man was frantically looking in the direction of the ambulance; he clearly couldn't see anything that deep in the structure from where he was, but he'd certainly heard it. Tom kept low, the top of his head peering over the ambulance bonnet to provide vantage.

"I heard you, I know you're there," the man called out, his voice high and breaking with excitement. "Let's just make this easy, come out, don't make me come and get you." He paused for a few moments. "Fine, have it your way," he spat. He started to walk towards the sound of the noise. Tom watched as he left the ramp and stalked towards him. Out of the corner of his eye, he saw a glimpse of movement, Kate had made a silent dash for it, he watched her running into the light of the ramp, and she was gone.

He smiled; at least he knew she'd got out. The man was closer now, just a few parking spaces and the ambulance separated him from Tom, he heard his rasping breathing with every step he took. He had the bat in his hand held out to the side, he'd slowed, but he kept coming closer. Tom darted to the rear of the ambulance, hoping he could use the vehicle as a barrier between them, make a run for it when the man checked around the front. He'd lost sight of him, but he could hear him moving. He pressed himself to the back of the ambulance and tried to steady his breathing, listening for any step, any sound to give away the location of the other man.

Tom felt a blinding pain enter his temple. As he fell sideways, he saw only the top of a wooden bat, he was sure he could see his blood on the end of it. His head exploded in pain, he fell heavily against the floor. The shock absorbed the main blow, but just seconds later, he felt it rip through his head. It felt like his head had cracked open, that pieces of bone would be showered all over the car park floor, he imagined parts of his skull and brain would be splattered up the side of the ambulance, that he was now dead. But he wasn't, the pain told him that, he could still think, he could still feel. He knew he was in trouble, but he wasn't dead yet. He forced himself to open his eyes fully and saw his attacker stood above him. The man hadn't moved again, he stood there, watching Tom writhe, the bat resting by his side.

"Said I'd find you," the man smirked. "Where's

the other? I saw two of you in the light."

The man glanced around, as if expecting to see Kate lay on the floor next to Tom.

"You tell me, or you'll not be tellin' anything ever again." The man laughed as he raised the bat threateningly.

The pain throbbed through Tom's head, he tried desperately to clear it, he needed to see through the haze to get himself out of this situation.

Kate had gone, he was on his own, and this man would kill him if he didn't do something soon. Gathering every ounce of strength he could, while the man appeared to be distracted looking for Kate, he raised his right leg off the ground, closed his eyes, and bent his leg back to himself, his knee resting near his chin, then forced all the weight he could manage back into extending it, connecting squarely with the man's knee. Tom felt his foot connect, he felt bone crush under his weight. The pain screamed through his body, he could hear it vibrating in his ears. He opened his eyes and realised the screaming he could hear was coming from the other man, he'd dropped the bat and was now lay on the floor too, clutching his knee, screaming in agony.

"You fuckin' prick," the man cried, his focus back on Tom. His gaze switched between Tom and the bat that lay on the floor between them. Tom made a jump for it. He missed, the other man got there first, using his good leg, he'd dragged himself to the bat lay tantalisingly close, and quickly scurried back. Sitting upright, he focused again on Tom and swung the bat in front of him a few times, connecting with only air. His breathing was laboured, the rage evident in his eyes, he wanted to kill Tom, and he was going to do it if he got the chance.

Tom tried to get to his feet. Stumbling, he fell, his head was swimming badly. The man laughed between groans and edged his way closer.

"That's it, boy, you're done," he spat on the ground as he used the bat to try and right himself, using it as a crutch to support his damaged knee. The next sound Tom heard was a sickening thud, followed by a blood-curdling scream. He didn't know that kind of noise could come out of him. He hadn't known it could have come out of any person.

But it wasn't Tom screaming, and aside from the pain in his head, he had no new injury he could tell. He looked up, Kate stood there, above the man, now writhing on the floor like a dying animal, her red axe sunk into the back of his calf. His jerky movements had made it impossible for her to retrieve the axe. Tom saw his opportunity and leapt forwards, taking hold of the end of the bat discarded on the floor. He turned it in his hands, gripped the handle as tightly as he could, aimed for the man's head, and swung. The blow connected, the force of it shaking the bones in his arms, the man went still. Kate clutched the handle of the axe, put her foot on the back of the man's leg and pulled, with a sickening pop, it came free. She held it in her hands by the handle. Blood dripped from the sharp blade.

Tom could hear only the sound of his heavy breathing, he was panting. His heart was racing so fast in his chest, he thought he might die right here and now from the shock. Kate's voice surprised him, it was calm and collected, the last thing he'd expected in the middle of this carnage.

"Are you okay, Tom?"

She knelt in front of him and inspected the wound on the side of his head. Blood had dripped down his face, he could feel the warmth running over his eye. She took a bottle of water out of her pack and poured it over his face, ripping the sleeve from her shirt, she started to blot away the drying blood.

"That was quite a hit there, Tom, can you see straight?" she asked.

He tried to reply, but no voice came out of his barely moving lips. His head spun and light flashed through his vision. He grunted and nodded his head, even that sent shock waves of pain through his body.

"We need to go," Kate said, the urgency in her voice clear. "We don't know if he was alone."

Tom tried to sit upright, his vision blurred, and he felt sick, falling back to the floor he shook his head.

"Go," he rasped. "Just go."

The last thing he heard before he passed out was Kate laugh as she shook her head. "Not going to happen."

When Tom finally woke, he could feel the comfort of cloth underneath him. His head had been propped onto a rolled up paramedic uniform. As he tried to get his bearings, he realised he was lay on a bed, not a comfortable bed, but a bed. The pain had dulled, there was a slight throbbing in the side of his head, but he felt a lot better than he had.

His eyes slowly adjusted to the dark, he saw the white plastic cladding the room above his head and the walls to the side of him. The plastic cabinets lay open above him, a single chair sat bolted to the floor next to the bed he lay on. He felt claustrophobic, the room was small, it was cramped, and he was the only one in it. He felt the panic threaten to overwhelm him. He took several deep breaths before the realisation hit him, he was inside the ambulance.

He banged as loudly as he could manage on the side, the back doors swung open with the creaking of metal hinges. Kate stood in the entrance; she looked tired, dark circles had appeared under her eyes, her hair sticking out from the usually tight neat ponytail at the back of her head.

"Hey, Tom," she sounded relieved. "Glad to see you're back with us."

"How long..." he started asking weakly.

"A few hours, I guess. Maybe longer." She exhaled. "It's night now, has been for some time, I thought this would be the safest option, with you out cold. Plus, it's about as far as I could drag you, getting you onto the bed wasn't as smooth as I thought it would be!"

"Have you slept; you look like you could do with..." Tom was cut off by a scream in the distance above.

"It started a few hours ago," she said grimly. "No one has been down here that I've seen or heard yet, but it's awful to sit here and listen to. I don't know who's screaming. I'm sure I heard some cries for help, Tom. What are we going to do?"

He looked at her, and felt ashamed. She'd been sat down here, alone and scared, as he slept. The screams were haunting her in the dark. He hauled himself off the bed, his head throbbed, but he kept his balance this time. He stumbled slowly to the back of the ambulance where she stood and put one hand on her shoulder.

"It'll be okay." She looked away. He thought he could hear her crying quietly in the dark.

Tom sat on the step at the back of the ambulance next to her. Her head was down, she didn't look up for a long time. Out here, without the protection of the ambulance walls to shield it, he could hear the horror in the city above. He heard screams carried on the wind. There was laughter, there was crashing, banging. It sounded as if the city had come alive here, at least the worst parts of it had.

"I'm going to take a look," he announced. Kate's face was filled with terror.

"You're kidding, right?" she was shaking her head. "What's wrong with you, can you not hear that?"

"We need to know what we are facing," he replied. "There's no use hiding down here. We might as well try to learn what we can."

"It's dark now," he continued. "They don't know we're here, if we stay quiet and careful, we can watch from the entrance, see what the city looks like at night."

Kate couldn't believe he was honestly suggesting this. Only a few hours prior he had the end of a bat dug into his skull, and that was by someone, she guessed, that avoided the people outside. Why else was he out and about on his own?

She was angry that he'd be so reckless, but she also knew he was probably right. No one knew they were here, it was the best way to try and figure out what they were up against. Thinking back to what happened to her in the building just down the road, she wasn't sure she really wanted to find out.

Eventually and begrudgingly, she agreed. So long as they stayed in the dark and didn't go out into the open, that would have been suicide. She held the axe close to her body; Tom picked up the bat that he'd used on the first man he'd ever killed a few hours ago. He didn't feel anything about that, he'd thought he would. He had thought he'd watch the fire in the man's eyes extinguish every time he closed his eyes. But he saw only darkness.

He didn't feel bad, he didn't feel guilty - he knew the man had deserved it. How quickly he'd accepted it worried him, he'd killed a man, and he didn't care.

Was he changing, was he becoming like the others, more primitive, less human, less civilised?

He chuckled lightly to himself. Where was the civilised Tom when he slept on a beach, eating tinned peaches with his hands, his stench as his only companion?

They silently made their way up the ramp leading to the ground floor of the structure, peering around every corner before venturing any further.

The sounds from outside were becoming louder, more distinct, but they didn't sound as close as the acoustics lower down the structure had made them appear.

Tom stood at the top of the ramp leading to the street, peering his head from the shadows to glimpse the sight outside. It was clear. The noise was crisper now, carried by the wind across the lifeless sky, he couldn't see movement.

Slowly, he edged himself out of concealment, venturing into the road. He kept to the safety of the campus buildings as they crept closer into the city. The brick buildings lined the street, their box-like appearance repeated as far as they could see. They provided some form of cover though, if nothing else. Kate followed behind, keeping in step with Tom, she glanced behind her, it was still clear.

There were no lights these days, the power went out months ago. The generators ran out soon after, the solar the only source left, but there was none of that here. Tom could see the glimmer of fire in the distance. He knew that's where the screams originated from, it was amazing how far sound could travel in the absence of the old hustle and bustle of the once-thriving city.

He continued to walk ahead steadily. As they approached the next side street, he skipped off down it, changing direction so they wouldn't be passing the halls again. Kate was pleased by that. She shuddered every time she thought of them, the less she had to gaze at that window, the better.

They carefully walked past smashed, burnt-out cars, piles of burn furniture, tyres and whatever else had been dragged to join the inferno, through the zigzagging streets.

Tom was struck by the contrast. A few miles across the sprawling skyline, where the textile factory stood, where he had first entered the city, the roads were clear and clean. Here looked similar to the shit hole he had originally left. Apparently, the gangs of reprobates inhabiting here never left the city centre.

They rounded the next corner, and he came to a halt. He thought he'd seen something up ahead. He peered into the darkness, watching, waiting silently. He saw a glint of movement up ahead, there was a man there. Tom could just make out his shape, silhouetted by the moonlight.

He was walking towards the centre of the commotion. He walked as if he had a purpose, he knew where he was going, he walked confidently and without fear. Without thinking, Tom followed him.

Kate ran from behind to catch up.

"Tom," she hissed. "What are you doing?"

He looked back at her in surprise.

"I... I don't know," he hastily whispered back. "But if we want to find out what's going on here, this guy is headed to it."

"Okay," Kate acknowledged. "Just stay back, and let's head in slower. Please."

Tom nodded in agreement and turned back to follow the road. He kept back as Kate had warned, but he walked quick enough to ensure he could keep the man in his sights. They followed the labyrinth of side streets to the centre of the city.

Screams filled the air here, they were clear, they were female, and they were in terror. The glow of the fire was getting closer; the flames licked high, Tom could see them over the top of the buildings between them. The noise was unbearable, screams mixed with laughter. There was still a low-slung row of shops between them, with one street leading through the middle to the source of the commotion.

They stopped as the man they had been following vanished around the corner to join the main crowd. Tom glanced at Kate and saw the terror on her face, he felt guilty for bringing her here. The journey across town had emboldened him. In a short time, he'd gone from hiding like a rat, to running into the most dangerous place he could imagine. He wanted to go further; he wanted to see what was around the corner.

CHAPTER EIGHT

Kate returned from the bathroom with the damp towels she'd tried her best to clean. The blood from Rose's leg had stained them a pale pink. She'd rinsed the worst of it off in the walk-in shower, wringing them dry as best she could. She knew this wasn't ideal, but she had no other choice, she was out of clean linen, everything she could find had been used, and it was all dripping with red blood.

Rose sat in the single chair in the middle of the room. The colour had drained from her face, and she hadn't uttered a word in the past half an hour. She'd lost a lot of blood, Kate was worried, she'd been trying to stem the flow since they returned upstairs to the floor of the building Kate was calling home, she hadn't realised just how bad it was. At least the bullet had gone clean through. There was an apparent exit wound on the back of Rose's leg. Kate wasn't medically trained, but she knew that was good, a bullet lodged inside could have some serious issues down the line, even if she could stop the bleeding.

When they had first returned and Rose was still

speaking, she'd introduced herself, thanked Kate for dragging her off the street and tried to console poor Matt, who was still shaking in the corner. That hadn't lasted long, she lost strength quickly, her voice turned to a whisper and then she was unable to get her words out at all. Kate had tried desperately to make a tourniquet, she'd only seen it on television in action films, she tightly wrapped a belt around Rose's thigh, but she couldn't get it to stay tight. They made it look so easy in the movies, *that was bollocks*, she thought to herself.

The bleeding from the wound was starting to slow, there wasn't as much blood dripping down her leg now, Kate didn't know if this was a good sign or not. Piles of bloody towels lay strewn across the floor, Kate had collected every one she could find. They had done nothing more than absorb copious amounts of blood. She wasn't sure if they were helping or not, she struggled to keep pressure applied with the blood making them slip from her hands.

She took the ones she'd rinsed out and twisted them in her hands, creating a thick rope out of them. Grabbing an old t-shirt, discarded on the sofa, she tightly wrapped it around Rose's leg, covering both wounds, then tied the towels as tightly as she could around them.

She looked down at Rose; it wasn't perfect. It wasn't even good. She needs a doctor. Kate was sure at the very least a wound like this should be stitched, she just had to hope it would heal, and that the bullet had missed the artery.

She headed to the kitchen to wash. The water was still running, although by now the slight cloudiness and sediment had become worse. Kate had a vision of water scooped from a stagnant pool every time she filled a glass.

She watched as the water ran red with the blood being cleansed from her skin, even under her nails were stained red. She scrubbed the best she could until the water ran clear, turning off the tap, she headed to check on Matt. He was in shock, she'd seen this before.

"Matt?" she asked calmly. "How are you doing there, Matt?" He didn't reply or look up. "Okay, come on sweetie, let's get you to a bed, you'll feel better in the morning, I promise."

She took his hand and gently tugged him off the floor, he took some persuading, but eventually he managed to stand and slowly limped to the bedroom she beckoned towards. She led him inside, lay him on the bed and then closed the door, hoping he would sleep.

She returned to the kitchen. The daylight had faded, the only light left illuminating the space she stood in was the reflection from the giant floodlights they still had active at the hospital gates at the far end of the road. The power had been cut off just after the shooting today, she knew it would never come back on.

She walked to the open window, it was getting

colder. She left it open to try and clear the vile stench of blood that choked her every time she inhaled. Glancing at the street, she noted how empty it seemed, she could still see bodies lay where they had fallen, she thought she heard the sound of wild animals moving outside, she had a sickening image of a fox, ribbing flesh from bone down below. She closed the window, pulled the curtains firmly shut and backed away.

Kate rested on the sofa in the living room that night. She wanted to be close to Rose, in case she stirred. She didn't know if she'd last the night, she'd lost a lot of blood, it didn't look good when she added her age to the equation. When she opened her eyes, the room was bathed in dull light, the sun trying to break through the heavy drawn curtains. She must have dozed off. She jumped up and cautiously walked over to Rose, who still sat motionless in the chair in the middle of the room. Kate held her hand in front of her mouth, she could feel her breath. *At least she's not dead*, she thought to herself.

She'd been proud of her actions that day, the lengths she'd gone to in order to save the other two, her chest swelled with pride, if only Rose pulls through. She walked to the bedroom she'd left Matt in the previous night, quietly cracked open the door and peered through, she could see him lay on his side on the bed, fully dressed but his eyes were firmly closed, he was asleep.

She heard the faint sound of music quietly

playing from the headphones around his neck, the phone they were connected to would soon be useless, with no way to recharge it. Closing the door as quietly as she opened it, she let him sleep.

Back in the kitchen, she flicked the kettle on. Nothing happened, she'd forgotten the power had now gone.

The cooker was gas, she suspected that would still work, and she was right, the hob clicked, the flame illuminated as she turned the knob and set about heating a pan of water over the blue flames. It didn't take long for the water to boil, rummaging through the cupboards, she grabbed the white cup she had treasured so much and spooned the instant coffee into the bottom. She added the boiling water from the pan gave it a quick stir. It tasted disgusting, but it was hot and wet, it would do.

"Any chance of a spare cup?" an old and rasping voice came from across the room.

Kate jumped in surprise, spilling half the hot liquid down herself.

"Rose!" she exclaimed. "I'm so glad you're awake. Of course, of course." She rushed to the kitchen and refilled her cup, taking a second for Rose and bringing it carefully back to the chair the older lady still slumped in.

"I'll warn you first, it's gross," she said apologetically.

Rose coughed as she tried to laugh.

"Take it easy, slow and steady," Kate said

soothingly. "How are you feeling?"

"My leg hurts, but I guess I did get shot," she inspected the towels firmly wrapped across her thigh. "You did a good job. Saved my life, thank you, girl."

Kate felt herself blush, she'd been proud of how she'd acted, it was nice for someone else to say the same.

"No, of course. It's nothing, glad you're still with us," she exclaimed cheerily.

"I have no intention of surviving two pandemic outbreaks, only to be killed by a child in an ill-fitting uniform, I'll tell you that for sure!" Her voice was getting stronger with every word she uttered. "How's the other one who was here? I don't see him," she asked, as she glanced around the bare room.

"It's okay, he's sleeping. I think he was in shock. I sent him away last night, I've checked on him this morning, left him sleeping."

"Good call, let him sleep it off, there was enough yesterday to break the best of us." Rose sipped the coffee she had handed her.

"You're right, this is terrible." They both laughed cheerfully.

That morning was the first time Kate felt hope since she'd been left alone in the halls. Matt didn't join them for many hours. They decided to let him sleep, there was nothing to get up for anyway, other than terrible coffee.

Kate had made the three of them breakfast; all

she had left was half a pack of noodles, that would have to do.

When he finally roused, Matt told them that he'd been staying in one of the student blocks just up the road. He, like Kate, had stayed put when everyone else left, but only because his family was so far away, and he wasn't able to get home to them. He was sure someone would come and save him, he thought when he saw the soldiers that day had come.

He told them that when he joined the first group, slowly ambling behind the soldiers, before the man attacked and killed one of them, they had been told they were taking them to a checkpoint in the city where they could be taken to safety. The death had changed all that. Matt reasoned that this must mean there was a place left safe, there must be somewhere all the soldiers are living, the government was rumoured to be still active in the city. Trucks were even seen rolling down the streets then. They must be parked somewhere, refuelled from somewhere. The glint in Matt's eye grew brighter as he talked about this magical rescue as Kate realised, he truly believed it.

"Matt," she started cautiously, followed by a long moments pause. "They shot people, they shot Rose here." Kate gestured to the older lady, sat back in the chair in the centre of the room.

"Yeah..." Matt muttered nervously. "But someone attacked them, they must have thought we were rioting, that we'd try to hurt them."

Kate shook her head. "I don't think it's like that,

I don't think there's anything left. I think they are going to keep it for themselves." She saw Matt's gaze drop, as his face fell.

"Look, I don't want to depress you, I just think you need to consider than no one is coming to help you, you're on your own, like we all are now."

"S'pose," came the sulky reply.

The conversation dropped markedly after that. Matt stopped participating, although he remained in the living room.

Rose agreed with Kate, she had seen clearly, felt clearly that the military was no longer there to be their saviour, she hadn't trusted them since they tried to ship her out to the camps, they had promised would save everyone. Few returned, Rose spoke of several who had managed to escape after the infection took hold inside. It was only rumours, she'd never spoken to anyone directly, but it was heard that the virus took hold inside the camps within days. Some speculated the government set it all up. They rounded everyone inside, knowing there were infected among them, then locked the gate. The perfect way to control the population.

"I was only on that blasted street yesterday because I was forced out of my home," Rose said bitterly. "A few days ago, I guess people got hungry, the governments giving nobody anything, a group of people showed up outside the house. They were breaking into them, seeing what they could steal. I'm not stupid, I know I couldn't stop them, I took what I could and left, hoping they wouldn't notice me. I only made it as far as here, I stayed in the old caretakers' house," she pointed up the road through the wall. "The one at the top of the street, I knew him quite well, I hoped he'd still be there. But he was long gone, left nothing in the house either, tight bastard. When I saw the people passing on the street, despite my misgivings, I figured I'd be safer to join them and... Well, you know the rest."

Kate nodded, she'd been listening intently, she'd wondered how Rose ended up outside her building, hobbling on that shot leg, but something else she'd said rang in her ears.

"Rose," she enquired. "You said you packed up what you could, what did you mean by that?"

"Any food I had left, tins, dried goods, things like that, I took it all," she replied. "But it's out there now," she gestured to the window. "I dropped the bag when the first shots started."

Kate walked over to the window and withdrew her familiar crack between the curtains, she looked out.

"Rose, do you know where you dropped it, what did it look like?" Kate was acutely aware she'd just served up the last morsel of food left that morning.

"I'm not sure. It can't have been long before you found me, it was a red and white carry bag, not too big, I had to carry it myself, but there was enough in it for a few days at least."

Kate scanned the scene below, she couldn't see anything. The angle of her window didn't allow her to see up the road against the buildings where she'd first seen Rose.

She backed away from the window and looked at Rose.

"I'll be right back," she declared, opening the front door and walking through it before the protests hit her ears.

She cautiously walked to the bottom of the stairs, her heart pounding faster the closer she got. She nervously glanced around the deserted street. Patches of red blood stained the ground like oil slicks, she could see the bodies of several people still slumped where they fell the night before, she felt the panic in her chest. She took a deep breath and walked through the double glass doors. She knew the bag must be on her left, that's the direction she found Rose. Carefully, she followed the wall of the building, pushing herself as far into it as she could, looking for the red and white bag Rose had mentioned.

It had to be around here somewhere. If Rose dropped it when she'd first begun to run, then it could be further up, it could still be in the road. *Hopefully, no one else has taken it already*, she thought to herself. She slowly walked further up the street, the sight was terrible, there were more dead than she'd first imagined, she couldn't see this far up from the safety of her window. The bodies lay in the road, bloodstains surround them, patterned across the street. Kate tried not to look at the worst of them, they made her stomach turn, and there wasn't enough food as it was to be leaving the little she'd eaten on the street for the birds.

She walked further up the road, slowly, surveying everything as she passed, they needed this bag. Kate hadn't told the others they had no food, but she'd thought about what she was going to do, her options were to ransack the nearby houses, but she didn't like the idea of that, and highly doubted there would be anything left anyway.

She saw it, tucked near a bush where it had fallen the night before, next to the road, there was the bag. It was precisely like Rose had described. She glanced around her one last time, then dashed from the security and cover of the buildings, ran to the bush and took hold of the strap on the top of the bag. It was heavier than she'd imagined it would be, she hoisted it around her shoulder, turned and ran back to the safety of the block.

Kate returned to the floor a few moments later, sweat dripping from her brow, she suspected from fear, the temperature had dropped dramatically today, and she hadn't run that far. She dropped the bag triumphantly in front of Rose.

"Silly girl," came her thanks. "There's nothing in here worth killing yourself for." Rose was incredulous at the risk she had taken.

"Let's see," Kate teased as she opened the zip. "We've got nothing here, so I'll wager that it was."

She opened the bag and started to empty the contents. Rose really had grabbed anything she thought might be useful, along with anything she could carry by the looks of the stuffed bag in front of her. There was food, boxes of pasta and spaghetti, tins of tomatoes, tuna and beans, a few bags of fresh vegetables and fruits, potatoes, onions, carrots, apples and oranges.

Kate estimated if they were careful, she could spread this well over a week, even for the three of them. It was much better than she'd expected, it'd be nice to have some fresh food again too. She put the food away in the kitchen, then returned to the bag that lay open in front of Rose to examine the rest of the items she'd saved from her home.

There were several photo albums, Rose had laughed when she pulled them out, it's funny what you save in a panic, she'd told her. She instructed Kate to dispose of these. They were only old sentiments, they wouldn't help them now. She'd also picked up a camping stove and several small bottles of refillable propane and a box of unopened firelighters.

"I just used to love the outdoors," Rose told her. "Not that I've been out of my house much recently, even before the outbreak, I didn't really do any of those things anymore, just got too old, I guess."

At the bottom of the bag was a flashlight and several boxes of batteries, Kate couldn't think of anything more perfect right now, after the food of course.

"Do you mind if I take these?" she asked, holding them aloft so Rose could see.

"Help yourself," she replied. "Not much good to me, stuck in this chair."

CHAPTER NINE

Tom motioned to Kate to wait where she stood and slowly crept further up the road. He knew his protection of the night was vanishing quickly, the fire illuminating everything around. Already he could see the glow of the flame bouncing off the road, their reflections clear in the glass shop windows, those that hadn't been smashed.

As he edged closer to the sound of the commotion, he came to the last building before the road veered off to the left, leading to the massive fire he had seen dancing in the sky. Peering his head around the corner, the sight that greeted him made his blood run cold.

There were people, lots of people, milling in the street. Some danced around the fire. Others sat on the pavement, watching. They were filthy; they didn't look like they had washed in a very long time.

Empty liquor bottles lay strewn across the ground, smashed glass littered the floor; Tom silently wondered where the alcohol had come from. As he gazed, mesmerised by the picture in front of his eyes, he counted at least 30 of them, just the ones he could see from this vantage point. They were all men, some large, some little. They all looked to have a wild glint in their eyes, the months of abuse, alcohol, whatever they could find to snort up their noses, inject in their veins, he suspected, had played havoc with their minds.

Several of them sat at the edge of the fire, Tom could see it was a high pile of old furniture, car tyres and whatever else had been ripped down by prying hands for fuel. Those sat closest didn't move much. He wondered if they were just too far gone, or maybe whatever they had forced into their veins that night had rendered them catatonic.

Another man danced in front of the fire, beating his bare chest as he jumped side to side, his ripped jeans covering his legs, bare feet connecting to the ground with every jovial leap.

As he watched the closest man to him pull a half-empty bottle of brown liquid from his coat pocket and drink from it deeply, the screams filled the air once more. He looked around, over by the fire he saw a figure with a dark hood obscuring their face, chains appeared to be attached their wrists and they were being dragged by a man wearing a leather jacket. It was a woman. Tom could see the torn, filthy dress she was wearing, the thin, bony arms, cut into by the heavy shackles of the chains. He noticed the scratches and bruises running the length of her arm, her leg briefly visible as the dressed riled up, he saw the same injuries and cuts, merging into a patchwork of pain, the evidence of the abuse her life had now become.

As she was dragged, she stumbled and fell, hitting the ground with a grunt.

"Up, bitch," he heard the man dragging her scream, he walked over to her and grabbed the hood concealing her face and tugged. Like a rag doll she was hoisted from the floor back to her feet, she fell again. The man aimed a kick into her ribs and Tom heard her cry out, several of the others laughed. The man joined the laughter and dragged her by the chains across the floor. Tom watched her fingers claw at the ground, trying in vain to stop her captor pulling her around to the other side of the fire. Then she was gone. The man had dragged her out of view; only her screams remained.

Tom took a step back, obscuring himself from view, his mind racing. He couldn't believe what he was seeing. His stomach felt heavy, his head light. He spun towards the shopfront next to him and threw up.

He returned to where he'd left Kate. She looked at him expectantly, he shook his head.

"What's going on out there?" she asked quietly.

"You don't want to know," he replied with a grimace. "It's awful, it's... brutal."

"How many?" she inquired.

"I'm not sure, maybe 30? Maybe more."

"What about the screams?"

"They have a woman tied up, I only saw one, but we've heard more. My God, Kate, what the fuck is going on here?"

"What do you mean tied up?"

"Chains on the poor girls' wrists, being pulled around like meat, I don't even want to think about why. Looked like she'd been like that for a while."

Kate's face hardened, she knew that without Rose and Matt, that could have been her.

"What can we do?" she asked sternly.

"I... I don't know. Nothing, I don't think. There's too many of them, although they looked to be out of it. I couldn't see what was around the other side, maybe we could sneak around, get a better look?"

Kate stood in silent thought, the next scream filling the air decided for her.

"Let's go."

They hiked back down the road, looking for a break in the shops, a side street that would bring them out further up the main road, away from the fire. They found what they were looking for, a small alleyway leading between the main road and the one they were on. It looked empty. A large industrial bin sat overturned halfway up, pieces of rusting metal poking out of the open lid. The glow of the firelight didn't reach this far, the alley was bathed in eerie darkness.

They carefully entered the alleyway, treading as lightly as they could, eyes alert for any movement, ears listening for the faintest sound. Tom didn't want to get jumped here, it was narrow and there was only the entrance and exit. If they did meet anyone in front of them, the only way to run would be backwards.

He held up his hand to stop Kate in her tracks, leaning forwards, he whispered: "give me the knife from your bag."

She obliged, he held the handle and pointed the blade forwards, he slowly continued to make his way through the darkness, back towards the main road. At the end of the alleyway, he paused. He slowly glanced up the road to his right, the fire now roaring in the distance, there was still no movement away from its flickering glow.

The road here was flanked on one side by the row of single-story shops and a now overgrown hedgerow the other. It looked like it might lead to a city park. Tom could just about make out the wrought iron fence, the hedgerow pushing its way through it, obscuring most of it from view. There was an opening off to their left, a gate which once would have been one of the entrances to the park. He pointed towards it, Kate nodded in reply, slowly they crept across the road.

He reached the gate first and pushed it open. It creaked as it swung inwards, he held his breath and listened, nothing. He saw no movement in the dim glow of the fire.

The park, like the rest of the city's green spaces, was overgrown, uncared for and unloved. He could see more empty bottles lying discarded in the grass. Holding the large kitchen knife in front of him, he continued into the dark. He wanted to get to the other side of the large hedge separating the road from the park and try to sneak up closer to the fire that way, hoping the hedge would provide some level of cover for them both. As they crept closer back up the road, closer to danger, the noise levels increased again. The screams cut through the air like a knife, it wasn't as muffled as the other voices. Tom paused, it sounded like it could be coming from within the park. He slowed his pace. Creeping closer, the glow from the fire illuminated the back of a man about 20 meters in front of him, knelt on the ground. The girl he'd dragged along the road was writhing on the floor in front of him. He was laughing, the hood had been removed from her head.

Tom could see the cuts and bruises extended all over her face too, clumps of hair seemed to be missing, bloody red welts where it had been pulled out. Kate gasped, she drew her hand to cover her mouth. Tom saw tears sparkling in her eyes in the dim light.

"We've got to do something," she whispered in his ear, her voice cracking under strain. He knew she was right.

"Okay, right," he replied, his heart raced. This wasn't him, he wasn't brave, he wasn't a fighter. But he knew what was right, and this wasn't it.

He let the rucksack slide silently from his shoulder to rest on the floor, crouched as low as he could and ambled forwards towards the man, who was now ripping at the dress with one hand, clumsily trying to remove his clothes with the other.

He was distracted, that was the only thing that kept Tom going. The man was a larger build, he looked about 40, ripped muscles bulging from his tight-fitting top. Tom would be no match for him if he saw his approach. He prayed the man was suitably drunk, or high enough, and too concentrated on the atrocity he was about to commit, to hear any of the tell-tale signs of Tom's approach. The soft crunching on the grass, the heavy breathing he was trying desperately to calm.

Tom held the knife at arm's length; blade pointed towards the back of the man now just feet in front of him. He saw how badly he was shaking, he tried to steady his hand. No good, it just made it worse. The man had removed his top now, Tom could see the white of his skin, the dirt that stained it, the muscles in his back moving as he wrestled with the screaming woman on the ground.

Tom took one last deep breath, then with all the force he could muster, he lunged forwards. He felt the blade slide through flesh and muscle as it entered the man's back. It was not like a knife in butter at all. Tom had expected it to be. It's what he'd always seen in films, read in books. There was resistance as the blade hit the harder parts of the body and came to a halt halfway towards the hilt. The force of the strike caused Tom to fall forwards as the knife stopped, he lost his grip and felt the pain as his hand slid down the exposed part of the blade. He jumped back, the man let out a howl and turned, he was up to his knees now. Beady eyes focused directly on Tom, the anger clearly etched into his face. He let out another great howl, Tom jumped at the primaeval noise as the man swiped at him with his large bear-like hands. As the man pulled forwards towards Tom, he slipped and stumbled, the knife still firmly lodged in his back. Tom jumped over his writhing frame and made a grab for it, he felt his hand reach the handle. Almost lying on top of the man, he took the blade with both hands and twisted it, as hard as he could. The man let out another howl of pain. Tom had to quieten him; if the others heard, they would all be dead long before sunrise.

He forced the man's head to the ground with his boot, he pulled at the knife handle until it came free and then plunged it over and over again into his torso.

The only sound in the air now was the repeated sickening thud of the blade entering flesh as Tom stabbed over and over.

He didn't know how many times he stabbed the blade back into flesh, he kept going once all movement had ceased. He only stopped when Kate rested her hand on his shoulder. Looking at her, he could feel the tears streaming down his face, his mouth open, extorted in an expression of sheer horror. He looked at the lifeless body beneath him and scrambled back to fall off the man, letting himself sink into the grass below.

It was several long moments later before the cloud fogging Tom's mind began to clear, the noise the other side of the hedge returned, they were still laughing and shouting, how had they not heard what had just happened. Were they so used to it, that they no longer paid any notice to the terrible sounds?

As the scene surrounding Tom came back into his focus, he noticed the blood dripping from his hands, stained up his arms, his sleeves dripping small red droplets to the earth.

Kate stood next to him, her head darting left and right, looking for the next threat. The woman still lay on the floor, her eyes glazed, but directed firmly towards Tom.

Her chest rose and fell as she sucked in air. Tom saw just how much trouble she was in. The cuts he observed from a distance were much worse than he could have imagined, her arm had been sliced so deeply, he swore he could see bone when she moved. Her nose was bloody and misshapen, clearly broken, her cheek every shade of blue and red, her left eye so severely damaged only the smallest slither allowed her to see.

Seeing Tom was observing her, she seemed to come back to her senses, the metal chain around her wrists had been removed, deep welts showed where it had dug into her skin as she was dragged across the ground.

She grabbed for the torn dress. Most of it had been entirely ripped off, but she managed to pull just enough to cover herself. Her skinny legs thrashed helplessly against the floor as she tried to stand, she was so weak, he wasn't sure she'd be able to. He offered her his hand, she flinched at the sight and sunk back into the grass.

Kate walked over, she gestured to him to keep a lookout and knelt next to the girl, now shaking on the ground in front of them.

He tried to get to his feet, his legs gave out from under him, and he fell back to the ground with a thump. He could hear his heart pounding in his chest, the blood pulsing through his ears.

Kate glared at him, he tried again. He was steadier this time, forcing every muscle to obey, he managed to clamber to his feet, he was shaking. Of course he was, in just one day he'd already doubled his kill count. He slowly walked a few steps away, looking towards the opening in the hedge where the man must have dragged the woman through. There was another gate, further up the road, just behind the fire. He shuddered, he wanted to get out of here and quickly.

He could hear Kate soothing the girl, whispering in her ear, he couldn't hear what she was saying. It must have worked, several moments later, the girl was on her feet, her arm propped around Kate's shoulder.

Tom took the axe and Kate's pack, retrieved his own and slung one over each shoulder. He wrapped the knife and placed it carefully in the closest bag. Holding the axe against his body, he carefully walked back the way they had come. Kate and the girl following noisily behind him as Kate half helped, half dragged her away.

They reached the iron gate leading back to the road, Tom glanced around one final time before pushing it open. Every squeal from its neglected hinge shot through the night like a scream; he was sure it would give them away. He held it open as Kate continued to lead and drag the girl out of the park. Once they were both through, he let the gate slide slowly back, coming to a rest against the post without a sound.

He looked back up the road, the fire could be seen in the distance again, people still milled around it. He was sure they hadn't known what had happened just the other side of the hedge they danced next to. The light was brighter here. He could see his hands, the familiar sight of blood hardening in the cracks of his skin, congealing under his fingernails.

Tom dashed across the street, aiming for the relative safety of the alleyway, out of sight of any eyes that might happen to glance their way. Kate and the girl made it in just after him, pressing them against the wall with his outstretched arm, he continued to lead the way, checking for any sign of danger as he slowly walked.

The journey back to the textile factory had taken much longer. The girl was in a bad way, she stumbled and fell several times. She couldn't keep up with the pace Tom and Kate had set on the walk into the city. The sun was hovering just over the horizon by the time Tom rapped his knuckles on the steel fire door of the textile factory they had started to call home. Matt took several moments to answer. Tom wondered if he'd been sleeping the other side.

"Thank god," the young man said with clear relief as he opened the door to reveal their faces. Faltering once more, his eyes settled upon the newcomer. Seeing the evident distress of the girl, he didn't say anything more but offered to help carry her inside. The girl had passed out entirely, a limp mass in Kate's arms. Exhaustion maybe, Tom thought. Kate and Matt carried her across the empty floor to the back of the factory and disappeared up the mezzanine floor to the rooms within.

Tom stood at the still open door, watching the sunrise for some time, he wasn't sure how long. The events of the day and night were starting to catch up with him.

He had killed two people in that time, in just 24 hours he'd taken two lives. They deserved it, he told himself solemnly. He let the steel door slam behind him and went to join the others.

Rose had already taken the girl to one of the free dormitory rooms. She needed rest, Rose had announced before she took over the situation. She still walked with a limp, so Kate had helped slowly manoeuvre the girl into the room and onto one of the spare bunks. She'd left Rose there to tend to the issues she could see, she'd had enough of blood for one day.

Tom sat at the steel tables in the kitchen area. Matt had placed a weak cup of coffee in front of him before walking off. He watched the steam rise from the cup and slowly wisp away into nothingness. He heard the chair opposite scrape against the concrete floor, looking up he saw Kate taking a seat directly in front of him.

"So, that went well." She sounded tired.

"Yeah, not exactly what I had in mind." He wondered if he sounded as tired as she did.

"At least we did some good. Rose thinks that girl is going to be okay. We just need to get her strength up. The rest will heal."

He rubbed the side of his head, his wound was still seeping clear liquid and throbbing profusely. The adrenaline of the last few hours must have dulled the pain, but now with only his thoughts to distract him, it hurt like hell.

"I guess we're staying put for a while longer."

"Going to have to," Kate replied, no vehicle and a new mouth to feed. That girl will be in no state to move for weeks, if she ever is. I don't envy what happened to her, but I suppose it's much worse than I could imagine."

Tom yawned.

"I think I need to head." He didn't want to think about it anymore.

"Me too, see you in a few hours."

She stood to leave, walking from the kitchen

towards her room.

Tom drained his coffee, it was cold now. He followed in the direction of Kate, more than anything, he wanted to wash the blood from his pores. He entered the shower, its cold water dripping on his skin like heavy rain, he discarded the clothes he had been wearing, they would never come clean.

He watched the water run red as it danced around his body, washing away the evidence of his actions, of the two people he'd killed.

Tom fell into a deep sleep almost instantly. He was in a meadow. He didn't know where the meadow was, but his wife was there, so was his baby girl.

A picnic set in a clearing in the middle. He was happy. He was truly happy and at peace. The sun felt pleasant on the back of his neck, his freshly pressed shirt collar smelt of lavender. His wife was giggling. Her flowing dress draped over her knees as she sat cross-legged on the blanket, cushioning the floor under her legs.

The baby was lay on her back on the same blanket, cooing softly as butterflies flew overhead, her stumpy outstretched finger grabbing for them unsuccessfully. Something was unsettling. Something wasn't right. He couldn't tell what, he looked around the meadow, it was idyllic, the blue sky and multitude of multicoloured wildflowers, it could have been out of a painting.

His wife spoke, but he didn't hear any words, the sound of a roaring inferno filled his ears, fire. He looked around, spinning on the spot, he couldn't see anything except the butterflies and long grass moving softly with the gentle breeze.

He spun around again, the blanket that his wife and baby had sat on was engulfed in flames, burning brightly, the heat was suddenly unbearable. He ran towards it, but the fire got further away with every step he took. His wife sat there, the flames slowly consuming her, she spoke, yet Tom still didn't hear the words. Her face turned to confusion, and then anger. He could see her mouth open in a scream.

Tom awoke with a gasp. Sweat drenched his body; his knuckles were white where he was gripping the edge of the sheets, his breathing heavy, his heart beating fast in his chest. He lay panting for several long moments, it was just a dream. But there was still something wrong, something he'd missed that he couldn't put his finger on.

Then it hit him, how could he not have seen it, her name was Julia. He'd seen her face. He remembered her name.

CHAPTER TEN

Tom sat in his favoured chair in the sitting room, the television on and the news reports playing out, like they had every day. He wasn't working now, the firm he was employed by had closed, the virus had taken hold of the country, and the government had instigated a total lockdown.

Shopping was restricted to once a week, only essential items were stocked, and even they were becoming harder to come by. Air travel had stopped across the globe, the only planes left in the skies ferried cargo between nations that could still afford to barter.

Across the world, they had reported over 20 million infections, over a million of them here at home. A lot of people had died, but a lot of people had also recovered. The death rate, according to the report still playing absently in the background, was averaging 10%.

That's a lot of death, he thought to himself. But there was good news too; infections were slowing, we're winning, they had decried. Soon, everything would be back to normal.

Tom no longer believed anything he saw in the

reports, the politicians taking the daily questions, statistics and figures being put onto the big screen for all to see. Graphs flashed up in a variety of colours, the arrows showed downward trajectories, proof the battle was being won, people in suits with balding heads would say while pointing to them.

There was even talk of easing the harsh containment measures soon, allowing children back to school, opening business again. He couldn't see it. Even here, in his house on the outskirts of town, he saw the daily queue of ambulances stream up and down the road, many of his neighbours had been carted away in them, he hadn't seen any return.

Julia, his wife of five years, walked into the sitting room.

"I'll make dinner soon," she said kindly. "It's nothing special, we don't have much, the rations haven't come again this week."

He could see the concern on her face, however well she tried to hide it.

"I'm sure they're busy, it'll arrive soon, it'll all be okay," he consoled her. She smiled and left the room.

Tom didn't believe his words. The rations had stopped; he knew that. He hadn't seen the distinctive brown trucks that had been delivering them to the doorstep of every house for weeks.

The independent milkmen still showed up, they were classed as essential workers and were exempt from the sweeping restrictions placed on the general public. They never had enough to go around.

There had been reports of workers being

mugged, killed even, for the products they were due to deliver, just last week in the early hours, a milkman had been stabbed to death. Whoever did it only ran off with three bottles. Someone lost their life for three pints of milk. It made him sick to think of it.

The days were all the same in lockdown, wake, wash, eat, sleep. There was nothing more. The internet and electricity still worked, although the reliability of both was getting steadily worse. Less and less content was updated, there was only so many reruns he could watch.

His baby daughter, Abi, had been home from the hospital for nearly five months, she was a quiet child, she didn't make much fuss and slept through the night. The time had flown by. He was grateful for that, both he and Julia could get a good night sleep. He'd heard the horror stories of parents who had to wake to calm their child every few hours, that was the part he was least looking forward to.

He picked up his phone and looked at the locked screen, hoping for the notification telling him to go back to work, the money was running out. He didn't know what they were going to do if this continued much longer. He hadn't been eligible for any government help, and his employer couldn't afford to continue to pay their workers, they had temporarily laid them all off after the workload dried up.

He sighed, he hoped this would all be over soon,

but there was something about the way the reports were being given, that over joyful tone from the presenters that made him think something wasn't right. If the infection rates were falling as quickly as they claimed they were, why did he still see ambulances screaming up and down the road, the drivers and paramedics dressed head to toe in an assortment of protective equipment. Long gloves pulled to their elbows, gowns and aprons extending down their uniforms, masks and visors concealing their faces?

He'd seen the army the night before, they drove down the neighbourhood, he didn't know why, he supposed they were patrolling. People were starting to become desperate. There had been reports on the news of riots, nowhere Tom could claim to know, but he'd heard rumours they were starting here, too.

People were running out of everything, with no food left to feed their families and no salvation in sight, they had turned increasingly desperate and then increasingly violent.

Reaching for the remote, Tom began his nightly routine of switching the television off, finishing the small glass of whiskey he allowed himself each evening, and then joining Julia and Abi for dinner. Julia had started making the baby food needed for Abi from the meagre assortment of vegetables they had left. She had a few jars in the back of the cupboard, but they were running so low, and with no replacements in sight, she wanted to make sure she could feed the child while they still had vegetables left to pulp.

As they sat down for dinner, a small stew of potatoes and sausage, he heard the rumble of a truck slowly passing the front of the house, the clang of the mailbox as a letter was dropped through. He reached for the letter and noticed the stamp mark had been replaced by the government seal, an official letter.

"Dear Occupant,

In response to the recent viral outbreak and severe negative effect it has had on the economic and humanitarian situation in the country, it is no longer feasible to attempt to contain this menace in our own homes. The government is, therefore, permitting the development of quarantine camps, mandatory for all citizens, with a maximum occupancy of 5000 per camp.

This will allow the authorities to accurately track and prevent the spread and further infection from the virus. This is a temporary measure. All services and amenities will be provided for, while you are resident in the encampments. Details of your allotted camp and designation number will be provided in due course. The camps are expected the take 21 days to become operational, after which point you will be required to report to the duty officer at the camp registration building on the date and time as advised in the follow-up letter.

Please be advised, this is a mandatory relocation programme. Failure to comply will be deemed unlawful and your case will be dealt with by the criminal courts should you not attend as requested.

This is for the safety of all citizens and will help to safeguard our country, and your very future.

WE ARE ALL IN THIS TOGETHER, AND TOGETHER WE WILL GET THROUGH THIS'.

Tom let the paper fall from his hands, watching it slowly float to the table in disbelief.

He looked into Julia's eyes; she had a quizzical expression on her face.

"But I thought they said we were beating it," she stammered. "I don't want to go to a camp in the middle of nowhere, Tom, we have a baby."

Tom looked to his daughter, cooing quietly in the pram pulled close to the table.

"We don't go," he said slowly. "We'll close the door, ignore them if they come, they aren't keeping records on who's where anymore. They don't know we're here, the letters are generic, they're not even addressed. No, we'll stay here."

He barely slept that night, he kept repeating the message over and over in his head, how were they doing this? They were issuing mandatory orders to force everyone into camps! This couldn't be right; it couldn't be legal. He knew things had gotten bad, but to resort to this? There had to be more to this; there had to be something the government was keeping from them.

How could these camps even work, forcing 5000

people into one confined area? They couldn't be sure no infected were let in; it wouldn't be possible. What would they do if someone was infected? Force them out, leave them wondering the wild like a dog, or would they just shoot them on the roadside?

The more he ran the situation over in his head, the more fault he saw with it. The planners must have seen the same flaws. The virus had a long incubation period, it was contagious throughout this period, even when the test returned a negative result. This couldn't work. It could only lead to more death.

For the next three weeks, Tom was on edge. Every time he heard movement outside, he expected the knock on the door, or the letter telling them exactly when and where they were to go, to fall through the mail slot. Their food was becoming increasingly low, the meat had long gone, the dried goods were nearly out, and the vegetables were starting to rot in the fridge. The power flickered off at more constant intervals now, and less than a week after the first letter arrived, the internet cut out.

Three weeks came and went. He heard nothing more about the camps; he heard very little about anything. The news reports had stopped, he flicked the channel on from time to time, but it all appeared to be old reports, showing those familiar graphs where the lines were heading down. He could have sworn one of them had a date stamp, dated over a month before the supposedly live report being played out in front of him.

He started to see some of the neighbours leaving their homes. They had their possessions strewn around them as they slowly ambled past his house. He didn't know if they had received information, or just run out of patience or food and decided to try and find their own way. He had no intention of stopping any of them to ask. He saw Julia less and less, she'd retreated into the bedroom after the official announcement and now barely came out, she stopped eating, although she did make sure the baby was fed each morning, using whatever they had left.

Tom had started exploring through the neighbour's gardens in desperation, they had nothing left, and despite being in the throes of winter, he hoped to find something, anything growing in the barren soil. He did get lucky once, a greenhouse with flowering kale, a few small stems of broccoli, but not enough to keep them all fed, just enough to keep them alive, for now.

He saw less people from his sitting-room window now, since the main exodus after the three weeks were up. He'd noted a few stragglers were leaving, he supposed this is when they too ran out of food and supplies. The trucks hadn't been seen down this part of the city since, either. The milkman had long since stopped his rounds.

The weather was becoming bitter, as winter began to extend its reach across the country, ice started to form on the windows. The power stayed on for an hour a day, if they were lucky. Any heat he managed to inject into the house in this time, the winter sucked it out as soon as things went dark. He'd taken all the blankets he could find, even some from the neighbours' empty houses to place on his bed. The three of them slept underneath them, cocooned in their protection. The days were becoming increasingly difficult, life increasingly miserable. He hadn't managed to find anything for them to eat in days, the gardens were barren, he'd taken to checking inside some of the abandoned houses, feeling guilt wash over him every time he walked uninvited into his neighbours now empty homes. As he suspected, they were bare.

He felt weaker every day. He watched the weight fall off Julia. Soon she was just skin and bone. Abi was faring slightly better. Tom ensured that anything they did manage to turn into food; she got her share first.

He was sat in his chair. Jumper pulled tightly up to his chin to keep the cold out, when Julia entered the room, he was surprised to see her, she'd barely left the bedroom recently.

"Tom," she croaked, tears flowing down her face "It's Abi, she's sick."

He ran from the room to his daughter's bedside, wrapped in the coats and blankets they had stuffed in the crib. She was crying, her cheeks rosy red, her small breath infrequent and staggered. She coughed, fear filled his veins, none of the hospitals were open, most of the doctors were dead.

He'd heard the virus was coming back, possibly worse than before, but he hadn't known for sure. He had to believe, to pray this was something less sinister. Julia was hysterical, tears dripped down from her chin, she whimpered rather than spoke, the helplessness showing on every inch of her face.

He felt his daughter's head. It was hot, very hot, her cries interrupted by tiny coughs. She choked as she tried to swallow between breaths.

He didn't know what to do, the fever was so high, but it was so cold out, should he remove the blankets, or wrap her up to keep her warm? He fetched some water and tried to drip small droplets into her mouth from the end of his fingers, hoping she would be strong enough to pull through. After several long hours, she fell asleep. She coughed a lot in her sleep, but her eyes had closed. She woke several times during the night; every time Tom heard her start to cry again, he felt relieved to know she was still alive. He'd returned to the sitting room, leaving Julia to comfort Abi, there was nothing more he could do.

The light was peeking through the open curtains when Tom woke in his chair. He listened for the telltale sign of a baby's cry; there was nothing. He stood and slowly walked to the stairs, praying to hear the quiet murmuring, the giggling from his daughter he'd become accustomed to. All he heard was the silence.

He walked up the stairs and came to rest at the door of the bedroom, from within the open door he could see Julia, rocking the lifeless form of Abi back and forth in her arms.

He'd cried, he'd screamed and bawled. He'd hit the wall in anger, he'd cursed the government, every deity known to man, none of it helped. Eventually he returned to the bedside where Julia still clung tight to the body of their baby girl. He hadn't tried to take her. He let her sit, gently rocking the child absently, her eyes glazed and soulless.

Julia didn't cry, and she didn't speak, she didn't make a sound, other than the cough that started deep in her chest by mid-morning. Tom cried again. His wife never once complained, she didn't acknowledge it, she just sat there coughing. She declined the glass of water he brought her at midday. He came back to see if she'd drunk from it an hour later. She was dead, the baby still firmly clutched in her arms.

He was lost, he felt empty, his life had lost all meaning in a little over 12 hours. He sat in his chair and waited for the cough to start. It didn't, he felt fine. This outraged him further, it wasn't fair, why should he be okay, while his family have to die like this? Where did they even get it from, they hadn't left the house. He'd later felt the guilt creep into him. Only he had left the house; only he could have introduced the virus to them. Many months later he'd decided that he must be somehow immune, asymptomatic, he guessed some people must be, or everyone would have been dead by now.

By the following day, he knew he'd have to bury his wife and daughter and say goodbye for the final time. The ground was frozen solid. He tried to dig through it, not even managing to break the surface. In the end, he'd had to settle for wrapping them together in a sheet, he tied cord tightly around it, and carried them both into the garden. Collecting anything he could find, he began to cover the bodies with stones, foliage, the branches from the evergreen trees that surrounded the neighbourhood.

He stood in the garden, his gaze fixed upon the mound he'd created as their shrine, tears rolled down his face. This wasn't a fitting end for them, but it was the best he could do.

A knock on the door made him jump. He hadn't heard anyone walk up the overgrown garden path, he hadn't heard the trucks rolling down the street. The man in the green military uniform, respirator mask securely tightened on his face had explained in a muffled voice that the camps had failed. The one meant to house this part of the city had never been built. Too many had been lost at the first ones to accommodate people, that the plan had been scrapped. The virus had mutated, and people were now falling in just hours. Tom already knew that. He'd seen it. The man continued to tell him that there was now an excess of accommodation further in the city and they were to move everyone there.

He'd have power and protection. Food parcels were still being delivered there. They needed to limit the scale of distance between the population now. To ensure they could keep everyone safe, keep everyone fed. The focus had shifted to containment. Tom didn't argue, he nodded and followed the man out the door, closing it behind him with a final glance to the garden where his family lay, cold and alone, their faces already melting into nothingness in the back of his mind.

CHAPTER ELEVEN

Tom wasn't sure if the sight of his dead wife's face in his imagination was a comfort, or a sign his mind was finally breaking for good. He was pleased he could remember her, remember his baby girl too, but the sadness that filled his heart threatened to consume him. He headed for the showers, wiping the last of the sweat from his brow.

As he passed through the corridor within the textile factory, he heard talking. Hushed, calm whispers coming from the room they had placed the girl into last night. Quietly, he stopped at the closed door and lightly knocked. Kate appeared; she opened the door just enough for her face to be visible through the crack.

"Not a good time," she whispered. "She's awake. Her names Chloe, but she's in quite a state. Rose and I have been trying to clean her up, calm her down, sorry if it woke you,"

Dark circles under her eyes gave away the truth that she hadn't slept that night.

"No," Tom replied kindly. "That's not it, I just wanted to check everything was okay. I was going to take a shower, then I'll look to set some breakfast, come join when you are ready, all of you."

"Thanks, Tom. Maybe we can tempt her out with food."

He wasn't sure if she was joking as the door silently creaked closed.

After he had showered and changed, he entered the kitchen. It was cold this morning. Usually by the time he got here, Kate had the stove on, the coffee was made and the heat from cooking had warmed the room through.

He searched through the cupboard, finding a pan large enough to boil the water. He pulled it down and headed to the sink to fill it. The water gushed out as he turned the tap. The water here was supplied by a rain collection system on the roof, gravity fed into the pipes that guided it to the taps. Tom was grateful for it, but it was another reason they had to leave, the summer would dry it out, replenishment would not be easy.

As the water boiled above the flame, Tom started to search the kitchen for something he could make into breakfast. He knew there were potatoes here. Kate had found several sacks of them when they first broke in, stashed at the back of one of the long storerooms. He was also aware that Kate had been taking the spring crops from a nearby allotment, so there should be some fresh vegetables around, with a bit of luck. He wondered if they might be able to find chickens, fresh eggs for breakfast would be a treat. Where would they find chickens though?

Anyone who kept them in these parts would have been sure to have eaten them a long time ago.

Maybe in the country though, some farmhouse somewhere, the occupants fled, or long dead. Far enough away from any of the failed camps, possibly there would still be chickens there, crops, freshwater. Kate's idea didn't sound too bad now. Maybe there was solar power; perhaps they could start a new life in the country. He was brought back to earth by the sound of the water boiling over the pan. He turned the heat down and let it simmer.

He poured himself a cup of weak coffee and set about peeling a handful of potatoes. He'd decided on the usual, fried potatoes and onions for breakfast. There was still most of the sack remaining, the cold and dark of the storage room had kept them edible.

He tried to replicate the spices Kate expertly used, it didn't quite smell the same, but he figured it'd do.

A short while later, he heard the door click. Rose stood in the entrance, Kate followed behind, helping an emancipated looking Chloe hobble into the room. Matt wouldn't be up for a while yet; he was not one for mornings.

Tom finished the dish he was preparing and transferred the contents into a large serving dish. Grabbing three empty porcelain bowls and forks, he set it all at the closest steel table and returned to pour some more coffee as the others sat. He placed a cup in front of each of them; Chloe gave him the slightest smile as she accepted the cup of steaming liquid then looked away. He didn't want to start the conversation, so he sat in silence on the corner seat at the table.

"Chloe here," Kate said. "Managed to tell us this morning that she too was a student, before all of this. Apparently, she was out on the road when the soldiers started shooting, she made it into another of the blocks and stayed hidden there for as long as she could."

She took a swig of the coffee from the table in front of her.

"She had nothing to eat, and when the water stopped, she had to go back outside. She ran into the group we met the other night." She looked sideways at Tom. "She's been kept captive by them since. We won't go into the details, but she'd like you to know Tom, she's very grateful for what you did."

He smiled. He could still smell the blood on his hands.

Kate offered to help him wash up once they had finished eating. Chloe had helped herself to a second portion at Kate's insistence; there wasn't anything left for Matt.

"She was a mess, Tom" Kate whispered as she filled the sink with cold water. "They kept her tied up, barely fed her. They raped her daily, all of them. And she wasn't alone, there's another two girls they had tied up there by the fire. She doesn't think they will make their lives any easier now we killed one of them and she's escaped, they might already be dead."

"How many of them are there?" he inquired.

"She thinks about 20 of the main group, others join them from time to time, but they stay in one place until there's nothing left, then move on. Most of the ones not part of their core are smart enough to make themselves disappear before the food runs out. They don't share well when things are tight. There's a network being set up in the city, all under the control of one man. She won't talk about him. If he's worse than the rest... God, Tom, I don't want to think about that."

Tom mulled this over as he washed the pan out and placed it on the drying rack. He'd seen a lot more than 20 of them, but maybe he could use that to his advantage. That meant the rest were just stragglers, like him, trying to fit in. It should be easy enough to turn them against each other.

He was thinking of the other girls, he desperately wanted to try and save them too, but even with just the 20, he was no match for them, what could he do? Maybe he could find a way to turn them on each other, then sneak in and free the other girls whilst they were distracted between themselves?

What had happened to him? He was trying to concoct these elaborate plans to rescue the damsels in distress from gangs of degenerates. How long ago was he on that beach, vowing to live his solitary life, and now he was breaking every rule he'd ever set for himself.

The thought of the young girls being held by these men though, it brought back the image of his own dead daughter's face. These girls are someone's daughter too, and he had to do something. They needed a plan, but first, he needed to know more. He hoped Chloe would talk.

He played over the best way to approach this in his head. Chloe clearly could now talk, and she remembered everything. But it was clear she didn't want to talk to Tom. Was it because of what she'd seen him do, or just because he was male? Either way, he'd have to try.

Rose hadn't left Chloe's side all day, he didn't want to push it with her there, she could snap, and he knew she would never let him question Chloe if she thought it might upset her.

Rose and Chloe were sat, quietly talking on one of the steel canteen tables. Tom saw his opportunity when Kate left the kitchen to shower. He walked over to the occupied table.

"Hey, Rose, could you do me a favour? I've just made some extra breakfast up for Matt. Could you go and wake him for me, you know he's better when you get him up rather than me?"

Rose looked at him; he swore he could see suspicion in her eyes.

"Don't worry, I'll keep an eye on Chloe here, it'll only be a moment."

Rose stood shakily from her chair and walked towards the corridor of the dorms without a word. Tom sat on her vacated seat, he had to be quick, before Chloe might break down, or before Rose returned and berated him for the questions.

"Chloe, look, I am sorry. I know it's hard, but I want to try and save your friends, and I need your help to do it."

She gazed down.

"You don't need to go back there. I just need to ask some questions. I need to know where they stay, where the girls are kept. Where they sleep, can you tell me that, Chloe, to help them?" He paused, Chloe looked at him, she gulped, he thought he saw her stifle a tear, then she told him everything he needed to know.

Rose had returned, and as expected, she viciously berated him for the barrage of question. She wasn't ready to talk yet, Rose had fired at him venomously. Matt was just upset there was no breakfast for him, he'd been dragged out of bed early for nothing.

Chloe had told him the fire he'd taken her from that night had been burning for days; they kept adding to it. They'd been in that area for a few weeks now, maybe longer, she wasn't sure. They hadn't come from too far before that, the other side of the city.

The de-facto leader was a man called Chester. He was a nasty piece of work, he didn't drink like the rest of them, he preferred to watch over everything with a sober mind. He'd been in the city since the beginning, she didn't know where. He'd set about recruiting the others once the army vanished, using them to loot supplies, food, water, women.

Chester had killed plenty of people that she'd seen, even a few of his own when he was in a bad mood. She'd been taken by him and a few of the others before he had full control of the city. They had seen her out looking for food, dragged her down the street and she'd been kept prisoner by them since. She'd been hiding in one of the blocks alone for a while before that. She'd been able to find food in the university bar, the alcohol had all gone, but no one had checked the small store cupboard under the floor. It's where they had stored the non-perishables for the bar snacks they offered to students. This had run out eventually though.

When she first saw Chester and the others, she thought they would help her, rescue her. They had done no such thing.

They already had one girl tied up when they took her, Chloe didn't know much about her, they weren't allowed to talk. Chester would beat them viciously when they did. The other girl had been captured more recently, he had found her in a nearby village outside the city.

Chester had seen movement in one of the houses on the outskirts, and when he went to check it out, she was trying to hide in a wardrobe. He forced her into his truck and brought her back here.

He had a black truck, with red writing down the side, chrome bull bars attached to the front.

Tom shuddered, was it possible it was his fault one of the girls had been taken? Had Chester seen him and by pure coincidence, she was hiding in the very next house? That black truck, Tom remembered reading the wording down its side, a landscaping company.

The story Chloe had told him vindicated his decision to run that day, otherwise he probably wouldn't be here today to try and make up for it. Chloe told him Chester had a rifle, he didn't use it often, preferring to use his fists. He'd taken it from a dead soldier during one of the riots. That could complicate things. Tom had hoped to use the day when they slept off their hangovers to quietly sneak in unseen and cut the other girls free. A sober and dangerous Chester would mean he needed a new plan. Although that truck of his did sound tempting right now.

He needed to speak to Kate, he wasn't sure he could do this at all. But he was sure he couldn't do it without her. A kitchen knife and an axe were going to be little help if Chester still did have that rifle.

Maybe they could find their own, there were plenty of armed soldiers towards the end, there must be something left. Tom didn't know how to use a gun, even if he did find one, he doubted it'd be beneficial to him. No, he had to think smarter, he'd stayed alive this long by trying to outsmart other survivors, he could do it again.

Tom and Kate sat around one of the tables,

they seemed to spend most of their time in the old canteen. There was a small break room, furnished with a single sofa at the very end of the corridor, but with the power off, it had no window to the outside world and constantly remained in darkness.

"They could already be dead, probably are," Kate countered, they had been arguing for the past half an hour over Tom's plan.

"Could be, sure. But might not be. I thought you of all people would want to find out. Look at Chloe, look at what they did to her. Surely we need to check?"

"And say they are, how are we going to get them out? You're now some kind of hero I take it, ride in on your white horse, kill them all and rescue the girl, right?"

"I'd rather not kill anyone. If we plan this right, we can get them out without anyone knowing we were there. It can work, Kate."

"And then? What happens next, this Chester guy just finds some more poor girls, takes them, do we rescue them too?"

Tom was surprised by her objections to the plan, he was sure she'd help. He was sure she'd want to, she'd seen what these men were doing.

"I just... Tom, I don't think there's anything we can do, and even if we can, it' a never-ending cycle, they'll just take more, hurt more. It won't stop, Tom."

Tom exhaled, she wasn't seeing his point. There was something they could do right now, they didn't need to worry about what happened next, as long as they tried today. He decided to change his approach.

"Okay, so we went out looking for a vehicle, right? We know this guy had one, so we go for that. If we can rescue the girls, then we do."

Kate frowned. "We do need a vehicle, especially now with Chloe, she's still pretty banged up. The more I think about it, the less I want to be in the same city as the men we saw. It's only a matter of time before they find us." She paused for thought. "Okay, fine. We'll go tomorrow morning, we're after that truck, anything else is a bonus. Just you and I, we use the main route we took, and we get out of there as soon as possible. We have everyone ready to go here so we can drive back, load up and be gone. You just need to think of where we are going."

Tom's survival mission had now become a rescue mission.

"There's something I need to tell you first though..." she whispered.

CHAPTER TWELVE

With the food recovered from Rose's bag, Kate figured they could stretch out another two or three weeks here. Hopefully, long enough for Rose's wound to heal enough to allow her to move. She hadn't had much mobility in the few days she'd been in the student accommodation. The injury was healing slowly, it looks looked red and sore. She saw Rose wince when she tried to sit.

All things considered, the three of them were doing quite well. They hadn't seen any movement on the street below, the army hadn't been since. Kate tried her best to keep everyone's spirits up. Matt still wasn't talking much, but he was accepting food, and Rose made up for both. She loved to talk. Rose spent the entire evening reminiscing about memories past, recalling stories from her youth, her travels in Mongolia, living in a Yurt for a year, her trek through Alaska, she even walked the length of the Nile in Africa.

She really was an interesting woman, thought Kate, it's a shame they met in the situation they did. Kate liked to hear her stories; they kept her mind away from the hopeless situation outside.

THE SURVIVAL OF TOM

Occasionally, Matt even sat with them and listened in, he didn't offer any comments, but the stories seemed to help him too.

Kate had learned a lot about Rose, but she didn't know much about Matt, only that he wanted to go home. Home was a long way, and he had no way to get there. He'd stayed in the accommodation provided by the university since the end of the summer. It was the first time he'd been away from home; Kate didn't think he liked it very much. He didn't speak of any friends he'd made here, she could relate to that, but she was older than the rest. Matt was their age.

He was 19, he'd taken a year out of education to travel the world, he'd spent a summer in Australia, Kate didn't think by the sounds of it he'd enjoyed that very much either. He didn't tell her what he'd done there, she didn't even know what he was meant to be studying, every time home came up in the conversation, he shut down.

Rose had better luck with him, he seemed to like talking to her, maybe it was due to the age gap, Kate thought. Part of her hoped so, either that or she just wasn't very approachable.

As Rose still couldn't move far, and Matt was a self-confessed terrible cook, Kate took to preparing the meals each day. She made it as varied as she could, but the options were limited.

It didn't matter, all three of them had felt the pain of hunger recently, any food was better than nothing. The company was also a necessity Kate hadn't realised she needed, she'd spent so long alone, to have the others, even when they didn't speak, it was wonderful. She didn't feel alone any longer.

Rose's leg healed more every day. After three days she was able to take short walks from the chair she'd been confined to, making it as far as the kitchen to wash up her mug. She was overjoyed at this, it seemed simple, but it's the little things that kept people going in these times.

It had been five days since Kate had seen or heard anyone down on the street below, a middle-aged woman, wrapped in a thick scarf, navigating the obstacles left in her path. Kate thought about calling out to her, inviting her in, but she didn't know who she was, or if she was alone. Besides, they didn't have enough food for the three of them, they could seldom afford another mouth to feed. Kate watched her walk up the road and disappear out of view where it snaked around the corner. No one passed after this.

Kate had let herself believe the city was now empty, its inhabitants dead or evacuated, headed to those camps which sounded so awful. The window was firmly closed. The smell from the street had been getting steadily worse, the decomposing bodies left to rot. She was continuing her usual morning routine, she'd made breakfast and was now washing up with the cold water. Matt had returned to the room he'd been allocated, Rose sat thinking in the chair when she heard the noise. It sounded like an earthquake after the week of isolation and silence, she dashed to the window and peered through the crack in the curtains, she heard the faraway hum of an engine, voices shouting over each other, her heart racing, she froze, watched and waited.

After a few moments, the front of a white rubbish truck came into view, the driver wearing a face mask and bright orange high visibility jacket. The emblem of the city council adhered down the side of the vehicle, the men working at the rear dressed alike in blue tracksuit bottoms and jumpers, the same orange jacket slung over their shoulders. Kate felt a strange sense of déjà vu. This exact scene had played out earlier in the outbreak, when the roads had been cleared after the first exodus. Although there weren't as many bodies to collect that time. The workers meticulously collected the discarded possessions strewn across the road and threw them into the back of the truck, the mechanical jaws doing their job and compacting it to mulch. They picked up possessions and bodies alike, two of them hoisting the dead by the legs and arms, unceremoniously tossing them into the back of the truck to be compacted with the rest of the rubbish. Kate watched in horror as she heard bones break under the force of the jaws, the men didn't appear affected by the sickening sound, perhaps they were used to it by now.

Following close behind was a smaller vehicle, the size of a large van with a transparent plastic tank attached to the back. Another man dressed in the same blue, with the same orange jacket, walked alongside the truck with a hose in hand, Kate realised he was washing the blood from the road.

She couldn't believe what she was seeing, the city was silent and here were sanitary workers cleaning the streets. Something was very wrong here.

Once they finished their work, they drove on to repeat the same actions further into the city. Kate watched from the window, nothing but the crows picking through what was left could be seen outside. Several hours later, she again heard the distinct hum of another engine roaring in the distance. It sounded different, not like the trucks that had rolled in front of her window. Dashing back to the crack in the curtains, she took her position, she watched and waited. A black car came speeding up the road, an executive saloon style car. Tinted glass blocking any hope of seeing who was inside. She noticed on the side of the car the same city emblem that she'd seen on the truck hours earlier. Could it be? Was this a government car? Was the government still alive, still in charge? Her mind raced with possibilities, who was this, why was the road cleared for them, who was coordinating all this and why hadn't they made anything public? The car stopped at the top of the road, its brakes squealing as it slammed to a halt.

Kate adjusted the curtain to get a better view.

Parked in front of the car was a black truck, engine running, it looked familiar. A man got out and knocked twice on the window of the vehicle, the tinted glass descended. She couldn't see from here who was inside. There appeared to be a conversation going on, then a package was passed from the car, the man took it, nodded his head and returned to his truck. Without another glance, he drove down the road towards Kate, she watched silently as the truck continued, increasing speed until it too veered out of view.

Kate didn't understand what she'd just seen. The meeting appeared planned, it wasn't a robbery, no one was hurt or killed. It was a transaction, between the government, wherever they may be, and the man she now suspected had caused the trouble on the street the week before. She wondered, was it all a setup? A reason to shoot down all those innocent people.

She wanted to know where the car had been going. The road it followed led onto the university hospital and campus grounds, the government had been holed up the other side of town, so she thought.

Rose was sleeping in the chair. Hoping she wouldn't wake her, Kate crept out the room as quietly as she could and headed for the street.

She made her way up the road as fast as she dared, keeping as close to the front of the building as she could, listening for any tell-tale sign of movement, engines in the distance, twigs breaking underfoot, breath on the back of her neck.

The removal of the debris and bodies made the journey easier, she wanted to know where that car had gone and who was in it. It couldn't have gone far, the hospital would have been visible from the end of the road where it veered off to the right. If she could make it there, she might be able to work out just what was going on.

She reached the bend in the road and peered into the distance; there was nothing. She didn't know what she'd expected. A car parked outside the hospital perhaps, people stood around, talking, spilling all their secrets to the open air?

She continued her route, she had to find out. She had to know who was in charge, what their plans were. She halted outside the main entrance to the hospital, where the road continued straight to the university complex, or snaked left into the car park. There were several tiers to the car park, one route went underground, the other to the multi-storey car park. It looked abandoned, the red and white barrier stood in place, she doubted it would move without power, it hadn't been used for a very long time.

The underground car park was reserved for hospital vehicles and staff, the barrier here had been broken off. Only a stub of it remained, it looked like someone had driven through it at speed, in something big.

Kate steadied herself and ambled towards the darkness. She kept to the shadows and crept as quickly as she would allow herself, keeping her breathing steady and her body pressed to the wall of the underground structure. She heard whispers in the air, a conversation from afar. She tried to pinpoint where it was coming from, but the acoustics of the structure made that impossible. The voice echoed around like a pinball, it could have come from anywhere. There was only one other option, there was a ramp leading down the ambulance bay, she thought she could see a faint light down there. There didn't seem to be any pedestrian access, just the ramp. Its walls scraped, the yellow paint from the ambulance bumpers dug into deep crevices.

She approached the top of the ramp cautiously and peered into the dim cavity below. There was light, she didn't know what from, but something was down there. She crept further down, conscious of her every footstep on the concrete ground. There wasn't much down there, a few cars parked neatly, they looked like they had been abandoned there for some time, an ambulance stood solitary in the centre, Kate supposed the rest had been left in the city, themselves abandoned when the driver became sick, or fled out of fear.

Just beyond the ambulance, the car she saw speed down the road earlier that day was parked, its headlights illuminating the structure. It was facing the grey wall, the side of the car to her and the ramp, the lights flickered off the grey concrete walls, she couldn't make anything else out. As she sneaked closer, the voices became audible.

"Why are we working with that degenerate?" a man in a pinstripe blue suit asked sharply. She couldn't see who he was talking to. "I can't believe we see this as the best option, give the city up to scum, let them clear it out, their way?"

"Because," came the reply, a female voice, she sounded older. "They don't cost us anything, and there's no risk. Let them clear this god-forsaken place, if we get lucky, they'll get themselves killed in the process. Heavens knows I don't want them left running around when we're ready to return."

Kate didn't understand, who was this and what were they implying? Why were they down in this parking structure, who were they waiting for? The sound of another droning engine made her jump. Glancing over her shoulder, she saw the headlights of a vehicle headed towards the ramp she was hiding at the bottom of. She dived for cover, hoping the running engine would cover any sound she made. She tucked herself behind one of the dust-covered parked cars, concealing her from both the parked car at the far end and the oncoming vehicle. She steadied her breath, her heart raced in her chest. The second vehicle appeared at the foot of the ramp, it was a car identical to the first. The same tinted windows, the same emblem down the door. It came to a halt in the space two over from the first, the engine cut out, Kate heard the door open and then slam closed.

"Is it done?" a voice asked. A man, Kate

recognised the voice, but she couldn't place it.

"Yes, Sir" the woman replied. Kate stood in horror, this was the leader of the country, meeting another official in a dark underground car park.

"Good," he said. "We'll let Chester think he's running things here. We'll deal with him on our return, did he take the package?"

"Yes, he was delighted, there was enough cocaine in there to keep half the city high for the rest of the year."

"That we may need to do," the man in charge replied. "Now come along, the plane leaves in an hour and trust me, you want to be on it"

The man in the blue pinstripe suit spoke up. "Sir, if I may ask, how bad is it, the second wave? I know it's tearing through every urban area, but what's the prediction?"

"We don't expect more than about 10% of the population to make it through this, and we don't want to be around when they figure this out. Most have already perished in the camps, that saved us some hassle, but the rest will not be happy when it passes."

Kate heard two doors slam, the sound of engines igniting and the squeal of tyres as both cars pulled off up the ramp and out of view.

She didn't know what she'd just heard, but she thought about it a lot in the weeks that followed. The government had just sold its people out and run for the hills.

She returned to the main road and headed back towards the accommodation block. She was trying to process everything she'd heard. She wasn't paying attention, she wasn't careful enough.

The first she heard of the men behind her was one of them stumbling on the pavement. His toe must have caught the edge. Glancing behind, she saw three men lurking further up the road, her blood ran cold. They were all staring at her, a deranged look in their eyes. All three appeared dirty, fanatical. A small evil smile drew across the face of the one in front. He couldn't have been much older than Kate, there was still youthfulness to him, his eyes a dull shade of grey, the stubble growing out of his chin casting a shadow on his face.

She marched forward as brisk as she could without running. *Don't run*, she told herself, *don't look like prey*. The building was only a few hundred meters in front of her, she could see the entrance in the distance. If she could get there, she could try to lock them out, it might buy her some time. She glanced over her shoulder; they were following at the same pace. As she got closer, she picked up speed. When she could see the entrance doors, she broke into a run, her lungs bursting with effort. The sounds of footsteps on the pavement told her they had done the same.

She reached the entrance to the accommodation just moments before them, she threw herself through the door and made for the stairs. She could hear them just behind as she ran up the stairs, taking them two at a time. Dashing towards the door she'd left slightly ajar for her return, she forced herself through with all the speed she could manage. As she turned to slam it shut, the head of a red fire axe wedged in the small gap before the latch clicked, she felt the owner the other side of the door readying his weight. With a swift shove, he forced the door wide open. Kate was flung aside as the force from the door hit her, she stumbled and fell to the floor. The three men burst in, hunger in their eyes, she wished she hadn't guessed what for.

She glanced behind her, Rose wasn't in the chair in the middle of the room, she couldn't see either of them. Hopefully, they had the sense to hide and stay hidden.

The men approached her, the closest glared at her, with the grin on his face becoming wilder the closer he got. He had the red axe in his left hand, the handle resting over his shoulder, the blade pointed menacingly at her. He hadn't spoken a word, he just fixated on her, that wild grin becoming more menacing with every silent step he took. Kate could feel the sweat beading on her forehead, the fear paralysed her to the floor where she lay. The man was licking his lips, his eyes looking directly into her soul. She saw the two behind, they were still by the door, their attention firmly fixed on the sight of her.

Breathe, she silently screamed to herself, *just fucking breathe.* She let out a low rasp of air, time seemed to slow, she felt her limbs coming back under her control. With a swift lurch, she rolled sideways towards the kitchen, she was on her chest now. Using her elbows propped under her, she forced herself off the ground and attempted to jump out the grasp of the man.

He threw the axe to the side and turned on her, she was scrambling for the kitchen, hoping beyond hope she would have time to grab something, anything, a knife, a pan, anything she could swing in her hand. She didn't make it halfway to the countertop. The rough hands grabbed her from behind, she felt herself tugged back, pain emanating from the back of her head where she was dragged by her hair.

She was spun by the force, she briefly saw the others had turned and were facing her, she was inches from the face of the man who had grasped her. He'd spun her around, her head now resting in the crook of his elbow as he held her close. She could smell his putrid breath; she saw the wild grin return to his rutted face. He opened his mouth to gloat in glory. The words never came out. The next thing Kate heard was the sickening wet thud, she felt the pressure on the back of her head release, the man fell to his knees. The red axe was protruding from the back of his head. In his place stood Rose.

CHAPTER THIRTEEN

It was sill early, the sun not yet visible over the trees in the distance.

Tom and Kate stood solemnly in the entrance to the factory, watching the quiet road in front of them. They wanted to get an early start, in case they had to face anything unexpected. They had tried to eat, unsuccessfully. Tom had just pushed the boiled potatoes around the plate, he was sure Kate had done the same. They'd taken only the axe and knife with them this time, they didn't want anything to weigh them down.

If Tom was honest with himself, he was having second thoughts this morning. His bravado had left him overnight, his mouth dry, he was terrified.

He glanced sideways; Kate didn't look much happier than he about it either.

"Okay," he murmured, his voice cracking, he hoped Kate wouldn't notice. "We should get moving."

"Right, but please, let's just take this carefully,

you remember the plan. It's about how quiet we can be - if we can't get them out of there, we leave, no arguments. There are three people here we need to look after, if we die today, they'll follow soon after."

Tom nodded, he understood. He hadn't been here since the beginning, but he felt at home, he had to protect these people and he couldn't help but wonder if the only way to truly do that was to show them that the world wasn't all shit, to rescue those poor girls if he could. To show there was some good left in the world, even after the apocalypse.

He was worried, he searched back through the cracks in his mind, trying to recall if he'd ever felt this before. It wasn't fear, it wasn't even anxiety. He was excited. And he knew why. Looking at the knife in his hands, he wondered if he'd get a chance to use it again. Part of him hoped so, the feeling of taking a life had woken something inside of him. Whether he admitted it aloud or not, he'd enjoyed the sensation. Once the shock had worn off, once the nightmares had stopped, he conceded that it had felt good. He tried to tell himself it was only because he knew by doing what he had, by killing those men, he would stop them ever hurting anyone again. He didn't honestly believe that though, it was to satisfy his selfish lust for destruction, a passion until recently he didn't even know he had.

It hadn't taken them long to reach the road in front of the university campus, where the fire had raged. It was nearly out now, smouldering lightly.

He wasn't surprised, it had burnt so high, so hot, it would smoke for days yet. They approached carefully, hugging the same building line they had used for their previous excursion, it was clear there was no one here now. No drunken figures lay on the floor, no shouting, no screaming.

Tom stood inspecting the base of the fire. He gagged, a charred, blackened arm stuck out from underneath the scorched remains of the fire. He didn't want to know who it belonged to.

Feeling the bile rise in the back of his throat, he turned and gasped at the fresh air behind him, his limited breakfast was threatening to make an appearance on him, the bravado was long forgotten.

Kate was examining the hedgerow, it was littered with debris, rusted cans, broken bottles, charred pieces of wood.

Ripped fabric stuck to the end of the branches, blowing in the wind like thousands of tiny flags, waving with every colour Tom could see. He tried to take in his surroundings, the street resembled a war zone.

Dried blood was visible on the ground at their feet, contrasting against the grey concrete in the glow of the sun, sparkling as the light reflected from its silky smooth surface, the dull red dancing with light.

Every shop in this area had been looted, the windows shattered, the doors pulled from their hinges. Tom could see the scorched facades where flames had licked their exterior, the insides burnt to a crisp. He was surprised the entire area hadn't gone up; it was only the old brick the buildings were set in that prevented a catastrophic fire from claiming this part of the city.

"There's nothing here," Kate had appeared at his side.

"They must have left just after we did. The fire's still hot, but everything else is gone. Any sign of the girls?" he asked.

"Nothing."

"Do we follow them?"

"How, Tom? We don't know where they went."

He gazed absently down the street.

"They can't be that hard to find – they seem to like a good fire; we wait till dark and follow the flame?" he suggested

Kate said nothing, he knew she agreed.

They spent the day resting in one of the burnt-out shops. The interior had been gutted, but the flames hadn't penetrated the store cupboard at the back of the building, the fire door doing its job. The room was empty, any hope of finding something useful dashed as soon as they had entered. All the buildings in this area had been thoroughly searched before being senselessly torched.

As the day dragged on, they sat mostly in silence, occasionally exchanging small snippets of conversation. Tom let his mind wander. He imagined the group of people they were searching for, slumped on benches, lay on the grass, their snores breaking the calm of day as they slept off the hangover of the night before. He imagined a man with them, sat in a chair on the grass, the sunlight bathing his face, his beady eyes surveying the open space in front of him. He imagined two girls, whimpering on the floor, their beaten bodies attached to the man's chair by chains. He felt the excitement of feeling the blade slice through flesh once more.

It felt like an eternity before the sun finally came to rest over the horizon. The silence had settled over the city, the sound of chirping birds had ceased, the buzzing insects retired for the night.

Tom and Kate had dozed during the day the best they could, they knew this would be a long night. They hadn't eaten or so much as sipped any water since early that morning; Tom could feel the headache threatening to erupt behind his eyes. He rubbed his temples as he closed his eyes tightly. It was nearly time to go.

Stood back on the road, they surveyed the distance for any sign of life, the dim glow of fire. They strained their ears, trying to make out any unnatural sound, a giveaway to the location they needed to head. There was nothing, it was silent and still. The stars twinkled overhead, the moon rising high into the night sky.

"We need to get higher," Tom said aloud, he'd expected to see something, he'd expected the night air to be cut by the screams, the laughter. The silence was disconcerting. He marched to the alleyway they had previously sneaked through just a short distance away, hoping for a way to reach the flat roof of the buildings either side.

The industrial bin was still sat on its side, the contents of misshapen metal strewn across the alleyway. He placed his hands under one side and heaved, it wasn't heavy, he managed to right it without exerting too much effort. Pushing it as close to the wall as it would comfortably roll, he looked up, it wasn't high enough. Glancing around for anything he could use to extend his reach, his eyes settled on a broken wooden chair discarded against the opposite wall, it only had three legs, but it might work.

He awkwardly balanced the chair on top of the bin, it wasn't ideal, nor what he might consider safe, but it gave the extra height he needed. Carefully clamouring on top, keeping to the side of the chair that still balanced on two legs, he reached for the flat edge of the roof. His hands comfortably slid over the brick. Gripping the best he could, he pulled all his weight up the wall, hoisting his arms over the ledge, the chair hit the ground as his fraying legs kicked out under him.

He pulled himself over the ledge and slid onto his stomach, panting with effort. Rolling onto his back, he looked up at the clear night sky floating alluringly above him as he caught his breath.

Straining to peer into the distance, his face fell

as he looked around. This wasn't the best vantage point, the taller buildings obscured his view on one side of the street, the tree's in the park concealing any sign the other. He frowned; this hadn't gone to plan. He glared to the rooftops in the distance, hoping to see the telltale glow of fire dancing from them, there was nothing. The moonlight shone bright, nothing else.

He lent over the edge and slowly dropped himself back to the bin lid, deflated.

"Kate..." he called out. No reply. He walked back to the main street and glared into the dim; he couldn't see her.

"Kate," he hissed quietly once more, again there was no reply.

He felt the colour drain from his face, the cold, sinking feeling striking deep into his chest. He frantically swiped his head side to side, hoping he'd just missed her crouched form, that she hadn't heard him call out.

He rushed back to the smouldering remnants of the fire further up the road, desperately searching behind every obstacle, praying she was inspecting something behind them. He stopped cold as he saw the red axe lay on its side in the grass by the hedgerow.

The dread grew inside him, without thinking, he dashed carelessly down the road. His running footsteps echoing off the pavement as he moved, heading deeper into the abandoned city.

His eyes were scanning the ground, searching

for any clue of what had happened, which direction to follow.

There - a shoe, it looked like Kate's, he wasn't sure, but he had to believe so. He barely slowed as he scooped it off the ground, he'd broken into a run now, the sound of his feet slapping off the concrete and his own panting loud in his ears, he hadn't been gone long, they couldn't have dragged her far.

But who, he thought to himself, who had dragged her? Had she screamed for help, was he too invested in his task to take notice? He cursed silently. He hadn't picked up the axe, he had only the kitchen knife and he didn't even know if he was headed in the right direction. He didn't know how many of them there might be, he was running blind into the abyss.

He was passing unfamiliar buildings, the strange shadows cast like monsters in the dark, taunting his every step. His pace didn't slow, he continued racing, following what he hoped was the correct route.

He fell, he hadn't seen the pothole in the road in front of him. His foot hit the uneven surface and momentum forced him forwards, a scream emanated from his throat from shock as his splayed hands broke his fall. He heard the knife clatter as it skidded in front of him. He felt the pain rip through his palms as small jagged stones tore into them.

The cut didn't seem too bad, but it stung. Lying face down on the floor, he brought his hands back to his face where he could see them clearer. He rubbed the small stones away and quickly examined the damage, nothing serious. He placed his hands under him and jumped off the ground, he wasn't going to let this slow him down, he searched around to retrieve the knife. A glint against the road in front of him. He grabbed the handle and held it in front of him, if anyone was nearby, they would have surely heard the commotion. He felt the throbbing pain in his knee, he'd check that out later.

While he took a moment to regain his bearings, he was sure he'd heard something, a muffled yell from the gloom in front of him. He glanced around, he'd left the single-story, redbrick and slightly run-down part of the city. Surrounding him here was tall glass buildings, cafes with fancy vinyl writing on the windows. High brand shops, long closed, but their gold and black signs still visible through the neglect.

None of the glass was broken, nothing had been taken from here. The road was clear too, the broken bottles and empty cans had been replaced by the occasional empty wrapper blowing in the breeze, weeds forced themselves through the small gaps opening up in the concrete. This part of the city was closer to the industrial area in terms of its cleanliness, he briefly wondered if the group he was trying to track had even been down this route, there was no evidence of their passing.

There it was again, he was sure he'd heard it this

time. A yell, muffled as if being shouted through a wall. From which direction? The glass building reverberated the sound, distant as it was, it sounded like it was coming from everywhere at once. He spun, trying in vain to narrow down the source, trying to track any hint of direction, of where he should head.

There it was again, it was Kate, it had to be - was she screaming, shouting, fighting for her life? He couldn't tell, he waited for the sound to occur again, he had to decide. It didn't take long, he glanced forwards, he'd been on the right track, it was coming from the gloom in front. He steadied his resolve, tightened his grasp around the knife handle and ran.

The muffled yell was becoming more consistent, it was getting closer. He was getting closer. He was running through a plaza, the financial district. Manicured streets and expensive fountains, long since neglected, the water no longer ran from the marble statues. He saw something, movement in the distance across a concrete clearing in the middle of multiple towering glass skyscrapers, some now pointless water feature set into its cobbled stone. The floor was uneven, he slowed, he didn't need another fall. It was becoming clearer, a silhouette in the gloom. A person being dragged, a rope tied around them, two figures dragging.

They were walking at a steady pace, Tom didn't think they had heard him approach. He was closer now, the silhouette was becoming more apparent. It was Kate, the rope strapped to her wrists, two men holding the other end. The jerky movement showed how hard she was fighting them, they dragged her for a few steps, then with a burst of power, the rope propelled her forwards, she stumbled a few steps before the process repeated.

Tom jolted off to the side of the plaza, hoping the glass-framed building would give him some sort of cover, conceal his movements as he tried to manoeuvre closer to them. The full moon was high in the sky, he could see the glass of the building opposite illuminated, if they looked his way there was little chance he wouldn't be seen. He had to be quick, it would be the only way to save Kate. How? What was he going to do, there was two of them, and from this distance, they both looked considerably bigger than him, he didn't think his physicality would be a benefit here.

He had only one option, he had to even the field, he had to make this one-on-one. The two of them would overpower him, punch him to the ground before they stamped the life out of him. He didn't want to die like that.

He briefly recalled the story Kate had told him about the young soldier, he wondered if his skull would splatter over the road. He hoped not, he'd been trying to keep his grooming to a civilised standard, it would be a shame for that to have been in vain.

He didn't have long to think, he didn't need long. He was nearing the men, he was less than 30 meters away, 25, 20. His pace steady, he crouched as low as he could, treading lightly. Ten meters, if he ran now, he could get one of them before they knew what had happened. Five meters, his heart beating in his ears.

He missed his chance.

One of them must have seen movement, he swirled around just as Tom was raising the blade of the knife towards his back. The man raised his arms in surprise, the rope wrapped around his wrist, they stopped when it met the resistance of Kate's weight the other end. The other man hadn't stirred, it was all happening so quickly.

Tom plunged forwards, knife outstretched, aiming for the heart. The man brought his arm down to protect his body, Tom felt the blade pierce flesh and swiftly stop as it hit solid bone. The man screamed, his partner turned just in time to see Tom pull the blade out of the man's arm and plunge it deep down into his shoulder.

He missed the bone this time, he felt the blade slide in cleanly, all the way to the hilt. The man screamed and grabbed unsuccessfully for the blade sticking out of him. The other man lunged forwards, Tom had no weapon, the man was squirming so much he had no hope of retrieving the blade stuck deep inside of him.

As the second man lunged, Kate drew her arms back as hard as she could. The rope still connected to the wrist of the first man, now down on his knees, his face contorted in pain. The rope tightened and her assailant fell over it. He crashed into the ground face first, a groan left his mouth. Kate moved like lightening, she straddled his back, pulled her wrists back and looped the rope around his neck. With all the strength she could muster, she pulled her wrists to the sky, the rope tightening around his neck, his fingers desperately trying to loosen it, his eyes widening with terror.

Tom watched, transfixed as the man's throat swelled around the thick rope, his face reddened, his screams became hoarse and then the sound stopped. The veins in his head expanded, his fingers clawed at the rope. The whites of his eyes reflected the moonlight as they rolled into the back of his head, his lips were turning grey, he stopped fighting, his hands fell limp and his eyes slid shut. He was dead.

Kate didn't release her grip, she kept pulling the rope as hard as she could, the strain in her arms discernible, not taking any risks that he might recover to strike them both down.

Tom was brought back to earth by the screaming of the man he'd stabbed. He'd managed to grip the handle of the knife, he was pulling it free from his shoulder. Anguished screams disturbed the night silence, like a wolf howling at the moon, the sound cut through Tom. It brought him back to his senses, he knew what to do. Leaping forwards, he fought with the man's hands for the handle, the blood making it slippery was still warm. Tom finally got a grip, he forced it back down into the man's flesh. The screams grew louder. Tom now had both hands on the handle, he twisted. He felt the blade cutting through cartilage, ripping into muscle, slicing veins, severing arteries.

He pulled it free, blood spluttered from the wound, he felt it spray on his face. His animalistic instincts taking over, he forced it into the man's neck, the screams stopped, the man on his knees slumped forwards, blood gushed to the floor, pooling at Tom's feet.

He'd asked for this; he couldn't have imagined it better.

Kate had remained stationary above the man she'd straddled, the rope had loosened but was still constricted around his neck, the other end remained firmly attached to the wrist of the other man, connecting the three of them in the grotesque carnage left before them.

Several long moments passed and neither of them moved, like statues stuck forever in their pose of death. The silence was eventually broken by Tom.

"What now?" he asked quietly. Tears began to flood down Kate's face.

"They're dead, Tom. The girls. They're dead." Her lip quivered. "They didn't take them with them, they slit their throats. Tom, they left them in the park.

"How..." he started, he didn't know how to finish the sentence. "Are you okay?"

She didn't reply, she didn't have to.

He cut the rope free from the dead man's arm then began to cut it loose from Kate's wrists, the blood from the blade staining the fraying fibres red.

Their mission had failed. They hadn't rescued the girls, they hadn't found any form of transport, they hadn't managed to get anything of use. All they had achieved was more pain. A red welt had appeared on Kate's cheek, it looked dark and angry.

She didn't know where the men had come from, it happened so fast. She'd been checking a pile of discarded clothes by the hedgerow, One of them had hit her from behind, so hard she didn't know anything else until she was being dragged up the road, a dirty scarf tied around her face, her wrists bound together, the loose stones tearing into her skin.

She's a fighter, thought Tom, they had dragged her quite a distance. He could see her ripped clothing, blood-stained where the ground had torn into her legs and arms.

She'd still managed to get to her feet. She'd even managed to yell. If she hadn't, he wasn't sure he would ever have found her again.

They sat in the grass at the side of the road. Tom had his arm around her, her head rested on his shoulder. He saw her chest rise and fall as she valiantly tried to stop the tears from falling. She was tough, but she was also kind, he didn't think she'd killed before. Both of them now had taken lives in such a short amount of time, were they honestly that different from Chester and the others they had gone searching for that night?

They sat in the long grass for a long time. Tom

wasn't sure just how long, but he could see the glow in the distance of the sun slowly rising, morning was approaching. The thirst in his throat was becoming unbearable, he knew Kate must feel the same. He looked down, she was asleep. Her head still delicately poised on his shoulder. He slowly lay her onto the grass, she stirred as he moved her, her eyes didn't open.

He awkwardly walked back to the men left dead from the night before. In death, they looked harmless. For the first time, he noticed their features, both of these men, in another life, he would have confidently walked past in the street, said hello to in the gym, shared a beer with at the bar.

His mind wandered to their pasts, their families sat around them as they prepared for meals, taking their children to the park, going to work. Paying bills.

These were ordinary people, once upon a time, they had an everyday life. Their families were likely dead by now, their jobs wiped out long before everything changed, their meals nothing more than scraps, bills hadn't been paid in a long time, the electricity and water companies kept the services running, hoping to keep custom at the end of the horror.

The horror never ended.

Tom unceremoniously searched their pockets, he didn't find much on the man who died at his hands. A packet of cigarettes, a lighter (he kept those), a scrap of paper, fading words which he couldn't read, it must have meant something to the man, he placed it back in his pocket. The other man was lay on his front, his head had dropped to the ground once Kate had finally been released from the rope, the rope that still threaded around his neck like a scarf.

Tom hadn't seen it in the commotion, attached to the man with a strap over one shoulder, a bag, not too unlike the satchel Tom had cherished in the early days. The man had fallen onto the bag, it was firmly wedged between the lifeless body and the ground. Tom took hold of the end of it and tugged, it slid out with little effort. He didn't want to move the man, so he cut at the strap instead. It came loose and without looking at what lay within, he walked away with the bag in his hand, back to where the sleeping Kate silently dreamt on.

He sat on the grass next to her head, waiting for her to wake, the bag now lay in his lap. Undoing the buckle, he opened it to examine the valuables inside. There was a large bottle of water, nearly full, the first bit of joy he had felt in a long time. Several packets of peanuts, the kind that flight attendants used to give out on aeroplanes, before they were no more too. He removed a cotton t-shirt, it looked clean, but no use to him, it was idly discarded to the road. Nestled in the bottom of the bag, muzzle facing him, there was a pistol.

CHAPTER FOURTEEN

They sat by the comfortably familiar metal table. Like so many times before, a steaming cup of weak coffee rested in front of Tom.

He'd retold their story, what they had seen, what they had done - most of what they had done, some things he wanted to keep to himself. Matt was pushing him to start again. He supposed this was the only form of entertainment available here, stuck in this red-bricked factory. How long had he been here now, he couldn't remember, it felt like years, he knew it wasn't.

He looked at the assembled audience of Matt, Rose and Chloe. She seemed to be feeling better and interacting more, she'd even said a few words to Tom since his return. Kate had gone to bed once they had finally crept back through the chain-link fence surrounding the factory, no one had heard from her since. He began recounting the night over again.

"Can I see the gun?" Matt asked eagerly.

"It's away," Tom replied, Kate hadn't been happy he'd kept it.

"But it's so cool," he retorted as he sniggered. Tom looked disapprovingly at him, recently Matt was showing his immaturity.

He continued through the tale, he told of the fire, now extinguished. The destruction left where that group had moved on from. The scene left behind how they might expect a slum in a third world country to look.

He told them of Kate's abduction, of the daring rescue, he didn't go into details. He told of the wait till sunrise and the slow, painful walk back. There was nothing of interest in that part, they had left once Kate woke. Walking in silence, heads down.

Matt seemed to get bored at the second telling, he'd pushed Tom for details on how he rescued Kate. After getting nothing, his interest waned and eventually he got up and left, muttering to himself about needing to be somewhere else.

Rose looked at him pitifully.

"You poor, stupid children," she remarked calmly. "How do you know they killed those poor girls?"

"Kate heard them, once she woke up. She thinks they hit her with the gun, sneaked up on her, it's where the injury on her face is from. When she came to, she heard them talking, about her, about her being the replacement. They knew she was awake, they goaded her, they told her how the other girls were no longer fun, no longer interesting, how she'd be the new toy. They were taking her to Chester."

"Scum," spat Rose. Chloe hadn't said another word, she sat in the chair at the end of the table, watching the steam evaporate off her coffee, eyes unfocussed.

Tom felt the pity in his chest, he didn't know if him rescuing Chloe was the reason they killed the girls, or if Chloe would have been slaughtered along with them, had they not. But he knew that she'd comforted them, huddled together when things got really bad. Chloe hadn't told them what happened to her, hadn't told Tom at least. He suspected Kate knew.

"Chloe..." he started quietly. "Chloe, I'm so sorry," at the sound of her name, she looked up over the cup, half a smile on her cracked, battered lips.

"Thank you," she said simply, her gaze dropped back to the steam.

The three of them sat in silence, the faint sound of birdsong floated in from the open windows on the main building beyond, the calming music soothing Tom's soul.

Rose interrupted his thoughts. "I need to go," she declared. "I'm too old for this, I need a lie-down." Without another word, she hobbled from the room. *Her leg isn't getting any better,* thought Tom, as he watched her leave.

He turned his head, to his surprise, Chloe was staring straight at him, the focus and purpose clear in her eyes.

THE SURVIVAL OF TOM

"I want to kill him." Her voice was so calm and quiet, Tom had to run the words over in his head again, he was sure he'd misheard. "That bastard. Chester, I want to kill him."

"Chloe, I'm sorry, I truly am, I know he hurt you, I know he hurt your friends..."

"He fucking killed them." Her voice still perfectly calm. "He's dirt, lower than dirt. He'll do this to anyone he finds; he'll use them, and he'll leave them bleeding in the mud, we have to do something."

"I don't know what we can do. He's not alone, we are." Tom couldn't believe what was happening. She was effectively suggesting suicide, at least his plans had a reason that started as something other than vengeance.

"The handgun, can you use it, do you know how?" she inquired.

"Well... no, not really, I've never held a gun in my life, in all honesty. I'm not sure how to shoot it, I guess point and pull the trigger?"

"I can." The focus in her eyes was clearer than ever. "I know about guns, I've grown up with them. Is it loaded?"

"I... I didn't check." Tom was starting to feel slightly embarrassed.

"Are there any bullets?"

"Yeah, a box, some loose in the bag too."

"Then that's enough. We go, we kill Chester."

Tom examined her face, her expression unlike anything he'd seen from her until now, the bruises were fading, her face had hardened, her resolve clear to see.

Looking into her eyes, he saw her clearly for the first time. She was young, maybe nineteen. Underneath the dark bruises, there was the face of a frightened girl, a girl who had experienced more in her young life than anyone should over a lifetime. She had light brown hair. He hadn't been sure at first, she was so caked in filth it had been impossible to tell. Her eyes shone with green fire, the sparkle truly back. He would help her. He would stop Chester from doing this again, he'd stop him taking the youth from anyone left in this rotting world. He had a new mission, Chloe was right. They'd have to kill Chester.

Tom had a problem. He didn't actually know who Chester was, he'd never actually seen him, certainly never met him and he didn't know where he was. He knew he was armed, but now so was Tom, although it was likely Chester knew how to use his rifle, Tom didn't have a clue.

Maybe he could throw it at him... No, that'd just give Chester another weapon. He'd have to learn, but with such a limited number of bullets, he'd better learn fast.

Chloe warmed to Tom after their conversation. She spent more time in his company, sitting silently with him, occasionally she spoke to him. He slowly learned more about her as she recovered. The deep cut on her arm was healing, she still winced when she made sudden movements.

Chloe talked Tom through the theory of using a gun. She had learnt how to shoot from a young age, her parents had been into shooting and ensured she was well versed in most types of firearms, she didn't go into much more detail.

She had told Tom, the handgun he'd found was a 9mm Glock 17 pistol, he didn't know what that meant or if it was important, as long as he could point it, and something happened when he pulled the trigger. The magazine had been full. Chloe emptied it and counted, 17 bullets in the gun. The box had contained 20 more, and Tom had found six loose in the bottom of the bag. Forty-four bullets, that was a good result, there were only twenty people he needed to worry about, after all.

They were cautious about firing live rounds, the noise would echo around the dead city, giving away their location to anyone within miles. Chloe removed the magazine, she would teach him using dry fire, Tom wondered just what this meant.

Standing in the empty car park, the weeds poking further through the cracked concrete than Tom remembered, Chloe talked him through the process of aiming and firing a gun. *That's simple*, Tom thought, *point and shoot*.

She was very in-depth; she really did know about this. Her voice was steady and confident as she explained the best way to aim to ensure he hit closest to the mark as he could, how to squeeze the trigger, not the jerky movement he was so desperate to try. He briefly imagined himself the protagonist in some faraway action movie. A Hollywood flick from the past, running down the road, shooting all the bad guys with ease, hitting his mark every time. He'd thought he was quite mature, until now.

Chloe's brief didn't last too long, after talking through the process and watching Tom aim and pull the trigger, the empty click of the hammer the only indication he'd done something right.

"That'll do," she said. "Not much we can do more if we aren't going to load it, now you can point, shoot, and hope for the best," she offered.

Tom smiled, he liked Chloe. She had a way with words and a good sense of humour, he was glad he was seeing the real her, not the broken shell of herself she'd been till now.

"Thanks," he said, offering a toothy smile. "There's more to it than I thought, I'm not sure Chester would have talked me through it on the spot, either."

She giggled; Tom blushed.

"Okay, let's go back inside," he instructed. He handed the pistol back to Chloe, who expertly inserted the magazine, and handed it back to him. He'd wondered if she might want to keep hold of it, if she might want to try and kill Chester herself. Despite her knowledge, she didn't seem to be very comfortable holding the small black pistol in her hands.

Kate still hadn't reappeared from her room; it was late afternoon and Tom was becoming worried about her. He knocked quietly on the door where he knew she might be sleeping behind. He'd had a nice day with Chloe, but he missed Kate, he'd grown fond of her company.

"Kate?" he whispered as he lightly rapped his knuckles on the wood door again.

No answer.

"Kate?" he tried slightly louder, still no answer. He slowly depressed the handle and cracked the door, just enough to peer around it. The bed was empty, Kate wasn't there.

"Kate?" Tom shouted as he reared around, looking up and down the corridor. He felt the familiar sensation of panic rising inside of him. He turned and dashed up the corridor, heading for the kitchen, hoping she'd silently crept out and would be found, toiling over the hob as he'd seen her do so many times before. He pushed the door open, it slammed off the wall, the kitchen was empty. He scanned the canteen; she wasn't to be seen sat at any of the long metal tables either.

Retracing his steps, he continued down the corridor leading to the mezzanine floor above the vast, empty expanse of the main factory. From his vantage, he could see the entire floor. Matt was sat with his back against the wall, his absent mind focused only on some faraway thought. His heart beat faster in his chest, he called out her name again.

"Kate!" The call echoed around the floor, bouncing off every wall and flying back at him, reverberating over and over above his head, *Kate...*

Kate... Kate.

Matt jumped, he hadn't seen Tom stood high above his head, he'd been so engrossed in his thoughts until the frantic shout ripped them from him.

"Dude, relax!" he shouted out angrily. "She's outside, she went out soon after you guys came back in, I think she wanted to be alone, but Rose won't leave her be. Stop screaming your head off around here."

Tom walked down the metal mezzanine floor to the glass window, he could see out of it from here. The height of the steel floor allowing him to scan the entire grounds that side of the building from his position.

There, he saw her. She was sat on the grass at the back of the factory, the chain-link fence at her back. He felt his heart beat slower, the calm sweeping over him. There was no entrance to the factory around that side. She'd mentioned once that she thought it was the safest place to be, anyone entering from the front where the gate into the car park allowed easy access, would be drawn to the building. No one would think to check the back where the weeds were slowly reclaiming the once manicured sloping hills that the fence was set into. He watched her silently through the glass. Rose was sat next to her, talking into her ear. He didn't see Kate reply. She was probably trying to console her from what she'd done with the rope, the man she'd killed. Rose had a way of calming people, she also had a way of being there when you wanted to just be alone. Tom could guess which this one was. Kate sat cross-legged on the floor, her head bowed, her blond hair fell over her face and trailed to the ground. It was usually tightly tied back. Her hair down, she seemed more vulnerable, a fragile display of herself.

The sight of the usually so confident and sure Kate, appearing downtrodden on the grass outside, saddened him, he hadn't seen her like this before. She always took things in her stride, moved on with that same wicked smile on her face, busting a joke about whatever issues they might be facing and working out a solution.

This was different though, as tough as she was, she was caring, loving, she had a hell-bent desire to help. He imagined that killing would have been hard for her. Whilst he'd found the perverse pleasure in it, he doubted she felt the same. She was too far away from Tom for him to see her face, he saw her shoulders moving rhythmically up and down. He didn't need to see the tears to know they were there. This was something he hadn't considered, if they were going to go for Chester.

For the first time since he'd met her, he wasn't sure he could count on Kate for that endeavour.

She didn't come back inside the factory, he watched as she sat on the grass, Rose had stopped talking now, both of them watching the sun as it began its nightly descent. Soon the night would take over, the darkness would return.

Tom was in the kitchen, he'd decided that the best thing he could do was to try to get some normality and structure back into the routine. At least, as close as he could with what their lives had become.

He had the large pan sat atop the blue flame of the cooker, pretending he was in a large, well-stocked kitchen, he would be creating the nightly feast for an army of hungry workers. Providing all the mouth-watering flavours they would ask for. The selection would be tremendous, there would be something to suit every taste.

He smiled in irony as he chopped the potatoes into bite-sized pieces. They were running low, they had them nearly every day, even rationing their portions, they would soon run out regardless. His mind wandered back to what their next move would be. Even if somehow they could rid the city of Chester, what's to say someone wouldn't take his place within days? Terrorising anyone unfortunate enough to be left within the confines of the city.

He thought once more about the possibility of an old farmhouse, deep in the country. The more this image pressed into his mind, the more he envied it. What did he expect, even if such a place did exist, void of people, free of the virus that had sucked humanity dry? The ground not poisoned by the rotting flesh of the dead, what then? Would he toil in the fields, bringing in the small crop whilst Kate baked bread in the farmhouse oven?

They still needed transport, that problem hadn't gone away. He hadn't seen anything that might be useful, not since the black truck back in the coastal village, the only way to get that depended on the other scheme, the one to end the tyranny of Chester. Tom stopped stirring the pan below him, why had this not come to his mind earlier.

He saw Chester, his truck at least, in a village, miles from here, in the middle of the day. He hadn't seen or heard the truck since he'd been here, there was no sign of it at the fire that night. With the silence of the fallen city, surely an engine revving down the main streets would have reverberated for miles. What if Chester wasn't even in the city?

Chloe had told him Chester was often around, but she hadn't specified when. With the torment she'd been through, what if Chester wasn't there as much as she'd thought? He'd travelled to that village, to the coast, that couldn't have been the only time. Maybe there was another way to do this, maybe there was a safer way.

If he could figure out where Chester was, when he left the confines of the city, he could strike while he was alone. Maybe he could draw him out.

The potatoes burnt as Tom's mind went into overdrive, there was a chance he wouldn't have to enter the city proper again, at all.

Kate had finally returned inside the safety of the factory long after dark. Tom had fed the others, he kept some on the stove for Kate, she declined the food he offered.

He made coffee; she was sat in her usual seat at the metal table.

"How are you?" he asked as he placed the cup down in front of her. She didn't respond, she showed no sign of acknowledging him.

"I know it's been rough," he continued. "I'm sorry you had to do what you did, but you saved both of us. We'd both be dead by now if you hadn't acted."

Silence.

"If you want to talk, Kate, you know I'm here for you." He meant it, he felt now like he had known her for longer than was true, she was important to him. It hurt to see her like this.

Silence.

He sat opposite in the spare seat, staring absently at the brown pale liquid in front of him. He wasn't sure how long passed; time became difficult to gauge without the light to guide it. His cup was empty, steam had stopped rising from hers a long time ago, a stale film formed on the surface. He took the cup and emptied it down the sink.

"It's not that I killed him." He heard the words float softly from the canteen. "It's that I got caught."

She didn't offer any more, Tom knew she'd said all she needed to. He moved to the vacant seat next to her and put his arm around her shoulder. She allowed her head to rest gently against his chest.

"You did great, you know that right?" he said softly. "You're a fighter, Kate, don't beat yourself up.

We're alive. It's my fault, I shouldn't have dragged you back, you were right, it was reckless."

He heard her take a deep breath.

"I know, I just couldn't stop thinking about Chloe, about what they did to her. I never saw the other girls, but I can only imagine how scared they must have been. Their last weeks on this earth, every moment of them just terror and pain."

Tom didn't know how to reply, he didn't argue about that. Nothing he could say would make her feel better.

His resolve hardened, the world was dead, the least he could do was try to make it more bearable. If he could save just one person from that fate, if he could make just one small difference, he had to try.

He started to tell Kate his thoughts from earlier, she listened intently. He saw her demeanour change, the sorrow leaving her as he shared what he believed now about Chester. The more he thought about it, the more he was sure he was right.

"Now you mention it, I think you're right," Kate said after she'd digested the information. She sounded more like the Kate Tom had come to know.

"I mean, we know he's in charge, but he wasn't there the other night, we haven't heard him, I know it's a big city, but you'd think maybe we would have heard something in all these months. I wonder where he goes, what he does." She paused in thought. "Do you think we could light a fire on the beach? If we added enough green stuff and made sure it smoked, it'd be visible for miles. I know it's a long shot, we don't know anything, but it might be worth a try."

"We'd have to walk back to the coast," he interjected. "It's a long walk, and we'd need to leave the rest here. I think Chloe will want to come."

"Then let her, she's angry enough at the world right now, that I wouldn't bet against her"

"So that's it, a beach fire? That's our big plan?"

"Why not?"

Tom had no reply to that. Why not.

Rose wasn't happy. She was never happy when they decided to put themselves in danger. Matt stayed quiet. He never joined in the planning conversations, terrified he'd be asked to help. As Tom had thought, Chloe insisted on accompanying them, if there was a chance to get even, she wanted to be part of it.

"How on earth do you expect this to work?" Rose said, the doubt evident in her voice.

"Do you have any idea how many miles of coastline there are? You don't even know he'll be anywhere near you - he could be at the other end of the country for all you know. This is ridiculous!" Her voice was rising as she spoke. "I've never heard a worse plan. If by some miracle, and I mean some miracle bigger than the second coming, you do manage to find him, then what? Hide in the bushes, jump out and shoot him, take the truck and drive off, then live happily ever after?" She was fuming now.

Tom felt deflated, she was right, there was no

way this would work.

"Why not just stay closer to home?" Matt sounded sheepish. "He may leave, but we know he must come back. So what we've never heard him, it's a big city. He runs those guys, right? Don't go to the coast, go to one of the nearby villages, closer to here. Much better chance of the smoke being seen."

Tom suddenly wished Matt would join in more, his idea might just work.

They studied tourists maps that Kate had pulled from a stand in a nearby petrol station. She'd remembered seeing them and dashed off when they had first started talking about location. Having something to do, something else to cast her mind to was bringing her back quickly.

They needed to be far enough away that walking to their location wouldn't be an option, it had to be somewhere the others would only try to drive to, but close enough that smoke would be seen in the distance. Judging where the fire in the street had been and making the best assumptions they could about how far the group would have travelled, they settled on a village just outside the city, so close it could have been a suburb. There were no natural obstacles in the way, the plain was flat, the tall buildings faced the other side of the city, they should be able to see, and be seen, for miles. It was riskier, there was no guarantee this way he'd come alone, if at all, but it was the best they had.

CHAPTER FIFTEEN

The cigarette sat burning in the grass, lay where it had been flicked, the last few drags slowly burning down in the wind. Chester sat on the hood of his truck, the black truck he'd lovingly cared for. It was his pride and joy. He'd brought it second hand; it was still the newest vehicle he'd ever owned, the vinyl writing down the side he'd put on himself.

He'd lost his job working in the car factory, they had made cuts due to slowing sales, and his name had been on the list. He'd worked there since he was a teenager, it didn't feel good to be cast aside so easily.

The money he'd been given had helped though, it was enough to buy this truck. He'd spent a bit of cash tidying it up. The rest he spent on tools, advertisement, everything he needed to get his new landscaping business off the ground. He'd always been passionate about gardening, he was going to see this as an opportunity, a chance for a new start.

He was nearing 40, he'd been in that factory for over 20 years. The hard work showed on his body. His rough hands calloused from moving parts

THE SURVIVAL OF TOM

all day, pain in his back shot up his spine when he reached up high.

He'd booked his first job, it wasn't anything fancy, but the beeping of the email that confirmed someone wanted his services, he'd been elated about that. He wished he had someone to share his joy with.

Chester was separated, he had two teenage children, a boy and girl, he hadn't seen them for years. He had had his run-ins with the law a few times down the years, nothing serious, a drunken pub fight, the minor traffic offences, the citation he was given when caught trying to sell small amounts of drugs on the street corner. In his younger days, He'd run up a substantial gambling debt, the bookie had agreed to let him off the money. He could never pay it back, but to clear his slate he'd have to pay in other ways.

Chester hadn't liked that, but he felt he'd had no choice, so he'd agreed and tried to sell the small bags of white powder in the desperate parts of town. He'd been far too obvious; the police had arrived within half an hour of his first attempt.

His employer had let him keep his job; he had a perfect record. The courts had taken leniency too. Community service, a few weekends picking rubbish from the hedgerows, he'd got away lightly.

He was married back then, his wife hadn't known about the gambling, about the drugs, she left soon after. Her and the children packed their things and walked out the door for the very last time.

He never saw them again. He'd had to move to a cheaper part of town after that, he couldn't afford to support himself without her.

He was at a low point in his life. The one-bed, small, pokey flat he rented was rife with damp, the distinct smell kept him up at nights. Not to worry though, things would get better, he was going to start again, working outdoors. He'd finally enjoy himself and his life. The cigarette was still glowing brightly as it finally burnt to the butt.

He slid from the bonnet of the truck, running his hand along the freshly polished wing as he reached for the door. Sitting in the driver's seat, he took a deep breath, turned the ignition and drove down the road towards the first job of his new life.

Business had been going well. He was making enough money to support himself, he'd moved from the one-bedroom flat to a small house on the outskirts of town. Most of his customers were out this way where the gardens were grander, and the population older. He'd been keeping busy and he was enjoying his work, he hadn't touched a drink in months, he finally felt like he was getting his life together, getting somewhere he wanted to be.

He entered the house of one of his regular customers. Originally, he would knock, wait for the older lady to amble to the door, invite him in and insist on making him tea, before he'd tackle the ever-growing list of chores in her garden.

These days, he let himself in. She'd been getting

steadily more unwell as the months went by, he'd be losing this job soon. *Horrible bastard*, he thought to himself, never mind the woman, worry about the money. He would miss her, but people died every day, she soon would be just another statistic. Hopefully she can keep going till the end of autumn, he silently berated himself again.

The weather was turning, the end of summer fast approaching, a slight chill entering the air as the sun set in the evening.

There was always a freshly made cup of tea waiting for him on his arrival. He was punctual, he could pride himself on that. Today the kitchen was empty, the cups still in the cupboard, the kettle cold. He frowned, he'd been coming here every week for the last five months, not once had old Miss Finn ever missed his entrance.

He heard a cough come from within the house. He paused. He'd seen the reports, he knew there was a nasty bug doing the rounds, he couldn't afford to be cooped up at home for two weeks or longer. He thought seriously about bolting, leaving her in her bed. But he'd grown fond of her, she was good to him, one of his first customers and certainly one of his more loyal.

He knocked on her closed bedroom door as he called out her name. He heard coughing in reply. Not a normal cough, not even a cough he might expect from a heavy smoker, although Miss Finn didn't smoke. This was a rasping cough, from deep in her lungs, it didn't stop. Steadying himself, he opened the door, she lay in her bed, floral sheets wrapped tightly around her. She tried to talk, every time she opened her mouth, another fit of coughs started.

He pulled his phone from his pocket and rang an ambulance, he knew she was in trouble, but he didn't want to get any closer. The room was sure to be full of contagions by now and he had other jobs. Most of his clients were elderly, the last thing he could afford was to kill them all off.

He waited in the kitchen for the ambulance to arrive. They didn't take long, two paramedics dressed in full protective gear burst through the front door. He pointed to Miss Finn's bedroom, without a word they wheeled the metallic trolley into the room. Within moments they were exiting the house, Miss Finn strapped to the metal bed.

He saw her look to him as she was wheeled out of her home, the fear clear in her eyes, mask strapped to her face. Miss Finn always paid cash, the money was on the kitchen counter, he put it in his pocket, she wouldn't be coming back, no sense losing a few hours pay. He thought about taking the purse left on the dining room table, but he wasn't that hard up, yet, he'd leave the sentiments for the family.

His work had dropped recently, after the death of Miss Finn, several other of his clients had become sick, more died. He solemnly crossed their names off the wall planner he had attached in his kitchen. Things were going to get tough.

It didn't matter too much after that, the lockdown started, he was forced to stay inside anyway. His money was running out and his work non-existent. He wasn't sure when it would come back, if it ever did. He pondered the situation, wondered how he was going to dig himself out of this hole. He had no savings to speak of, everything he'd squirrelled away was used on the deposit for the house he'd moved too, and he was sure he'd soon be evicted from that, he couldn't afford the rent any longer.

Shops were still open, provisions could still be brought, but only if you had money, Chester didn't. He tried to do the right thing, to sit indoors, to busy himself with newfound hobbies, daytime television, the monotony of lockdown life.

He was out of tea, even using each bag twice, his supply had run out a week ago. That was a shame, he did like his morning tea. He sat in his kitchen, looking at the wall planner, drawing pins holding it in place. Only two names remained not crossed through, only two clients left out of the 14 regulars he'd had just a week previously.

He did miss the work, the money too. Deep down though, he missed the people, he'd liked them, most of them were far too elderly and fragile to keep their gardens in proper order. This wasn't what he'd intended to do. He wanted to make beautiful rock gardens, tend to vast manicured lawns and pruned fruit trees, but it had paid the bills and kept him busy.

He walked to the drawer where he kept the keys of clients who trusted him enough to let himself in. He had eight in total, seven would now open doors to only empty houses, the owners never to return. He rested them on the table and looked at each one. Seven of them were now gone, after all... He pocketed them and walked to the black truck.

This was a new low, even for him. He drove to the closest and parked outside, the neighbours had seen his truck there every week for months, they wouldn't think anything of it. An old friend helping to clear the rubble, helping console the families. He let himself in the front door, he hadn't been here for a few weeks, no one else had either.

This house had belonged to a man who had lived alone, easily into his 80's. He was pushy, he wanted things done exactly as he liked them, Chester used to laugh him off. Despite his cranky attitude, he'd liked him, he didn't mess about.

He checked the cupboard first, there was plenty of food stocked in them, old people always did hoard food, even before the outbreak. He cleared out what he could, placing it in old plastic shopping bags, he'd got enough here to last him weeks.

He walked into the dining room, on the mantle taking pride of place was an old brass pocket watch. Chester had admired it in passing, he didn't know if it had any value, but he'd always liked the look of it, he figured a pocket watch gave off an aurora of cool, if cool still meant the same thing these days, he was getting older.

His truck loaded high with the possessions he'd taken. He thought he'd feel more guilt at robbing the dead. No, it turned out he was fine with that.

Over the next few weeks, he meticulously cleared the other six houses he knew to be empty. Each time he entered confidently, acting like he was supposed to be there, taking anything he wanted or liked and driving home with the hoard.

His cupboards were full, bursting with tins of various foodstuffs he'd collected. Boxes of teabags sat on the kitchen counter; he wasn't planning to run out of them again for a very long time. He'd taken the jewellery too, any money they had lay around. Anything he thought might be of value once this was over.

It was so easy, no one had stopped him, no one had questioned him. He saw one of the neighbours once, walking their dog on the street outside. He'd stopped, but only long enough to mutter how much of a pity the passing was, and that he hoped the whole virus thing would go away soon, before scurrying off to complete his walk.

The streets were quiet, people were staying in. Autumn had passed and the throws of winter were taking hold, the cold snaked through the country, ice formed on the windows, snow fell from the air. Fuel was getting harder to obtain - the government had announced that all reserves were to be kept for emergency vehicles, people should ration what they had, they wouldn't be able to get any more. He hadn't seen any of the emergency vehicles, he wondered where they all were, needing all this fuel.

Sure, he was in the suburbs, maybe the city proper was a bustling metropolis of police forcing people off the streets back into their homes. Ambulances ferrying the dying between overwhelmed hospitals, the dead to the mortuary.

The power was intermittent, at first Chester thought they had cut him off, he hadn't paid his bill this month. It soon became clear it was everywhere. The city was hit badly by the virus, its ageing population bearing the brunt of the first wave. After the worst of it was over, it looked as if things would get better, the future seemed brighter. Soon after, the second wave hit like a tsunami. It slaughtered old and young alike, no distinguishing between sex, race, religion. It was swift, deadly and brutal. To Chester, it was beautiful, nature at its finest.

The situation escalated quickly, more and more people died in droves. Bodies were burnt in giant furnaces, or shoved into the mass graves hastily dug on wastelands. Evacuation to the country had been announced. It failed. Chester had learned that the promise of safety and protection had forced many of the city residents to flee. Heading for the rumoured saviour far too early, hundreds of thousands had swamped the camps designed for 5000, the virus had gone with them. None returned.

He saw more opportunity, more empty houses. There wasn't likely to be much left in the way of food, everyone had been slowly starving, Chester wasn't interested in food, he had plenty, he wanted anything that might be valuable.

The police were stretched thin, their numbers dying just as quickly as everyone else. No one tried to stop him. He started with the nearby houses, aiming for the larger ones pressed up against the main road.

He took the high-end televisions, loading them one by one into the back of the truck, the expensive electronics, anything with a value when the world returned to normal. He didn't fully realise at this time that would never happen; he was collecting junk.

He took the jewellery, the gold and silver pendants that would be melted down. Gold was always a strong currency, whatever happened to the rest of the world. He found the lack of people disconcerting, other than the occasional vagrant pawing through the overflowing bins for a morsel of food, he didn't encounter anyone for weeks. He noticed the silence slowly descending over the city. In the beginning, he could hear sirens in the distance, the blue lights reflecting through the night sky, they had all gone now. Through his window he watched the stars, nothing unnatural to break their glow.

It wasn't enough for Chester, he had everything he thought he'd ever wanted, all the equipment he could never afford, riches beyond his wildest dreams in the precious metals and rare gemstone looted from the back of sock draws, exquisite jewellery boxes and the occasional wall safe. The less likely it appeared people would return, the less value he realised these things truly held.

He thought back to an old friend still living in the shanty, congested area of the city. A man he's known for many years. Living, that might be his first problem now, he chuckled to himself. He'd met Benny just before he was arrested for attempting to sell drugs. Benny was a user and supplier in the area. He was a young man, probably somewhere in his mid-twenties if he had to guess. He'd been injecting heroin into his veins for half this adult life and the effects were stark on his slight frame, the welts on his skin and bruising around his arm showed all to easily the abuse Benny had put himself through for his fix.

He walked to his parked truck, the fuel tank nearing empty, he'd need to do something about that soon. The engine ignited and he started towards the towering skyscrapers on the horizon. The roads were clear, fuel had been rationed long before. The cars that usually choked the city roads like ants were now stationary in their parking bays. He didn't bother to check any of them, knowing their tanks would be dry.

It hadn't taken long to arrive outside the rundown block where Benny resided, the deserted streets void of traffic. He walked to the main entrance and went to knock. He noticed before he did, that the lock had been forced in. Lightly pressing the door, it swung open with ease.

He climbed the stairs, the filth here worse than he'd seen before. Rubbish had been discarded along the corridors, used needles sat menacingly on the filthy lino flooring, he jumped several steps to avoid the used condoms stuck to the grime covering every surface.

Benny lived on the third floor, the brown door full of scratches, dents where someone had tried to force their way in. He tried the door, it was locked. It was an old door, like most things around here. He put his shoulder against it and pushed, it gave easily.

The door swung open; the smell hit him instantly. He didn't need to see it to know Benny was dead, and not recently.

He forced himself into the small flat. Benny's lifeless, decomposing form was doubled over on the sofa, needle still resting on his rotting arm.

"Fuck," he said aloud. He wasn't surprised, at least this meant there should be some gear left around here somewhere, assuming he hadn't shot it all up in one last drug-filled bender before he died in a pool of his own vomit.

The small bag of brown heroin on the coffee table still contained a tiny amount of powder, he put it in the pocket of his jacket. That wasn't what he was here for, but it was a start. He searched the cramped flat, it didn't take long before he located what he was looking for. A bag of white powder hid under the sink in the kitchen, Benny didn't have the best imagination. He looked at the wrapped bag in his hand, it was the size of his palm, that would do.

The city was empty, but he knew it wasn't deserted. Plenty had refused the exodus, the evacuation attempts, the relocation attempts. There was sure to be a host of recruits left in the dead city. His ambitions had grown, he wanted to rule it. The police and army still inhabited the city, although those he did see seemed to get younger each day. He could do this, but not alone.

He concocted his plan, he needed to find the withdrawing junkies, those begging for a final fix, starved of the drugs that gave their lives purpose. He knew most of the dealers would be dead, or in jail, if people were still being kept locked up…

When the lockdown had first started, arrests of dealers and suppliers had skyrocketed. They stood out, easy pickings for the police. He searched the flat block he was in, opening door after door, calling into the dark, waiting for the strangled replies. No one did. A few bodies littered the damp flats, some of them were in a worse state than Benny's had been, the building was dead.

He'd spent a lot of time in this part of the city in his past, he knew where to check.

He was pleased his memory of the seedier areas was still perfect, it didn't take him long to find signs of life, the dregs of society crawling in the undergrowth, starved and dazed.

They had been abandoned, living in the new wilderness of overgrown wastelands. It was easy enough to band them together, there weren't many left. This part of the city had been hit hard by the virus. The authorities pulled out, they didn't need to keep this area running, it provided nothing to them.

Within an hour, he had half a dozen men, dressed in ragged, unwashed clothing, listening intently to his every word, their eyes following the bag of white powder he held aloft.

He'd promised riches to them, no more sleeping in the dirt, no more withdrawal, he could provide all they needed, they just had to follow him into the lawless new world.

The new followers had eagerly joined him. He provided purpose, he promised shelter. He promised food, he promised drugs, alcohol and girls. He promised them their utopia. Chester was a proud man, he wanted to be in control, but there had to be some rules, there had to be some order. He had to figure out how to keep things in control. The cocaine would only last so long, even if he rationed it out, he couldn't have more than a couple of hundred grams in that pack, he needed more.

Chester had reversed his black truck through the glass door of a fancy, upmarket hotel towards the centre of town to temporarily house his new crew of misfits, he hoped the water might somehow still work, they needed a bath, badly. Glass and the aluminium frame lay strewn across the ground.

After he'd collected the keys from the metal case

behind the deserted reception desk, he handed them out, along with a small line of cocaine to each of the six people that followed him here. He hoped there were still beds in these rooms. Either way, it was a step up from the dirt, he was winning regardless. He sat in the lobby as the others slowly made their way to their allocated rooms, the lack of light hindering any progress. He would need to sort that out too, to keep order, he needed to be able to see.

He sat on one of the red plush chairs, reserved for travellers to rest their weary feet as they waited for their rooms to be prepared. He lit another cigarette, he was alone now. He watched a fox walk across the road through the glass window, the moonlight reflecting from its eyes. It startled, glanced behind it and ran into the darkness. He walked to the glass, intrigued by the sudden movement from the fox. He saw the reflection first, the glass and metal used in the construction of the vast building around them glowing like a kaleidoscope, the angles of the sloping glass sparkling brightly in all direction.

The headlights grew brighter, and the sound of the rumbling grew louder. He could see the shape of the truck's cab as it got closer, the green canopy back concealing whatever lay inside. He stood by the window, watching as it passed, disappearing into the distance. It was an army vehicle. As it had passed, he saw the green uniform of the driver, heading towards the hospital in the centre of the city.

He sat back into the plush chair and mused silently to himself, that was worth checking out.

The rising sun had returned the glimmer of daylight to the foyer. Chester opened his eyes, his back twitched as he moved, sleeping on the chair hadn't been his best move. He glanced at the watch strapped to his wrist, it was early.

He walked to the black truck; parts of the door he'd rammed through the night before rested on the roof. With the scraping of metal, he drove back onto the road. He turned and followed the trail of the truck that had ambled past the night before.

He didn't want to conceal himself, to hide and watch like a rat. He was going to be in charge, and everyone would know it.

He stopped the truck at the entrance to the hospital. The road split here, the left fork went underground, right into the towering multi-storey car park used for visitors. He turned the wheel to the left, depressed the accelerator until the engine screamed in fury then allowed the truck to leap through the barrier. The shattering of plastic, the thud on the roof as it bounced of the truck and flew to the ground.

The soldiers, dressed the same in the green camouflage uniformed, looked up in unison, they hadn't expected a large black truck to be hurtling through the gloomy structure, they didn't move. He slammed on the brakes, the truck screeched to a halt, the roar of the engine echoing off all four walls, deafening the occupants within. He wanted to talk, that wouldn't help, he cut off the engine, the silence cutting through the musky air.

He climbed down from the truck, heard the sound of rifles being raised, he put his hands up to his face and slowly turned to show he was not a threat, yet.

"What the fuck are you doing here?" one of the soldiers had approached him, he had his rifle pointed at his chest. He looked older than the others, but still a young man. Chester smiled.

"I'm only here to help." His deep voice rough and demanding.

"We don't need no help, fuck off," the soldier replied.

"No?" Chester asked. "Are you sure? If I had to guess, there's maybe a dozen of you down here in the dark, why? There's half a city left out there," he motioned to the city above, half was an overestimation, but he liked the way it sounded. "And they aren't too happy with you lot, feel like you've abandoned them, looking out for number one, whoever that is these days?"

No reply.

"Fine. Why are you here and who's still in charge? Last I heard the government had collapsed, yet here you band of wannabes are. I'm going to guess sent by someone."

The man's face in front of him flinched, he was on the right track. Still no reply. He continued his monologue.

"Okay, let's make this simple, I want you to tell whoever you still report to, that I want to meet them, soon. They want to keep hold of this city, that's their business, but I can promise they'll find it a damn sight easier after they speak to me. Tell them, I can be their most valuable asset, but payment will be needed."

"You want cash?" the soldier finally spoke, surprise in his voice.

Chester laughed.

"No, I don't think cash has too much value anymore. I want cocaine. I want a lot of it, clean. If they want this kept under control, then they bring me what I ask for. The road," he pointed towards the ramp. "Tomorrow, midday, I want them to bring it, I want to know who's left."

The soldier still had his rifle training on him, the others watching intently.

"I don't care how they get it, police evidence room, whatever they have stashed at customs, as long as it turns up. They do that, I'll ensure you lot are left alone. If not, well your drive through town might not be so pleasant next time."

"I'll tell them," the soldier replied. "But I reckon you'll get the same answer, now fuck off."

Chester smiled, he'd made his point, they'd turn up tomorrow.

CHAPTER SIXTEEN

Tom had spent most of the day pacing the wide-open expanse of the factory floor. The more he ran their plan over in his head, the worse it sounded. He was doubting himself, how had he become the hero all of a sudden? He couldn't do this, why didn't he just run away, leave through the steel fire door, run down the road and never look back?

Why? He asked himself. He was quite happy on his own on that beach, why had he had to meet Kate, why had he had to care for these people? Why was he going to run off on his potential death march? To kill a man he'd never met, to save some hypothetical woman he couldn't be sure existed at an undetermined date in the future?

All he'd wanted to do was live a nice life, a quiet life. The farmhouse popped briefly back into his mind. Maybe he could talk to Chester instead, surely he was reasonable? The paving slab stained with blood floated to the front of his vision. Maybe not.

"Hey," he spun around, Kate had been watching

him from up high on the mezzanine. "What troubles you?"

Kate was as confident as ever, any doubt she had of herself previously had floated away, Tom was pleased to see it.

"Nothing, nothing," he replied. "Just... I don't know, this seems daft. I mean, what are we doing, when did we start playing judge and jury?"

"You've seen it, Tom, you've seen what they do. It's the lowlifes he carries with him, they're the worst, but you have to cut the head from the snake to kill the body. Besides, we want his truck, don't we?" she asked.

"I guess," he replied carefully. "I just worry that we've jumped into something we can't win. Chester doesn't even know we exist and what, we're now out to kill him?"

"He knows. We've killed three of them, maybe four, I don't know who the man in the car park was with." Tom's head throbbed at the memory. "I think he's probably out for us by now too, it's only a matter of time, he'll find us. We can't be more than a few miles away, even now."

Tom thought about her words. He guessed she was right, but running still seemed the sensible option.

"Anyway, the worlds gone to shit, if I... if we can do just one thing right, maybe it won't be so bad. Then, Tom, I promise we can leave, we can go to the middle of nowhere, we can live it out till we're old, peaceful and happy."

They had settled on a location; they just needed a time.

They wanted to start the fire early in the morning, the smoke would remain visible in the daylight, the hope was most of the others would be passed out asleep. They wanted to draw Chester out, not his entire gang. The weather would be important, it had to be a clear day, the cloud cover minimum so the smoke could travel further. They didn't want their efforts wasted by a poor line of sight.

Kate had lost the axe. It lay where it had been dropped by the park in the centre of the city, there was no getting it back now. She'd tried other weapons, none of them felt as comfortable. She eventually settled on a length of metallic pipe, it had reach and looked deadly enough. She didn't want to be left with only a knife, you had to be too close to your victim. She didn't want to see the white of a person's eyes as she tried to drain the life from them. Besides, she'd seen the knife stick in flesh too many times to be sure she could quickly get it out, if it came to it.

The three of them would go, Tom, Kate and Chloe. They agreed Chloe would sit in the open, bait. Tom would hide nearby, the gun trained on the space they hoped Chester would arrive from. Kate would wait the other side, behind whatever cover she could find. A last resort, they hoped she could cause surprise and confusion, if it was needed.

Chester was sure to be drawn to Chloe, he'd recognise her, he'd want to know what had happened the night she escaped. They didn't think he'd be happy that she'd left, he saw her as his possession by the end. He didn't like to lose his possessions.

Chloe was the only one of them who had met Chester. She'd painted him as a ruthless monster, but articulate. He could talk and charm his way to wherever he wanted to be, but as soon as your back was turned, like the snake he was, he'd strike. She'd been adamant about that. They shouldn't allow him to speak if it came to it, just bury the bullet into his skull.

Tom's nerves were on edge. He wanted this over with. They agreed they would leave that night, they'd need to be there by sunrise if their plan was going to work, they couldn't risk arriving late. They packed a bag of supplies. After the last excursion, Tom made sure they had a little food and water. He took the knife, the same one he'd previously forced into a man's neck, folded in the familiar cloth and carefully placed it on top of the pack, it would make a good backup if he needed it.

They said their goodbyes to Matt and Rose, she still wasn't happy with them, and they walked out the gap in the chain-link fence for what they hoped wouldn't be the last time.

The journey was arduous, their agreed location a walk of several long miles.

They had to skirt around the city, they didn't feel safe crossing through the centre. The labyrinth of side streets where anything could strike at them from the dark, unseen and deadly.

It was early afternoon when they first departed the factory. They were barely halfway to their location and the night was setting in. The hills in the distance were shrouded by dark, Tom could feel his bearings slowly eroding. They continued the route they had planned; they didn't talk much. Chloe had walked on, a hard resolve in her eyes. Tom wasn't sure she knew where she was headed, but she strode so confidently, he followed her silently.

By the time they neared their destination, the chill of the night had set in. Tom felt himself shiver, he hoped it was just the cold.

"We're nearly there," Kate announced. "We should think about finding somewhere to rest up, we'll probably need it by morning."

Tom couldn't argue with that, the travel had worn him out. It was late in the night now, he could feel his eyelids drooping. Stifling a yawn, Tom peered around for anywhere that might provide basic shelter for a few hours. The village had become one of the affluent areas at the very end of the city, grand parks and oversized gardens separated the large townhouses, nestled between thatched roofed cottages. This had been a village once, since swallowed up by the growing metropolis on its doorstep.

Tom woke as the sun began its daily ascent into

the sky. They had sheltered in a disused bus stop, set back from the road. Its slate roof and stone walls reminding Tom of the similar buildings that littered the coastlines. He'd spent plenty of nights near those. It felt familiar, it felt safe.

"Kate, Chloe," he whispered, Kate stirred. "Kate," he said, slightly louder. Her eyes crept open, blinking as they adjusted to the light. Chloe remained asleep, curled up on the stone bench. She looked innocent in her sleep. Tom felt the familiar surge of pity, she hadn't deserved any of this.

Kate was getting to her feet, he held his finger to his lips. They could be in for a long day, he left Chloe sleeping as they crept out.

"We'd better get started."

"Okay," she replied. "The trees in the park, let's see if there's anything over there, dead branches would be best. We can use the hedge for the green."

He scanned around, behind the bus stop was a large green park, old oak trees adjourned its boundary, a once neat hedge connecting them. As he walked towards the nearest tree, the size of the task dawned on him. They needed this fire to burn for hours, maybe longer.

The bracken littering the ground was a good start, but it wouldn't last. They hadn't brought anything to help them collect more wood. The thick branches of the oak trees would be of little help, he wouldn't be able to break them free.

He paused, they thought their plan had covered

everything, everything except the obvious. He glared around the park, there wasn't enough fuel there, he let out a large sigh. It would have to do.

Tom and Kate spent the next hour collecting the broken, dead wood from the ground, they had a large pile in the middle of the park. He took the lighter from his pocket and carefully held the flame to the edge of a dry branch. It caught. The flames licked slowly up its side, growing ever larger before jumping to the branch stacked on top. Larger still they grew, consuming the foliage at an alarming rate.

"It's never going to be enough!" Tom said exasperated. "It'll burn itself out too quick."

Kate didn't reply, she was furiously ripping green leaves from the hedge. He watched the speed the fire engulfed the rubble. The flames were high, the roaring deafening. Then he heard another sound, a thud of something hitting the ground. As he turned, he saw Chloe behind him, a pile of broken wood lay at his feet.

"I figured we'd just use the fences and furniture from the houses." She shrugged as she turned, Tom watched her kick another white-painted post loose from the nearby garden. *Clever lass*, he thought to himself, wondering why neither he nor Kate had thought of that.

The three of them collected broken fence panels, dining chairs and small coffee tables they could pull from the abandoned houses lining the street.

They added them to the pile, ready to keep the fire burning, for as long as needed.

The flames now roared high overhead. They didn't need the greenery after all, the paint from the fences and the fabric seats from the chairs spewed dark plumes of black smoke high into the sky. If anyone was looking, there was no way they would miss the signal.

Tom once again started to doubt the plan, another eventuality they hadn't considered. They were trying to draw out Chester, the smoke would be seen in all directions for miles. What if they drew out someone else? He didn't want to think about it, not everyone left in this world could be bad, but he would wager a decent portion of them were. To survive this world, you needed a nasty streak.

With the fire roaring, they retreated to their agreed positions, Chloe sat, cross-legged on the grass in front of the fire, Kate chose the nearby oak tree, crouching behind the thick trunk. Tom backed himself into the overgrown hedge, a clear line of sight to both Chloe and the approaching road. There they waited in the hope that this might work.

It had taken longer to prepare the fire than they had anticipated, the sun was high in the sky now, close to midday.

How long had the smoke been billowing into the air, an hour, two? He listened for the approach of an engine, some tell-tale sign of life rushing towards them. He didn't know how long he'd been crouched there, his legs were aching. His mind wandering, he found it hard to concentrate. Forcing himself to stay still, it dawned on him, it had failed, no one was coming.

"Tom!" The sound of Kate's voice startled him, he looked round to the tree where she'd hid, she was stood in the open, a shotgun pointed at her back.

Tom didn't recognise the man stood behind her, he could see him well enough, it wasn't Chester. The man was older, his chequered shirt tucked into blue jeans, work boots on his feet. His expression curious, not threatening.

"Gun on the floor, lad," he said gruffly, looking to the handgun in Tom's hand.

"You don't understand," Tom protested. "There's likely to be someone coming, someone bad, we can't be here in the open. We're all dead if we do."

"Then you'd best drop the gun, so we can all get out of here quickly," came the simple reply.

Tom saw no other option. He threw the gun to the floor between them, the man ambled over, pushing Kate lightly with the barrel of his shotgun until they stood over the discarded pistol. He slowly picked it up, checked the magazine and slipped it into his belt. He stepped back away from Kate; shotgun still pointed up.

"I'm Bob," he stated cheerily, with a smile across his large face. "Let's get out of here, then, follow me." He motioned to the three of them. Kate looked at Tom, he simply shrugged, what else could they do now?

The man led them away to the back of the park, through a green peeling gate, out into the fields beyond.

"Saw that fire of yours from a long way off. Trying to get yourself killed, I guess?" His voice was kind, despite the gruff undertone. His large greying moustache and beard muffling the words slightly as they came out.

"The opposite," Tom replied. "We were hoping to draw someone out the city, someone whose been killing people as he pleased."

Bob grunted in reply, pushing overgrown brambles out of the way as he traversed the edge of the fields.

"We were only after one man," Tom continued. "I swear, but we have others to look after too, whatever your plan is here, we need to leave."

"Not safe anymore," Bob replied. "Thanks to you lot. That fire will draw every reprobate for miles, trust me, there are more than I think you realise."

Tom mulled this over in his head, he hadn't seen many others on his travels, he assumed most were dead by now. But he'd stayed hidden for a long time, it made sense others could do the same.

He felt the hairs on the back of his neck prick, could it be he'd been watched, through twitching curtains, eyes peering over dark hedgerows, staring out from the dark?

Bob continued to push through the overgrown

brush, keeping tight to it as he strode confidently on. Kate followed directly behind him, Chloe in the middle and Tom at the rear.

They had followed without much persuasion; the man had slung the shotgun over his shoulder. Other than when he took Tom's gun, he hadn't threatened them, he hadn't really forced them to follow him, but they had anyway.

Tom thought about this, he couldn't explain why, but he trusted Bob, the man he'd only met moments before, who had a shotgun pointed at his friends, the man who took his only protection from him. The knife in the rucksack popped into his mind.

After walking the muddy, uneven ground of the fields for a further half an hour or so, they arrived at a large old house, set in the centre of a flowing meadow, with a growing orchard located in the front garden. Tom smiled, a farmhouse, perfect.

The city was still visible on the horizon behind them, he could see the plume of black smoke still plummeting high into the sky. Chester was sure to have seen that, everyone was sure to have seen that. Another flaw they hadn't considered.

Bob knocked on the old wooden door, it cracked open, two eyes peered through the gap. The door pushed back, the sound of a chain being removed, it opened fully.

"Bob, you've brought back guests, again." The grey haired woman stood in the doorway sounded agitated, Tom got the impression they weren't the first group to be hounded to this front door.

"Everyone deserves a chance, Carole," he replied. "Anyway, these are the ones who set the fire." He pointed behind him.

"So that was you lot," Carole's eyes narrowed as she studied them. "That seems... short-sighted," she finished.

Tom felt slightly embarrassed. "Sorry," he stammered.

Carole stood in the kitchen, waiting for the electric kettle to boil. The lights from the ceiling bathed the room in unnatural light. Tom was awestruck, he hadn't seen working electricity in so long.

Bob and Carole had lived here long before the virus first infected the world, they liked to be off grid anyway. They had installed solar panels several years ago. They were still connected to the mains, but they liked to keep their reliance off others as much as they could. A borehole on their land supplied the water. For as long as the panels held up, they were completely self-sustained here.

Bob had told them it was difficult in the beginning, people fleeing the city had called on their door, begging for shelter, food or water. He'd let them in originally, but before long they had been overwhelmed, too many stood by their door, helpless and hoping for salvation.

Bob had blocked off the public footpaths that led through his land, hoping the masses would divert to the main road where the orchard and high hedges hid the house. It had worked to some degree, less people banged on his door late at night, but it was still too much.

They had to turn people away, people Bob was sure would now be dead. The creases in his face deepened as he retold the story, it weighed heavily on him that he hadn't been able to help them all.

A few of the early arrivals had stayed, he'd found them a bed, fed them the best he could. Some got sick, he'd buried more than he cared to recall in the field across the way. Others left as winter set in, and the food started to run short. Several ran out in the dead of night, taking anything they could carry with them, he lost a lot of precious supplies that way. Eventually the flood stopped, no one came from the city, no one returned.

For the longest time, Bob had assumed it was only he and Carole left, that everyone else had died. He was grateful that neither of them got sick, he didn't know how they avoided it, he wore long black gauntlet gloves and a thick apron whilst burying the dead. Disinfecting the area with pesticide, although he didn't know if that would have any impact on hundreds of thousands of virus spores blowing across the land.

One night as he watched the stars sparkle up in the sky, he'd noticed the glow of a fire in the distance, then another and another. He had a good vantage point from his house in the field, the hill behind blocked the view down to the coast, but looking towards the city, his land was slightly elevated and he could see a large part of it off in the distance. The fires were burning from various locations, all burning with different intensity.

He'd immediately headed off to investigate the source. Bob believed that everyone still had good left in them, they just needed a reason to show it. The first night, he'd found a group, warming themselves around the fire, starved and nervous, he'd taken them all back to his farm.

"That was fine," Carole said firmly, dragging Tom back to the conversation. "Until the first time someone tried to kill us off, keep the farm for themselves! Did he stop? No, of course he didn't. Just the very next week he brought more stragglers back, offering them board! It never worked out. Most people left in the world now are broken." She eyed the three of them suspiciously, now sat around her kitchen table, fresh cups of coffee steaming in front of them. The coffee Carole had was wonderful, flavoursome and rich, not like the industrial catering stuff Tom had become accustomed too.

"You've had many here?" he asked curiously between sips.

"Yes. Less of them recently, but Bob has brought more than one or two strays home in his time. I begged him to stop. No offence," she nodded her head towards Tom, he shrugged in reply. "People seem to have lost it, I just want to live out the rest of my days in peace, not worried someone will cut them shorter than they may naturally already be."

Bob let out a roaring laugh. "That's no way to look at life," he bellowed cheerily. "The world may be over, it doesn't mean our manners have to be."

"Perhaps." Carole sounded curt.

Bob liked to talk, he was a jovial man Tom learned, always seeing the good in life, in the situation. How he'd survived this long, Tom would never understand. He had seen the house on the approach, he could see why it might be missed from the road, high hedges surrounded the boundary. The house was in a valley outside of town, it couldn't be seen until you got close, despite its elevated setting. Carole had explained that they couldn't use the power after dark, they didn't want to give their location away. Bob was okay bringing people here, but only at his invitation, on his terms. He'd learnt his lesson, but the desire inside of him to help was too strong to stop completely. Tom wondered if he'd keep trying to help until the day he died, which might be closer than he thought if he didn't take more care.

Carole seemed much more against the idea, she was obviously the more practical of the pair. Although, even she admitted with their advancing age, collecting the crops of the coming years would get harder. Although if it was only the two of them, they would need to harvest much less. They had let the fields furthest from the property fall into disuse, the weeds claimed them back quickly.

Bob had ploughed the closest field over the winter before the frost took hold of the ground, preparing them for the spring when he could start to grow grain. He hadn't scaled back completely. He had the seed, might as well try to create as much as he could, in case anyone else might be in need.

They even had a few animals, a couple of milking cows remained, chickens for eggs, and a goat that lived in the front garden. A pet, Carole had scoffed as she told how Bob couldn't bear to slaughter any of his animals. The animals would outlive them, she was certain of that.

"So, why were you trying to burn half the town down?" she asked Tom, as she turned her attention back to him.

"We weren't exactly," Tom replied. "We were hoping to draw someone out. A man, he's being doing some pretty unspeakable things recently. Poor Chloe here," he gestured to his side where she sat. "He had her tied up, beaten, half dead. We wanted to stop him, so he couldn't hurt anyone else, we wanted to make that small difference."

Carole studied Chloe; the faint bruises still visible around her eyes.

"Still, stupid move. Setting that fire," Carole said disapprovingly. "There were lots of fires in the first days, weeks. Bob went to check them out. To see if there was anyone he could help. Sometimes there was. Sometimes, he barely got away with his life. Other times, he was too late. Whoever set some of those fires met a very ugly end. Bob thinks the fire gave them away. I guess maybe to the same person you were after. I begged him to stop going, it's only a matter of time before he finds them, or they find him..." She trailed off.

"That's just one group," Bob interjected merrily. "There's plenty of people we could be helping, we should never stop trying, eh. You once told me that, Carole."

She smiled weakly at him.

"Aren't you worried, about what might happen to you, to your home?" Kate asked.

"It's worth the risk," Bob replied. "Like you, I'm just trying to help one person at a time."

"What made you come to us today? How did you know we wouldn't be a threat?"

"Well, I didn't for sure, that's why I had the shotgun. Between you and I, I feared the worst when I saw the gun on young Tom over there." Bob motioned his giant head in Tom's direction. "But it all turned out okay, didn't it? You three seem like good eggs." The grin back on his face.

"We can't stay," Kate said firmly. "There are others we need to get back too, they're on their own, they don't know what's happened to us and if the fire does draw people out, they could be in danger."

Bob sat in thought, a moment of silence passed.

"Okay," he said finally. "So let's go get them."

CHAPTER SEVENTEEN

Tom sat in the passenger seat of Bob's truck. It wasn't the sleek, polished black one he'd dreamed when he closed his eyes. Bob's truck was red with white stripes running up the wings, it was much older. The interior bare, creaking at every turn, every bump in the road.

"She's old, but she's reliable. Pulls much better than this modern rubbish," said Bob, sensing his disapproval.

Kate and Chloe had stayed at the farm, Bob had agreed to take Tom back to the factory to collect Rose and Matt, along with any possessions or supplies they had left. It hadn't taken long for the decision to move to the house to be made. They were running out of everything at the factory, the gas had been spluttering, the food suppliers dangerously low. The safety he'd enjoyed now felt like it was on borrowed time.

Bob had been thrilled when Tom and Kate had agreed, Chloe didn't say much. Tom wondered if she was disappointed she hadn't managed her reckoning with Chester. They had jumped into the old truck, locked up in a barn behind the farm, and started the slow drive to town.

Bob had a large tank of agricultural diesel, plenty enough he proudly announced to run his truck for years. Bob was perfectly prepared for this, thought Tom, and almost enjoying it too much. The drive to town took longer than he imagined, the roads outside the farm were pitted and neglected. Bob drove slowly to avoid the potholes, ever-increasing in size, the obstacles strewn on the ground amongst the decaying bodies of the countless who fell in the weeks and months before.

Outside of the beach, since he'd left his city home in the early days, Tom hadn't seen the dead in these numbers. Rotting corpses had become the normal, especially in the country. People fled, they never made it too far. As Tom watched the scenery pass him by, he wondered if this was repeated up and down the country, deserted streets littered with decomposing husks, the animals stripping the soft flesh, white bone glistening in the sunlight.

With the numbers who had perished in the second wave of the virus, and those who died of exposure or hunger, Tom realised that the lack of bodies he'd seen must be the exception, not the rule.

The early deaths were hurriedly buried or burnt, in giant furnaces hidden from view. As those who disposed of them started to get sick, there would be no one left to give them the same send-off. He imagined a country covered with bodies, lay head-to-toe, in various states of decomposition. The stench began to fill his nostrils again, he swallowed hard, trying not to gag.

Bob had talked for most of the journey, he did like to talk. Tom listened, for the most part, offering his comments on rare occasion. Bob seemed quite happy to ramble on and Tom was happy to let him.

He began another story; Tom suspected the facts were clouded with fiction at parts. Some of Bob's stories were far-fetched, other downright unbelievable. He told of the time he found a young family on the outskirts of the city, cornered by ravenous wild dogs. How he'd fought them off with his fists, taking a good bite or two in the process. Tom suspected fiction. He then told of the young couple he'd come across, they were trying to warm themselves by a small fire they had started with broken fence panels (why did everyone think of that except Tom?), freezing to death in the depths of winter. Bob had taken them home and warmed them through, prepared them food and offered them a bed. They had been sick though, they died within the day. *Fact*, thought Tom glumly.

Bob then said something which made Tom take note, he sat upright, sure he must have misheard. Bob repeated his statement.

"I've met Chester." His face was no longer joyous, deep creases formed in his forehead; his eyes were hard.

"Wha... Why didn't you say anything?"

"Carole would have had a fit if she knew. Nasty piece of work that one. I saw them in the distance, maybe ten of them. They looked rough, looked like they could do with a good meal. I tried to talk to them, see if I could help. Course I didn't know who they were, what they were capable off back then, I've learnt more from the people I've met since. I've seen what they do to people."

Tom was in disbelief; Bob had met Chester and knew all about him.

"Why didn't you let us kill him!" he almost shouted.

"Because he woulda' killed you!'

"We had it planned out, it could have worked."

"But it likely wouldn't. I got you, didn't I, and I'm not a psychopathic lunatic. Not today, anyway." He smiled again. "Truth of the matter is I've had to be much more careful these days, never know who's hiding under his wing. I can't risk him finding my home, imagine what he'd do to poor Carole."

The truck lurched sideways as the wheel struck a pothole.

"What happened when you met him?" asked Tom.

"Well, like I said, he's a nasty piece of work. All charmin' and what not at first, trying to get information out of me I reckon, wanted what was mine. Wanted to know who I was with, how many people, where we stayed, what we had. He offered drugs, silly bastard, I haven't taken drugs in my life. Mind you, reckon that's how he gets those others to stay with him, doing what he tells them."

"Kate saw him once, she thinks the drugs are coming from whatever government is left."

Bob mulled this over. "Figures," he said simply.

"So?" asked Tom. "What then?"

"Well, then he starts to turn, musta' seen I wasn't going to tell him anything, he gets real nasty, had a rifle with him. Military one I think, looked like he probably knew how to use it – all his cronies start getting up close too, I didn't like the feel of it."

"How did you get away? How come he didn't kill you?"

"Cos I punched him in the nose and ran!" He laughed, the smile back on this face, the seriousness now gone.

"That was it? You hit him, and he just let you leave?"

"I can throw quite a punch. Don't think he was best pleased about it mind, think he's been out looking for me since, I've seen him leaving the city a few times, he checks around the villages. He's out as far as the coast now. Lucky our place is well hidden."

The clouds were intensifying overhead, the clear sky replaced with a grey blanket of mist, rolling high above their heads. The rain thundered on the windscreen of the old truck, each drop hammering into the earth.

Bob slowed as the road in front was quickly submerged, with the drainage no longer maintained, it didn't take long for the road to run like a river. Tom suddenly felt grateful they were in the old truck, high ground clearance and oversized wheels, knobbly tread forcing the water to part as it rolled on. They were coming into the city; the rain didn't let up.

"At least the rain will stop anyone hearing us drive up!" Bob shouted as he raised his thumb to the end of his balled fist, his booming voice barely audible over the sound of the relentless pounding from every inch of the truck as it was assaulted by the elements.

"True," Tom replied.

"Eh? Didn't catch that!"

"Nevermi..." Tom was cut off mid-sentence, even with the falling rain obscuring the view, he could see the smoke, snaking high into the air, the black contrast to the grey sky. It was coming from the industrial area. *Please God*, he thought, *don't let it be coming from home.* He pointed furiously to the plume growing ever closer.

"THERE!" he shouted. Bob nodded to show his understanding and pressed the accelerator to the floor.

They sped into the industrial estate where the old textile factory was located. As they approached, Tom could see the factory, the windows high up the exterior had cracked and buckled, flames licked the red brick wall like the tongue of a serpent.

"Fuck..." he whispered to himself; this was bad.

They skidded to a halt at the entrance to the gap in the chain-link fence, water flooded through the car park. Tom couldn't stop looking at the running water on the ground. Right in the entrance, even through the haze of the storm. It ran red.

He knew what he was about to see long before he could bring himself to lift his head. He watched, mesmerised, as the swirl of red followed the water and diluted into nothingness. Forcing his gaze up, his heart broke, every emotion he'd been trying to bottle up broke free, tears rolled freely down his face.

Tied to the fence, head lolling at an angle, was Rose. Her throat slit, blood covered her clothes. He could see it trickling down her lifeless fingers, joining the water below.

Tom scrambled for the door, he felt something holding him back, turning, he saw Bob had his hand placed on his shoulder, he was shaking his head. He shook him off and pulled himself from the car. He ran over to Rose, his shoes slapping through the rising water with every step.

She was tied at the top of the fence, her arms spread, wrists bound. Her legs were loose, she swung gently in the wind, she was the crucifix in the storm.

The sorrow overwhelming him, Tom fell to his knees, this was his fault.

Bob gently walked below the lopping figure of Rose, withdrew a lock knife from his pocket, reached and cut her free. She fell onto his shoulder, without a word he carried her to the back of the truck, wrapped her still-warm body in a large blanket and carefully laid her to rest.

Tom had seen something fall from her mouth as she'd dropped, he reached to pull from the water a small bag of white powder, a pair of headphones wrapped around it. He held them in the palm of his hand as Bob returned, the rain lashing off his face, anger replaced sorrow.

Matt, he suddenly thought, he'd forgotten about him. Glancing over to the building in front of him, he tried to put the image of Rose out of his mind, he would have to mourn later, Matt was still missing.

If he was inside, was there any hope of him still being alive? What else could have happened to him. Rose was displayed so prominently, if they had Matt, wouldn't they have done the same to him? The headphones, they were Matt's, they had taken him. Tom felt bile in the back of his throat, he retched into the water flowing around his feet.

"We've got to go after them," he said hopelessly.

"We can't do that now," Bob replied, sympathy etched on his face. "We don't know where they are, there's only the two of us."

"We can't leave him. God knows what they'll do to him. They can't be far, this happened very recently." The feeling of dread, now so familiar, returned. This *had* happened recently, the blood still seeping from the slit on Rose's throat as they pulled up, if only they had been just moments earlier, they might have been able to save her, to fight them off, to stop Matt being taken.

"We need more bodies, and we need more guns," Bob shouted over the sound of the falling rain. "I have a couple, we can get Kate, maybe Chloe, then we'll go look for your friend. I promise."

Tom felt useless. If they went back to the farm, they might lose Matt forever. They couldn't be far by now, but he didn't know which direction they had travelled, the storm sure to have hidden any tracks.

He didn't know how many there were, had they come on foot or had the black truck belonging to Chester parked on this very spot? They might be half a mile away now, or they might be long out of the city. They wouldn't have heard the engine roaring in the distance, not with the storm that was still raging overhead.

Tom was deflated, he was broken. He clamoured back into the big red truck and sunk into the chair, eyes closed, tears staining his face. He didn't recall much about the trip back, the storm had passed, the sky cleared.

A rainbow in the distance floated majestically over the rolling hills. The truck pulled slowly into the barn, the noise cut off and the sounds of the birds returned, floating in from the open door. Tom finally opened his eyes.

Kate was stood outside, watching them, her face unreadable. She didn't yet know what had happened. She must have guessed something was wrong; they had returned alone. She couldn't see the body wrapped in the back of the truck. He didn't want to tell her; he didn't want to see the pain etched on her face again.

As she moved closer; her head turned slightly to the side in question. Tom shook his, eyes down. He nodded towards the back of the truck, better to get it over with. He watched in the door mirror as she slowly walked over to the covered mass in the back of the truck and pulled the corner of the blanket free. He heard her scream. In the mirror, he watched her fall to the ground, hand clasped to her mouth, eyes wide in terror.

She didn't move for a long time. Bob had excused himself and headed for the house. Tom was sure he could hear him and Carole arguing from the closed bedroom window a short time later.

He must have told Chloe. She came running to the barn, dropping to the ground next to Kate, her arm around her shoulder. He couldn't hear what she was saying.

Bob had returned, he didn't talk, but removed a shovel hung against the barn wall. Nodding briefly to Tom, he turned and headed into the meadow on the other side of their home, where he'd previously indicated he'd buried the dead. Tom finally forced himself to move. The day had drained him, it took every sinew of effort just to push himself upright, his legs felt weak, his head swimming. He didn't head towards the grieving women at the back of the truck. He needed to give them time. He removed a second shovel from a nail on the wall and followed where Bob had walked.

He had already started digging a fresh grave, freshly turned mounds of earth lay on the floor. Tom pushed the shovel into the ground without a word.

The storm had fully passed by the time they had finished, the hole was shallower than he would have liked. Birds sung in the meadow. Butterflies scattered overhead. He felt the sweat running down his chest. In this wildflower meadow they had dug Rose's final resting place. Tom wondered if it was purposefully selected by Bob, a white rose bush rested at the head of the grave.

Kate had allowed Bob to effortlessly collect the fragile body in the blanket without a word. She followed as he solemnly walked, the bundle resting in his arms. Chloe hadn't said a word as she followed soundlessly behind. A gasp escaped her lips as he laid the bundle into the shallow grave. He stood back and bowed his head.

Carole had left the house to join them, the five of them stood to the side of the grave.

"Anyone want to say anything?" Bob asked.

Tom couldn't think of anything to say. He'd gotten to know Rose, her dry humour had made him smile, the way she would chastise him for the smallest things, he missed her. She'd been part of his new family.

"I will." It was the first time Kate had spoken

since they returned. "Rose saved my life, she was a good person. She was a kind person. She didn't deserve this. This world wasn't right for Rose, but she tried to make the best of it. She always looked out for others. She was caring, she had the loveliest soul of anyone I have ever met. I'm pleased I was able to know Rose; she made my life better, even in this horrible world. She survived the deadliest virus ever seen, and came out the other side stronger. She was shot by those she thought were there to protect her, but never cursed them, she never wished them harm. She never spoke of vengeance or revenge. She once told me she hoped the young man who shot her would be okay. It couldn't have been nice, shooting an old lady, she prayed for his soul. I laughed at the time, I never believed in turning the other cheek. Rose did. She felt the world would come together again. She tried to keep us all safe. She didn't want us to go yesterday, she made that clear. She was right, if we hadn't, she might still be alive..." Kate trailed off.

"Or maybe you'd all be dead along with her." Carole's voice was cold. "The bastard who did this wanted to make a point. He's still got one of you. My guess is he is going to use him to get the rest."

Kate collected a handful of the soft earth, throwing it into the grave.

"Then let's go find out."

" It's almost certainly a trap," Carole said.

"I know."

"You don't know how many of them there are, or

where they are."

"Doesn't matter."

"You don't know if they have weapons, or what they might already have done to your friend."

"Which is why we need to go."

"Then I'll go get the guns." Carole walked back towards the barn.

CHAPTER EIGHTEEN

Chester sat in his truck on the road adjacent from the hospital, the engine running. He'd parked sideways, it would be impossible to be missed.

The street had been cleared since he was last here, the bodies removed. He'd watched the carnage unfold, he sent several of his men out to confront the soldiers. He figured they'd end up dead, but as long as he stayed out of the firing line, it was the perfect solution to create further division between the surviving people and the government meant to be caring for them.

He hadn't expected the paving slab crushing the soldiers head, although he had to agree it was a nice touch, sure to get the reply he was after. He had been right, moments after the crushing blow, he'd watched the man shot by the other soldiers. He hadn't known the man long, hadn't bothered to learn his name. He'd blindly followed instruction, eager for the chance to fight. He could use a man like that, but could he control his anger? Probably not, it was better this way. He wanted the rifle, that was the goal. They had gone too far though. Like a pack of wild animals, they attacked the one soldier, forgetting about the rest, still armed.

After Chester had seen the second soldier shoot dead his man and then run off to confront the others, he'd calmly walked up the road, approaching the blood-splattered ground, he reached for the rifle and slung it over his shoulder.

He briefly admired the result the paving slab had had on the soldier. His head unrecognisable, white bone glistened from the ground. He heard the approach of the other soldiers before he saw them. Turning, he walked back to the safety of his waiting truck.

He could see the road from here, and if he needed to, it would be easy enough to get away. He watched as the massacre started, people ran, they were shot down. He laughed; this was better than he could have expected.

He took interest when he saw a younger blond woman running from the safety of one of the buildings. What were these building, student flats? He'd thought, maybe she'd been there since the beginning. He'd have to send someone to check them out once this settled down. The woman had dashed across the road and spoke to a boy huddled against the opposite building. He looked terrified before she led him out of sight. He could have sworn just before she stumbled out of view; she'd looked directly at him.

It was nearing midday; the time he'd told the soldier their boss was to turn up. He hoped this would work. He'd been so confident and sure of himself, but he doubted it deep down. He hoped he'd done enough. There was nothing to stop those men with their rifles surrounding his truck, shooting him dead if they wanted to.

He'd guessed they were all new recruits, anyone with experience had been deployed to keep the peace in the early days. Most of them had got sick and died when the virus ravished the world. Other had been killed in the riots, when they first opened fire on the innocent people, they had become the enemy.

He'd watched the riots from the safety of afar, he knew the people were desperate. He guessed the authorities were too, the only outcome was bloodshed, and he had no intention of being caught in that. He'd heard of the violence in other cities around the country and the world. Those which had no strategic value, which didn't house the elite, were left to die. The infections ran rampant, they'd be lifeless soon anyway. The government had pulled out, brought their last remaining troops back here to defend what they had left, to maintain the illusion of power and safety.

The virus was still active, he'd seen people sick. He'd avoided them. With the volume of dead, it was losing access to hosts, the spread was slowing.

He wondered if it would die out when there were no longer enough to infect. Probably not, the incubation period was so long. As long as there were people left alive, it would continue its spread until every last one of them had perished. He'd just have to enjoy himself till then.

He was careful about those he built up around him. He needed those desperate enough to follow him, but he couldn't have dissent. He wanted them to obey. The drugs had helped, but he needed something more long term.

They were staying in the hotel he'd claimed as his own. He had more with him now, they turned up at night, starved, begging for help and mercy. He invited them to join him with open arms, promising a new life, promising safety and security.

He didn't care for them much, they were the dregs of society, likely to be more trouble when he really needed them, but it was a start. The first who had questioned him, a younger man, barely out of his teenage years, had demanded to know what they were doing, where they were going and how they were going to survive. He'd been high at the time, but Chester couldn't allow it. They had been in one of the long corridors on the upper floors of the hotel. People were milling around, watching the confrontation, waiting to see who would act. Chester acted first. He grasped the man by the scruff of his shirt, forced him to the window overlooking the street at the end of the corridor and with a powerful blow, he pushed him through it. The glass shattered, the scream grew distant as he fell, the wet, sickening thud on the road below, and then silence. He didn't say a word, he didn't have to.

This wasn't the first man he'd killed, and it wouldn't be the last. No one questioned him since, obedience was swift.

Chester hadn't come alone, he'd brought three of his henchmen with him. Once this meeting was over, he wanted them to search through the accommodation either side of the road. He'd dropped them off and told them to lay low until things were clear, then search through the buildings. He also wanted to know if the government car left, if a helicopter did arrive, he wanted people here to report back to him.

He glanced at his watch, midday exactly.

He heard the rumble of an engine approach, it was travelling fast. He felt his heart race and took several deep breaths to calm himself. He had to remain confident, he had to show he was in charge, or this would never work.

A dark saloon car came hurtling around the corner, slamming its brakes and skidding to a halt, just feet from his parked black truck. No troops, no guns pointed at him. He smiled. Perfect.

He rapped his knuckles twice on the tinted glass window and waited patiently as it rolled down. He tried to mask his surprise as he found himself face to face with a woman sitting in the back of the car. Her grey hair pulled tightly into a bun at the back of her head. She was wearing a neatly pressed black suit and a white blouse with a frilly collar around her neck.

"So," she started, eyeing him suspiciously. "You're the one who thought he'd gate crash my soldiers, are you?"

"Yes, ma'am," he replied with a smile. "I think we can be of help to each other here."

"How so?"

"Your mob aren't best liked at the moment, nor trusted. I think there's more people left here than you realise, and I don't think you have the resource to deal with them. I can. People feel abandoned while you drive around in your fancy cars and clean clothes. How long will it be until they want what you have? There's enough of them, trust me, they will take it."

The woman took a moment to think.

"We are still in control of this country," she said firmly. "We have enough to keep that control too. Once the vaccine is in production, people will trust again."

"And how long is that going to be? Do you really think people won't have starved to death by then, killed each other off, died of this fucking virus?"

"It's closer than you might think. But it's true, we have seen some... issues in other areas. Some protests have had to be... shut down, shall we say."

"I heard about them, so did almost everyone else. Shooting dead half your remaining population doesn't win the populist vote, you know?"

"And what do you want, why do you offer to help, Mr...?"

"Call me Chester. I want this." He raised his arms, outstretched around him. "All of it. I'm not daft; I don't for a moment think you lot plan to stay here, I'm surprised you're here now, to be honest."

"Quite," came the curt reply. She clearly didn't want to be here. "It is true, the government is retreating to somewhere... more remote. There are just a few loose ends to tie up first."

Chester nodded, he didn't care about their plans here.

"The helipad, right? That's why you picked the hospital. There's fuel stored underneath and escape up top. If you can get over how many died in there, it's not a bad plan."

No reply, he was right.

"So, you're obviously up to something, planning to make a quick getaway once it's done. You've no protection right now. So I gather there isn't enough of you left to provide it. There must be other places around this city where they're needed, deemed more essential? I'm offering you the chance to roam these fine streets in peace, then you can fly off to who-gives-a-fuck-where. I just need what I asked for."

"Yes," she replied questioningly. "Why did you request that, anyway? Why not guns, ammunition, money, food?"

"Everything runs out eventually. But trust me – people will take drugs over food these days, anything to escape. I also suspect there's more cocaine locked up around the country than there is food. Besides, if I had demanded food or guns, would you be here now? I don't get the impression you might part with things you still need."

She smiled. "Okay, Mr Chester. You have a deal." She reached to the seat next to her and withdrew a large wrapped package from a plastic bag. She handed it over. "Five kilos, confiscated at the border, there's more if you prove your worth."

He smiled. "One more thing. The fuel supplies. If this is going to work, I'm going to need some. Can't be walking now, can we?"

She examined his face.

"Fine. We'll have some dropped off."

"Pleasure," he bowed his head, took the parcel and walked back to his truck. He sat and watched as the saloon car sped off and disappeared into the underground car park. He headed in the opposite direction.

He was surprised at how easy it had been, he'd persuaded a government official to hand over a substantial quantity of illicit drugs, with little guarantee that he would keep to his word, or that he ever had any real power in the city.

The truth was, at the time, he didn't. His small gang of addicts and vagrants had been holed up in that hotel, spending their days high, avoiding the real world.

He needed to expand his operation, he needed more people, he needed more fear.

He was aware his plan had flaws, to gather as many people as he could, risked gathering the remaining infected, letting the virus spread through the survivors at a terrifying pace.

He hoped by now most of the infected had died off, alone in their homes, the virus within their dead cells expiring with them.

He would still have to be careful. He'd use the others to do what he needed. He'd avoid contact with anyone they managed to draw out. Anyone who wanted to join him, he'd welcome with open arms whilst he figured out if they had any use, any value. Those who didn't, well he could deal with them as he needed to.

Chester was enjoying his new role. Leader, Tyrant, Drug Baron. His followers had been elated with his return, or more accurately the haul he returned with. They were willing to do whatever he asked of them now.

They left the hotel, he needed somewhere more open, more visible. The fortitude of high-rise buildings standing around them would obscure their presence, he didn't need that now, he needed them to be known.

He counted the men walking in front of his rumbling truck. Thirteen, he had thirteen followers left. Nowhere near enough. This city had once been inhabited by millions. Many died, many more left during the evacuations, but there must still be thousands more scurrying around its abandoned streets, hiding in its lifeless buildings.

He wanted them all. He'd seen the assortment of people following the soldiers blindly down the street by the university. Old, young, male, female... He would have a job for all of them.

They lit the first fire on a scrag of wasteland, it was flat, the skyscrapers now in the distance, it would be seen in all directions for miles. He had instructed everything flammable to be pulled from the nearby houses, closed shops and dilapidated warehouses. The fire needed to be big, it needed to burn for days. He'd see who opted to come to him, before he went looking for them.

The first group appeared from the darkness a short time later, a family. The parents holding hands of two small children, they couldn't have been much older than ten or so. Their clothes were filthy and ripped. The parents were quiet, they had approached cautiously. From a distance, Chester had watched as they spoke to one of his men on the road. Something had been said, some offence caused. He watched his man raise his arm and strike the woman with the back of his hand. Her husband had valiantly tried to protect her, the knife plunged into his chest stopped him in his tracks, he dropped to the floor.

He heard the woman scream, she'd let go of the hands of the children, they had run off into the darkness. The woman was being dragged by her hair towards the fire, other men whooping with delight at her torment.

He watched as the last glimpse of the children vanished into the darkness, they wouldn't survive long on their own, there was little point in chasing after them.

He turned his attention back to the woman, still being dragged by her hair. Her dress had been ripped, what was left of it, he saw a flash of her bare skin in the firelight, he felt the lust burn inside himself.

The woman hadn't survived the night. Chester had ensured he had his time with her first, she'd whimpered, screamed, tried to fight back. His hand had stopped her, the red marks spreading across her face. Once he finished with her, he'd left her to the wolves, the others weren't as kind as he'd been, he wasn't sure if she died when they had finished, or at some time during. They didn't seem to care.

This hadn't been the best start to his plan, he couldn't take control if they killed everyone they met. The body of the woman had been tossed into the fire, he could smell the burning flesh from his vantage point. He had done what he wished, but he had to ensure the rest knew they could only do what he allowed them to.

He picked up the rifle and looked down the scope. He steadied his aim on Jamie, a young man he'd first found crawling around the undergrowth, track marks snaked up his arms.

He pulled the trigger. The deafening crack

silenced the whoops and calls of the men. Jamie fell backwards, dead before he hit the ground.

He walked closer to the fire, the muzzle of the rifle smoking in the cold night air.

"This is not a fucking free-for-all!" he shouted, examining the face of each person in turn.

He pointed to the man earlier killed down the road, then back to the burning corpse of the woman in the fire.

"How the fuck will we take this city if we kill every fucking person we run into?"

He paused to gauge their reactions, he had to be sure those closest to him would be loyal to the end.

"From now on, anyone who kills, rapes or robs without my permission," he placed a boot on the body lying on the floor in front of him. "God fucking help you. Now someone get rid of this fucking eyesore." He indicated to the body under his boot.

The silence descended, the twelve remaining people stood aimlessly around the roaring inferno, the buzz wearing off from their earlier hit, the shock sobering.

More people did arrive that night, a lot more. As instructed, none of them were harassed on arrival. They were brought one by one to him. He said his greetings and promised them protection, whilst judging their worth as they passed before him.

By the time the sun rose, his numbers had surpassed 30. Not all of them would be suitable, some held no value to him. They were too old, too infirm. Others he questioned if they could live by his rules. If they couldn't, then they would die by his rifle, it was all the same to him.

He would repeat this show all over the city, swelling his numbers, his power, his hold over all those left.

CHAPTER NINETEEN

The five of them squeezed into Bobs truck, Carole had insisted on coming. She was well versed in using a rifle. There was no way she was staying at home alone with the chance none of them would return.

They had spent a sleepless night in the old farmhouse. Tom wasn't sure why Bob and Carole were helping them, they had known them for just a day and yet here they were, about to risk their lives to rescue, or at least to try and rescue, someone they had never met.

Tom had questioned Bob that morning.

"Why don't you stay here, stay safe?" he'd asked.

"Can't do that," came the simple reply. "I told you before, got to help who we can, where we can. What are we if we don't try?"

"But you're risking everything, even Carole. This is a trap; we know that Matt might be dead already."

"Might not be, too."

"And you're happy to run off into a lawless city?

Just five of us, against, God knows how many?"

"I know how many, quite a few. Chester has his main group, that's probably about ten folks he trusts. All around the city he has outposts, people holed up in old hotels, factories and what not. They all report back to him. It's like a network, I reckon by now he's well over a hundred following him. Some women too, but not the pretty ones, he likes to keep those for himself. As you know."

The chilling feeling returned to Tom's chest.

"How do you know all this, Bob?"

"I see a lot; I speak to people. I see them leaving sometimes, they join him because they think it's safer. When they learn the truth, they try to leave. They're not all bad, Tom." With a mournful look in his eyes, he paused as he drained the remnants of the tea in the cup in front of him.

"Some of them are just too caught up. There's an old factory on the outskirts of town, probably a dozen of them in it, they are meant to be watching the routes into town, making sure the government doesn't come back mob handed. Or watching for people returning, not that there are many of them. They don't like what they do, they don't like Chester. They feel they have no other choice. I go see them once a week, I'm always careful like, but I like to make sure they're okay. They invite me in, make me a cuppa. They're not bad people, Tom," he reiterated.

"Can you be sure?"

"Can we be sure about anything these days? No, probably not. For all I know they tell him every time

I show my face. But I'm still here, so I think that's unlikely."

"And that's where we're going?"

"Yeah, first. I'll see if they've heard anything, seen anything that might help us find him. We'll need to be careful. I say they're not all bad people, plenty of them are, mind you."

"Does Carole know about them?"

"Course!" Bob replied. "I might not tell her every little detail, but she knows where I go, what I do. She wouldn't stop me, even if she could. She acts hard, but she's a heart of gold. It was her idea in the beginning that we should do what we can to help people. I wanted to lock us away from it all, she wouldn't have that. Didn't turf you lot out, did she?"

Tom smiled. "I suppose not."

He was surprised at how much they had lived in their little bubble. The city was bustling with life, it seemed, and they never saw it. Perhaps they were better at keeping to themselves than he'd thought.

The truck lurched down the pitted road, the squeak of the suspension vibrating through the cab on every bump. Bob had quite a collection of firearms, the typical farmer armoury, a few rifles and shotguns. He passed the handgun he'd taken back to Tom, along with the magazine which he'd removed. The shotgun he'd used when they first met was resting over his shoulder, Kate and Carole grasped small rifles. Chloe had refused them all. Tom couldn't figure her out; there must be more to this than she was letting on.

They approached the edge of the city, slowing as Bob turned onto a dirt track leading to what Tom guessed was also a textile factory in years past. The city had a history with the textile industry.

The truck came to a halt in front of the brown loading dock doors built into the side of the building. It was much larger than where Tom and the others had been staying, huge chimneys extended from its roof.

The loading door slowly opened; the sound of a chain being pulled as the door crept towards the sky. A man with mousey brown hair approached the truck. He wore thick glasses, resting across the bridge of his nose, his short auburn moustache dominated his face. He waved a greeting to Bob as he came closer to the truck.

Tom could see he was probably a similar age to himself; he had a machete strapped to this belt, but no other obvious signs of weaponry.

"Bob," the man said happily. "Wasn't expecting you, how..." he faltered as he noticed the others and the guns in the truck. "Everything okay?" His eyes had narrowed.

"Just fine, Adam, don't you worry." The usual jovial voice boomed back.

"What's going on, Bob?" Adam asked, clearly worried.

"Nothing to be afraid of, just need your help is all. After some information if you could indulge us."

"What information?" he asked curiously.

"Your man, Chester, know where he is?"

"No, I haven't heard from him this week. He doesn't come up here much, thank god. Why?"

"He killed an old lady yesterday, took a lad too. Making a message, I think. Wants us to go get him, so likely won't make it too hard."

"Wants you to go get him? Bob, he's been looking for you for months, why now?"

"No, this lot," he gestured to Tom stood close behind. "Not sure he knows Carole and I are helping, would like to keep it that way too."

Adam looked past them, out at the city stretching far into the distance.

"They'll be out there tonight; he's not done yet. Probably got half the survivors here under his control, long way to go though." Adam paused in thought. "There was a lot of noise last night, bigger than usual, over by the hospital. Fire going larger than we've seen in quite some time. Thought it was a bit odd, they've been there recently."

"That's grand, Adam, could be very useful."

"Yeah, no bother, just be careful out there, big man."

Bob nodded and returned to the truck.

Safely inside, he turned to Tom. "What do you reckon, back to the place you wronged him?"

"Makes sense," Tom replied. "If we were going to look for him, I guess that's where we'd start. This has escalated quickly though. Why has he done this, I've never even met the man?"

"Doesn't rightly matter, you took from him." He

nodded towards Chloe. "That's as bad as anything you can do these days, short of punching the fella in the face in front of all his cronies!"

"Okay. So, what? We just roll up to the old hospital, hope he's there. Hope that he hasn't set a trap and doesn't just shoot us before we can get out of the car?" Kate interjected,

"This is getting ridiculous, we need more to go on. We're walking to our deaths here. And if that happens, we've killed Matt too, assuming he's not dead already." The frustration on her face clear to see.

Tom sighed; she was right. This was ridiculous. They would almost certainly be walking into a very brutal and untimely death. Or rather driving into it. Even worse, they'd know they were coming long before they got there.

"I go," he said simply. "I'll walk from here, I'm less likely to be seen alone, maybe I can get closer, at least find out what's going on."

Kate screwed her face in frustration.

"Because that's a lot bloody cleverer," she scowled. "We'll all go, but we can't just rock up in a great bloody truck. There's only one road leading to that hospital. Even on foot, we'll struggle to get in unseen, trust me, I spent enough time watching it."

"Could do with one of those green trucks," Tom said absently.

"What trucks?" asked Bob.

"I was just thinking aloud, the big military ones, we know Chester and his guys aren't well-armed that we know of, and they have some kind of deal with the government. Bet they'd let one of them roll right up to him."

"Hmm. Then why don't we get one?" All eyes turned to look at Bob, his face turned red. "You know, there's plenty of them, down by the camp..." He pointed to the distance behind him.

The camp had been the first failed evacuation point for the city, the trial run. It was built to contain 5000, hundreds of thousands had turned up. There was no refuge from the virus. Tom had heard of the camps, many times. He'd heard of the squalor, the deprivation and with the speed the virus ripped through them.

They were not the safe haven that had been promised. Some suspected they were built for population control. With the virus raging throughout the world, supply chains had dried up. Air travel ceased overnight, freighters were turned around at borders, left to fend for themselves on the open sea.

Roads were closed, everything was locked down. Food was running out and supplies drying up. The healthcare systems had long since been overwhelmed. A lack of basic provisions, medicine and protective gear saw an unprecedented level of infection amongst the doctors and nurses, an unprecedented level of death.

With no work available, the population couldn't be cared for. The migrant workers that picked the food from the fields never came, the native population unwilling or unable to take the task. The government had tried to shrink the geographical area they were spread over.

Thousands, like Tom, were relocated to the cities. Housed in dark and dingy flats, hostels and the houses that once belonged to the victims. It wasn't enough, they still didn't have enough food to go around. This was when the camps started to crop up. They had been trialled unsuccessfully before this. They decided to give it another shot. Thousands were built around the country, evacuation orders issued and the population moved. Too many of them blindly followed.

"How far?" Kate demanded.

"Not too far, maybe five miles, it was between here and the coast"

Tom must have walked right passed it on his journey inland.

"If we leave now," Bob continued. "We can be there in maybe half an hour, the roads aren't that great."

Without another word, they climbed back into the red truck, Bob reversed onto the road and turned, facing away from the city, he sped off.

He was right, the roads headed to the camp were terrible. They had been damaged by the winter onslaught, still littered with the possessions dropped by the travellers heading to their supposed salvation. Bones poked from the earth where they lay. There must have been thousands of dead on the road here, Tom stopped counting as the bodies mounted.

Bob stopped the truck a short distance from the camp entrance. Bodies had been pushed to the side of the road; they lay piled on top of one another. Some were stripped to the bone, others still clothed. They piled high, blocking the view out over the fields to the horizon.

Tom tried to block out the smell, it was impossible.

The gate in front of them reached high into the sky, the fence extended around the perimeter. He really didn't want to see inside.

They exited the truck and walked towards the gate. Tracks dug into the ground, the wheels from the massive army trucks rolling in and out. The giant green gates were locked, a thick chain holding them firmly closed.

"Bob," Tom asked. "How do you know there's anything left in here?" He was studying the chain; it hadn't been touched in a long time.

"Over there," Bob pointed to where the gate and fence connected. There was a gap where the oversized hinges had been bolted on. "It's not pretty though, out here is a party compared to what I saw in there."

He retrieved a pair of large bolt cutters from the back of the truck and handed them to Tom. "Up to you though."

Tom took a deep breath and walked to the chain, he forced the bolt cutters together around the lock, with some effort it finally snapped. The chain fell around his feet. He steadied himself and grasped the giant handle, pulling with all the effort he could muster, the gate retreated enough for him to peer his head through. Bob hadn't been lying, for the second time in two days, he left his lunch on the floor.

The scene in front of his eyes was worse than anything he'd experienced during the apocalypse so far. He'd heard the rumours, but the truth was far worse. Every part of the ground he could see was littered with the dead. They might have been trying to get out, or maybe there was just far too many of them and they died where they fell.

He covered his mouth and nose as he tried to carefully step around the limbs blocking the path. He could see up ahead three of the large green army trucks, parked in a line next to one another.

As he walked through the mound of dead, he noticed several of them bore the evidence of bullet wounds, a shot to the back of the head. Had they been trying to get out, or had they been infected, was this a last-ditch, futile attempt to stem the flow?

Corpses in green uniform lay by the trucks, the soldiers died too. He could see the rows and rows of green metal containers stretching far along the camp. Larger canopies housing tables and cooking facilities. *So, they really did intend people to live here*, he thought, the intention was good, to start with.

He stood in the middle of the horror, he couldn't accept what he was seeing, he knew this scene would be repeated up and down the country, thousands of times. The camps had been a disaster, he already knew that. The scale of just how much of a disaster they had been was now hitting him.

This was a massacre, people followed like lambs to the slaughter. Their deaths must have been terrifying, watching those around them die. If they were fortunate, they would have been one of the first to go.

He thought about those who were infected on arrival, the gates padlocked from the outside. Would they have had to wait it out in here, watching all around them die, knowing they were next? Would they have slept next to the corpses of their families, their loved ones, the stench of rotting flesh growing ever stronger? With no way out and the impending infection settling in their lungs, were the bullet holes in the bodies by gate a mercy after all?

He imagined himself being here, if he'd left when he was first ordered, taking his wife and child from his prior life. They would have been locked in a camp like this, watching those around them die. He would have had to wait, for how long... Would they have sat here for the full incubation period, what was it, up to three weeks, in this hell? Would it have been any different from what had actually happened?

He'd watched his neighbours die, he waited for

the sickness. He watched his family die in front of him. This was just in closer quarters, he supposed. He wouldn't have been able to bury them, or to lay them to rest. They would have been left, rotting with the masses strewn around him. For once, he was grateful for his past.

There were no keys in the trucks, there had to be an administration building around here somewhere. Somewhere for people to register their arrival and for the troops to sign in. Tom was sure the keys would also be kept there. Another thought struck him, there were soldiers here, there might be an armoury, too. He thought about looking for it, but they had enough weapons for the five of them, they didn't need any more.

It was evident the camps hadn't been ransacked yet, he couldn't imagine even Chester was desperate enough to enter a place like this. Although he'd likely be more than happy to send someone he felt was expendable. Tom prayed to God the virus was extinct here, with the vast amount of dead, the fluids that would have seeped into the floor, if it wasn't, he was already dead. No, it must be. Everyone here had been dead for months at least, there's no way it was still active. He prayed silently.

He saw the admin building across the camp, the other side of the gates he'd entered from. It was a solid wooden building, the black corrugated iron roof discolouring from the months in the open, this place hadn't been built to last.

He entered the wooden door and stepped inside. It was musty and damp, the room was almost empty, dust danced in the stream of light from the window. There was a row of metal lockers against one wall, each housed the green camouflage uniforms used by the army recruits. He took one from the hanger. *You never know*, he thought to himself.

Attached to the wall next to the long wooden desk was a small metal case, a simple box with a key lock on the front. No keys, though. It didn't look that secure, he tried to pry it open, he couldn't get a grip on it. Looking around the small room, he noticed a heavy paperweight at the edge of the desk, that should do, he picked it up. He used the weight in his hand to bash into the side of the metal box, several swings and he heard the lock pop loose, he pulled the door forwards.

The keys were there. Three sets hung in a neat line. There were other keys too, smaller ones, they looked to be for filing cabinets, or small padlocks. He didn't have time to worry about them now, he grabbed the three for the trucks.

He dashed back across the open ground, in his eagerness he took less care, he nearly tripped as his foot caught in the ground, glancing down he saw he was stood on an arm, he didn't want to think about who's, or where the rest of the body was.

He unlocked the truck door and climbed into the cab. Turning the key, the engine spluttered and died. He waited a few moments then tried again. It spluttered again, but didn't start. *Damn*, he thought, moving on to the next one, same result. The third, same result.

He returned to the others, still stood outside the gate.

"They won't start," he announced solemnly. "Think the fuels gone bad."

"No problem," Bob replied, he held a plastic bottle in front of him. "Stabiliser, should get them up and running again, come on, let's go see." He slapped Tom on the shoulder as he marched passed him.

Bob had emptied the plastic jug into the tank on the closest truck, sitting in the cab Tom heard the engine spluttering as Bob turned the ignition. It spluttered for a long moment, his heart sinking with every passing second.

It fired, the sound filling the air, black smoke poured from the exhaust. He heard Bob whoop in delight, he jumped into the passenger seat.

"Okay, let's roll!" Bob was enjoying this too much, he accelerated the truck towards the gate, Tom heard bones crack under its wheels.

Bob lifted an army issue rifle from the seat behind him. "Lookie what I found," he smiled. Tom didn't mention the thought of an armoury, they'd never leave this place.

The truck lurched through the gate, the bumper forcing it fully open as it thundered through. The others jumped into the back of the truck. Hid by its green canopy, they started the journey back to the city.

The trip back was uneventful, it took longer in the slower green army truck. It rolled over the debris effortlessly, roaring along as they approached, the plumes of black smoke barrelling towards the sky.

They entered the city cautiously, watching for any movement, any sign of danger. They saw none. Tom was sure they would have been seen by now, the noise of the engine, the black smoke, it starkly contrasted against the silent landscape.

Still they saw no one.

They approached closer to the hospital and university campus, they edged past the building where Kate had once stayed, she looked mournfully to the window, the small crack in the curtains where she left them.

They rounded the corner and saw the remnants of a massive fire blocking the road. It was still burning, the glow dulled by the sunlight. It was huge, larger than the one on the main road adjacent to them they had seen previously, when they had rescued Chloe.

Bob slowed the truck, the road was blocked, he wouldn't be able to get passed.

"We either turn around and try to come up the other side, or we walk from here," he said, his face deep in thought. "Either way, this isn't going to work. Got us in though."

Tom sat in thought. He'd never met Chester; Chester had never met him. Maybe, just maybe, he could pull this off.

"I've got an idea," he looked to the others. "We think... We hope Chester is going to accept the army, or some kind of government in. He knows they are still around and needs to keep things quiet with them, or he has some real issues, more than just us." He held the uniform he'd pulled from the locker aloft.

"So, the army shows up?" his suggestion wasn't a great one. It might get him in, but not the rest, and then what, he'd have one rifle, which he didn't know how to fire, and no way out. They might be able to get some information though, to see if Matt was even still alive, how many of them there were, what fight they were likely to put up.

"I don't like it," said Kate. "There's no guarantee they'd let you walk out of there, even if they didn't figure it out."

"There's a truck out here, full of soldiers for all he knows, he'll be keen to avoid any problems now, I'm sure of that." Tom didn't really like it either. "I don't see what else we can do."

"We don't even know where they are, they could have already seen us," Kate said.

"No, I don't think so. If they knew now, I think we'd be dead already," Tom replied.

"Speak for yourself!" Bob scoffed.

Tom jumped out of the truck, freshly dressed in the green uniform, rifle slung over his shoulder, handgun tucked into his belt. He confidently walked past the fire; he could feel its heat still radiating on the side of his face.

He stood at the entrance to the hospital car park, where the road split, and waited. It didn't take long before two men appeared. They had come from inside the hospital stood in front of him, its glass facade providing the perfect viewing. They both had rifles strapped to their backs. Tom tried to stop the panic enveloping him.

"What?" the closest spat.

"I've been sent to discuss the current arrangement with Chester," Tom replied, hoping his voice sounded as confident as he intended it to.

"He's not here." Came the blunt reply.

"What?" Tom blurted out, more in surprise. "What do you mean he's not here?"

"What does it sound like. He's. Not. Here. Gone away, someplace else."

"Then who's in charge right now?"

"Don't matter," the man replied lazily.

Tom had a thought.

"Alright. When he returns, tell him we've the next shipment of cocaine waiting for him."

"Erm, just a sec," the man stuttered, that had caught his attention. He beckoned Tom towards them.

He followed the men back into the hospital. He saw four others as he walked into the main reception, two snoozing in the waiting room chairs, the others arguing in the corner.

"Where's the drugs?" the man who had escorted him inside asked. "We'll take them here, till Chester gets back," a smile spread across his face. Tom noted he was missing several teeth, the rest were yellow and jagged.

"No, that wasn't the deal." He saw an opportunity too good to miss. "What we agreed with Chester was it gets handed to him, and only to him. The last ten kilo was the first of many shipments."

"Ten kilos..." the man repeated, his face contorted in confusion. "You didn't give him ten last time, he told us!"

"I don't really care what he told you," Tom snorted. "I don't care what he gave you, or decided not to give you, but I know what he had."

The man looked in a rage, it was working.

"I'll take it this time," he shouted, grappling for the rifle on his back.

"Don't be stupid," Tom said simply. "I'm not alone, and I see six of you, and two guns. By the way, where did they come from, we didn't give Chester guns?"

"Found 'em."

"Found them? Where?"

"From your lot, a load of you, dead out there!" The man laughed

"You kill them?"

"Nah, virus most likely," the man replied. "No blood or nothin'."

Tom thought this over. "How long ago was this?"

"Dunno, few nights?" the man replied.

"Had they been dead long?"

"Not by the looks of em, still fresh." The sickening smile returned.

Tom shuddered, he hoped the man was wrong. He hoped the virus hadn't killed that recently, that would mean it was still ravaging the planet.

"Give me the drugs!" the man demanded.

"Okay, alright. They're in the truck, follow me."

Tom led the two men back to the road; they were nervous and jumpy. Not a good combination for junkies holding guns.

"You need to put them down," Tom commanded as he gestured his head to the rifles. "If we get around this corner the others see you pointing those, they'll shoot you."

"What others?"

"The others I'm with, I didn't come alone. I told you that. My colleagues won't take kindly to two men pointing guns at me as the first thing they see."

The men mulled this over silently, then hoisted the rifles back over their shoulder. These two were not that bright, Tom decided.

He whistled loudly as they approached the truck, he noticed the eagerness in the men's eyes grow the closer they got. Kate stepped down from the cab.

"Kate," Tom said with authority. "These men will be taking the shipment on behalf of Chester today." He winked. "But we need to be sure they are who they claim to be, that they do work for him."

"Course we are!" came the reply. "Been with him since the start, you can trust us."

"Hmm," Kate started, catching on. "Okay, so tell

me, the factory the other end of town last night, Chester told us he'd burnt it down."

"Yeah, that's right," the man replied greedily. "Burnt it down, slit the old bitches throat and left her hanging."

"And the boy?" They were so focused on the promise of drugs, they spilt everything.

"Dead too, tied him up whilst we set the place on fire, watched him burn," he giggled. "He screamed, he cried," the laughter now near hysterical.

"Told us everything, all the people he was with, Chester's gone to find them, wants them dead, wants his girl back!"

"Where's he gone?" Kate nearly screamed, Tom saw the tears forming in her eyes, the rage etched on her face.

"He thought they'd come to the fire last night, they didn't show up, too scared. Thinks they've run off to the countryside, he's gone following tracks from the fire they started to trap him!"

The first crack of gunfire turned the man's expression to surprise as his companion fell, the second dropped him to the floor. Tom stood behind him, handgun stretched, the muzzle smoking.

CHAPTER TWENTY

Chester had learned a lot recently. The government had fallen, they were in the process of withdrawing everyone they considered to be valuable, taking them to one of the secret bunkers in the wilderness, somewhere no one else could go. They had fuel still, that was evident, they must have had food, too.

It was nearby, he didn't know exactly where. Those very important had been flown further away, a remote island off the coast of the country. The rest were posted closer to the city, they could maintain access as required.

He wondered how large the bunker must be, he'd seen helicopters in the sky a few times since his first run-in with the woman in the car. He wondered if she was in one of them.

The soldiers were leaving, he saw less of them on the streets, not that they were a common sight anymore.

The evacuations had failed, everyone already

knew that though. The concentration of people moved to the cities had caused the exponential spread of the second wave. The government thought they might be able to control it; the squalled conditions only excelled its spread.

Fearing for their own safety, the government had withdrawn long before it was officially stated. Those left were the junior officials, the replaceable. No wonder the woman he'd been meeting those months before was so cranky.

Chester had worked fast in the time that followed. People were happy to accept a leader, someone to take care of them. Someone to guarantee them a future. Before long, he had hundreds following him. He couldn't walk them around the city like sheep so he set up outposts where he housed them. He'd checked in on them when he needed to, to show he was there for them, whilst he assessed their value.

He needed the food to feed them all. The drugs wouldn't do it anymore. Most of the new followers were just the lost and the lonely, they weren't induced by cocaine, like his originals were. He thought long and hard about this. The winter months had passed, he knew a thing or two about gardening. It wasn't quite the same, but he knew what he could grow and when, they had to act fast if he wanted a harvest this year.

He needed to think further ahead, he needed to think about how he was going to consolidate and keep power. Fear did a good job, but it was flawed. Tyrants are always felled by those they oppress.

He kept a tight-knit group around him, it was better if he used them to enforce his message, he wouldn't directly be seen in the violence that way. He could still indulge when he felt the urge.

He still had problems though. There was the farmer, the big man who had broken his nose in the early days. He couldn't let that go, he'd have to find him, have his revenge. He'd tried, he went out alone, looking for signs of him. Not only did he want him dead, he wanted to know how he was keeping himself alive.

He was clearly farming, which meant the land hadn't been decimated by the millions that trampled everything in their path as they fled. Most of the farmland surrounding the city was destroyed, nothing would grow there for a long time to come.

He hadn't been successful. He'd travelled as far as the coast, down to the beachhead, no sign of him. This frustrated Chester, how could a man so big, hide so well?

One day. He'd get him one day.

There was also a new threat. People had attacked some of his men a few nights back, he didn't know how many. They'd taken one of his girls. His favourite girl, they'd killed one of his men that night and those he sent to search for tracks hadn't made it back.

They'd been found a few days later over in the financial districts, they were both dead. He'd been quite impressed by the brutality of their murders, but it made him nervous, someone was out there, someone possibly as feared as him.

These new people had caused fear in his group. They had never been seen. Silent, they killed in the night, and they seemed to be targeting him.

It was this that had forced Chester's hand with the weaponry. He hadn't wanted to arm his men, should they ever revolt, but he saw no alternative. He knew of a cache of rifles, left by the army when they gassed those new recruits. It was an experiment, they had thought they could drop an airborne disinfectant, it should kill any trace of the virus. It had killed much more than that.

He'd found this out during his next meeting with the woman in the underground carpark, she was quite chatty once you got past the cold, hard-arsed exterior.

The scientists thought it had a chance, it had killed the virus in the lab, even massively diluted. Why they tested it on their own, he didn't know, maybe they had infected them with the virus first?

He hadn't been happy about rooting through the bodies, so he sent others in this place. Like normal, he watched from afar. Ensuring they did as they were instructed, but not getting close enough to put himself in danger. He stayed away from the men for several weeks afterwards, watching them for symptoms. The spray must have worked, none of them got sick.

Now he had an army.

His meetings with the government had become less frequent, more of them fled to safety as the days drew on. He always attended these alone, he didn't want the others to know what he'd agreed. They were happy to let him run the city, although they had made it abundantly clear he worked for them. He was happy for them to believe this, it kept them out of his way.

He wondered where he should claim as his residence once it was all his. He thought about the grand diplomat houses, in the affluent part of town, but it didn't feel right.

He set his sights upon the new age industrial lofts that had been converted from old flour mills and failing textile factories. once so prevalent on the edge of town. They were modern, many had some form of solar power, one of their green credentials selling points.

The land was flat here, and the buildings didn't stretch high into the sky, it would provide good cover and allow his scouts to see any incoming threats. Not yet, though, he still had work to do in the city. Maybe he'd check them out later though, he hadn't been in that part of town for a long time. He'd have to make sure it was habitable, clear out any stragglers left sheltering there.

He sat back and thought about how quickly

things had moved. Was it really so recently he was gardening for old ladies? Now he nearly had an entire city under his control.

He thought about Chloe, the girl that had been taken from him. He liked her, he liked the way she screamed. He'd had the others killed as a message, whoever took her had to know there would be consequences, for everyone. His world was no utopia, but people would be fed. As long as they listened, as long as they obeyed.

He'd enquired of the grey-haired lady the last time she met with him about the state of the world. The news had been gone for a long time now. The electricity was down, the internet a relic of the past.

She'd told him things had gotten worse, there were pockets of survivors everywhere that they knew of, but they couldn't feed them. Other countries had fared just as poor, some still had functioning governments, others had descended into lawless chaos.

He wondered which category she put this country into.

The virus had become a worldwide killer, there was no refuge to be had in the hotter climates, they were decimated just as quickly as the colder ones. The latest estimate was 80% of the world's population had already perished. Not all had been infected.

Maybe some were immune, maybe some didn't die once infected. The world would survive, but no one knew what it would look like in years to come, when the pandemic was consigned to the past.

Most of the surviving populations would succumb to hunger, or would be taken by other disease caused by the medieval sanitation conditions left when the modern machinery stopped. People of the modern world weren't equipped to feed themselves, without the conveniences of life, most wouldn't make it on their own.

They still had reports of infections coming through. They were slowing, though, not enough people to spread it anymore. Travel had ceased, people stayed far from one another, it would pass. They had to ensure they were still here when it did, to rebuild the world in their image.

Chester didn't trust them, but the current arrangement worked in his favour.

The events of the last week had unsettled him, someone had killed three of his men, four if you included that crazy bastard who followed them from a distance. He'd been slaughtered, head bashed in down the hospital car park. He hated that place. He found it dark and claustrophobic. He spent a lot of time there, the government and army had used it as their base, until the fuel stores ran dry. The grey, soulless walls gave way to the evil deeds that had since been carried out there. The so-called vaccine tests that had killed the subjects, he'd seen their bodies wheeled out on stretchers, burnt in the nearby mortuary.

They'd stopped the trials after the 'incident'. There had been a breach. Somehow, the virus had escaped the isolation wards. It took several scientists catching it before they realised. They abandoned the hospital to its fate. The risk was too high. Their beeping machinery had been taken away. He was sure it'd be back. There was too many potential subjects left here they could test on. They would run out soon enough where ever they hid themselves.

He chuckled, he really did get off on this stuff, who knew.

He wanted whoever had killed his men, they worried him. The guys they had taken out were some of his best.

Sure, they were drug-addicted reprobates, but still good at what they did. The killings in the financial district had been a form of art, the rope wrapped around the neck, the knife wounds, deep into the shoulder and neck, He couldn't have done it better himself.

He had visions of trained mercenaries. A thought struck him, maybe the government was done with him, maybe they had sent them in to undermine him, maybe to kill him?

He was getting paranoid, he could feel it. Power was taking its toll.

Better to be safe than sorry. He knew one day he was likely to find a knife in his back, he'd followed that road and put himself firmly on this path. He wanted to make sure that day was as far away as possible, and if he had his way, the knife would be in the front, he wanted to look into the eyes of his killer. He chuckled, was he losing it?

He needed something to take his mind off things, maybe he'd go and check out the industrial area today, after all. It would do him good to get away from this for a while. Modern-day shopping therapy.

He called two of his more trusted from the small group around him and instructed them into the back of his black truck. He loved that truck. He could have taken something newer from the showrooms around the city, enough were abandoned, but they wouldn't have been the same. This truck reminded him of him. It looked vicious and mean. It was perfect.

He sped along the empty streets, taking the corners at speed, listening to the tyres scream as they slid across the road. He loved this new world. They reached the industrial part of town quickly, it was deserted, but it was clean. That would be a nice touch, the lack of litter, the lack of the dead, would be pleasant.

He'd have to remember to ensure it was kept that way, decaying flesh on the lawn didn't scream grandeur. He brought the truck to a halt in the middle of the road and scouted around. There wasn't much here, he was sure he remembered it...

trendier.

Storm clouds were forming overhead, growing ever darker. A crack of thunder rumbled through the air, the flash of lightning in the distance.

A glimpse in the distance caught his eye, movement. He held a finger to his lips and crept up the road. There was a textile factory at the very end, a smaller one, it looked disused.

Peering through the chain-link fence, he saw a young man disappearing through a steel fire door.

Now he was interested. He beckoned to the others to join him. He didn't know who was inside this place, but he wanted to find out, as long as he could send someone else in first.

He studied the exterior of the fire door, there was no obvious way in, it only opened from the inside. At the top left corner, he noticed a small indentation, someone had forced it previously. He took the machete from the hand of the man stood next to him and forced it into the small gap. With a bit of pressure, he heard the latch click, the door swung open. He'd have made sure it was more secure, that was a rookie mistake.

Quietly, he sneaked into the building. There was an empty expanse in front of him, black mezzanine flooring ran up both sides, a door in the centre leading further into the factory. He was getting excited now, anything to break up the monotony of the day.

He followed the mezzanine, creeping as lightly

as he could on its steel frame. He liked to stalk his victims, it made it more fun when they finally noticed him. Pushing the door ajar, a darkened corridor lay inside. A stream of light showered through an open door halfway down, he heard soft voices floating on the air, a young man and what sounded like an old woman, they were laughing. *How sweet*, he thought, it sounded like they were alone, only the two of them here.

For the briefest moment, Chester held the image of the old women he'd worked for, the woman he'd watched wheeled out on the stretcher. They loved to talk, he thought they enjoyed his company, even with his thug-like appearance.

He had to let go of the past, it served no purpose in the world he was building.

Chester peered through the open door, the corridor concealing him, he saw an older lady, probably in her 70's. She was talking to a young man, a boy really. He had to still be a teenager, they were both smiling, laughing. A charming smile broke across his face as he positioned himself in the frame of the door.

"Folks!" his voice boomed. "It's a pleasure to meet you both."

The older lady dropped her cup, it shattered on the floor.

"Well, that's a meagre greeting, but I'll take it," he continued, walking into the canteen area, arms outstretched.

The boy spoke first. "It's you... you're... Chester."

The colour drained from his face, his hand was shaking.

"I'm flattered!" It was true, he hadn't expected that, his reputation was growing. "And what can I call you then, young man?"

The boy stumbled, trying to get his words out, a sound close to a cat in pain left his lips.

"You don't say a word to this scum," the older lady spat. Chester saw the hatred across her face. Now he was curious. She stood and pointed a long bony finger at him. "I know who you are, I know what you've done. You should be ashamed of yourself. That poor girl, poor Chloe, the state you left her in. You are the worst kind of person." She physically spat at his feet.

Chester shifted his head slightly to the left. "Chloe?" he asked.

"The poor girl you beat, raped. Nearly left for dead."

"She was here?" he was pointing around the room as he spoke. "She here now?"

"You'll never see her again, you'll never hurt her again." The older lady stumbled forwards with every word, she was stood in front of him. She was considerably shorter than him, she stared into his eyes from below with nothing but hatred on her face.

"You were the problem with this planet long before the virus ended it." She poked him in the chest. "It's only a shame it didn't take you."

"Huh," he hadn't expected this. "So, you took the girl, murdered my man? I don't believe it."

He placed his hand on her shoulder. "And I don't think that streak-of-piss crying to himself at the table did either." He shoved her aside, her frame tossed across the room, she hit the floor with a cry.

"Boy!" Chester snapped. "Start talking, or you won't like what comes next. What's your name?" As he approached the boy still sat at the metal table, he thought he looked vaguely familiar.

"M... Matt," he cried out. The tears were flowing freely now.

"Matt? I've some bad news for you."

He slapped him on the shoulder laughing, his hand wrapped around the white headphones around Matt's neck, he ripped them free. "You seem to have pissed yourself!" He roared with laughter.

Matt had talked, he told Chester everything. What Tom and Kate had done, about the four people they had killed, how they rescued Chloe, how they tried to save the others and how they were trying to use Chloe to ambush him right now. He still had the maps they had studied the night before; he gave everything to Chester.

His enemy had a name, Tom.

He ran it over in his mind, committing it to memory. He had something special reserved for Kate, he wanted her alive, for now.

The old woman whimpered on the floor where she'd fallen.

Chester was done, he had everything he needed, he knew where Tom was now, trying to set a trap for him. As he walked out the door, he leaned into the men guarding the door.

"Burn it, kill them both. Leave a message, I want it known it was me."

The white headphones now in the hand of the man with the machete. He stopped a few steps down the corridor. "Leave this, somewhere they'll find it if they make it back." He tossed a small bag of white powder over his shoulder. They obviously knew about him; the drugs should make the message loud and clear.

He returned to his truck and watched the flames lick out the factory windows, his men were in the car park, dragging the old lady by the arms. He watched as they tied her to the fence, her legs beating uselessly against the metal as she thrashed in protest, screaming obscenities at them. The machete raised; blood splattered the ground. The sky opened and the storm released its rage.

It didn't take long to find the park on the outskirts of town where the fire trap had been set, the smoke was visible for miles around. They'd done a good job, he had to give them that.

He had approached carefully; he still didn't fully know who he was dealing with. There was no sign of them. The fire was burning itself out, helped by the torrential rainfall. They had left hours ago.

They had tried to call him out, and now he would

do the same. His message, however, would be much louder. If the swinging body of the old lady – he suddenly felt guilty about her death – didn't do it, then his fire would.

He remembered why the boy looked familiar, the same tears staining his face as he hid by the wall whilst the soldiers executed the people on the road by the university accommodation. The woman who had pulled him inside the nearby building. Matt had told him, that woman was Kate.

CHAPTER TWENTY-ONE

"What now?" Kate asked simply.

No one spoke, Tom shook his head.

Bob kicked the rifle free from the dead body. "Military issue, they all got em?" He looked at Tom.

"Just these two that I saw. I'm not sure though. I thought he only had the one. Sounds like they found them on a group of dead soldiers."

"Not hard to find," Bob replied. "Enough of the poor souls perished with these still on their backs. There was a barracks here too. Not enough people or space to take them all with them." He paused. "Adam didn't have one, so maybe he's either only armed those he really trusts, or he doesn't have enough to go around. Either way, don't reckon leaving them lay around is smart."

He collected the two rifles and placed them into the back of the truck.

"And the others?" Kate asked, she indicated towards the hospital towering in front of them.

"What do we do with them?"

"There's another four in there, at least. If they

heard the shots, they could be coming right now anyway." He glanced nervously up the road, it was clear. He noticed Bob's hand edge to the shotgun resting behind his shoulder.

"We can't let them leave, if they've seen us, how few of us there are, that could be the end of it."

The grim realisation was slowly spreading through the group. To keep safe, they'd need to deal with the others still sheltering in the hospital.

No one wanted to be the first to suggest it, the silence was deafening. The birds chirped merrily in the distance, their goading song reverberating through the empty streets.

"I'll do it," said Bob grimly, this was as serious as Tom had seen him since they'd met.

"Don't be silly," Carole snapped back. "You can't get four people with a shotgun, they might be armed too, remember?" she rolled her eyes.

"Well... I reckon it'll be okay!" The smile returned to his face.

"No," Tom interrupted. "It should be me. I brought us here; I started all this. I'll do it."

"Tom, how?" Kate asked.

"I'll go back to the lobby, I'll tell them we need their help, as soon as they leave, I'll shoot them in the back." The words sounded worse when they came out of his mouth.

"You need to get four shots off before they realise... I don't know Tom, there must be anoth..."

"We all do it." Chloe cut her off. "Tom, draw

them outside, we'll wait by the entrance. As soon as there's a clear shot, we kill them."

Tom tried to think of a better option, he couldn't. "Okay, we all happy with this? Happy enough at least?" sober nods of agreement answered him. "Right, okay." His head was swimming. "I'll draw them out. Then I guess... Boom." Kate glared at him.

The plan worked perfectly. Tom walked into the foyer of the hospital, two of them still snoozed on the waiting room chairs, the other two had stopped their argument, they eyed him suspiciously. He called out that he needed their help to unload the extra supplies they had agreed to hand over. The others were unloading it now, they just needed more hands. They followed eagerly. The promise of meagre supplies drawing them to their death.

They walked out the glass doors, they had taken no more than a few steps into the daylight when the first crack sounded, followed soon after by more. Tom counted more than four, many more. The men lay dead on the street, blood pooling around their bodies.

Bob dolefully collected their rifles, adding them to the growing pile in the back of the truck.

No one spoke. They walked in silence back to the truck and climbed in. The engine roared to life and the truck vanished down the street.

"That was messed up." Kate broke the silence first.

"They deserved it," Chloe counted.

"I know Chloe, I know. But it doesn't feel right, that was an execution. We can't sugar-coat it. We killed those men in cold blood."

"It had to be done, you know that." Carole had rested her hand on Kate's arm.

"Yeah," she paused. "I guess."

The journey back to the farmhouse was finished in silence. Bob had dropped Tom, Kate and Chloe at the door, he and Carole were going to get his truck back from the camp where they'd left it.

Chloe had excused herself, leaving Tom and Kate alone in the living room of the old farmhouse. The streaks of light forced their way through the cracks in the curtains.

"How are you?" Tom asked when they were alone.

"Not great. What's life become? It feels like we're no better than the bastard we are trying to kill."

"Maybe not. But at least when we kill him, we know he can't hurt anymore."

"And then what, Tom? What about whoever takes his place, do we kill them too? How long until we play God and we try to kill anyone who might have the potential to do these things?"

Tom lent in towards her, he kissed her pale lips. He felt her kiss him back.

The time that followed, Tom would forever remember. Maybe it was sorrow, maybe grief. Kate had kissed him back, he lay her down on the dusty sofa beneath them. She let him guide her, moaning softly at his every touch.

Bob and Carole returned an hour later. The low rumble of the army truck could be heard long before it could be seen. Bob eyed Tom and Kate suspiciously as his massive frame walked through the door. Tom blushed.

"Keep the truck then?" he asked, deflecting any onslaught of questions.

"Yeah," Bob replied slowly. "Never know when it might be handy. Always wanted one, anyway."

"I told him to leave the bloody thing."

Carole had appeared by his side. "Nothing like a great big green truck to get you seen. But no, he was having none of it. No use arguing sometimes. Tea?" She wandered off to the kitchen.

"Well, it's true! You do never know!" Bob smiled.

They had settled in for the night shortly afterwards, it had been a long day. It had been a strange day, even for Tom.

He was losing count of how many people he'd killed. How many he'd murdered. He didn't feel bad about it, he didn't really feel anything about it. How long had it been now, how long since he felt secure in his previous life?

That was fading to a memory, a dream remembered for just moments after waking. This was life now. This was the world now. He drifted off to sleep.

He woke late the following morning, the sun high in the sky, he heard voices from the kitchen below. He was the last one up, the rest were sat around the long wooden table in the kitchen, empty cups told him they had been up for a while.

"Morning, sunshine!" How was Bob so cheery all the time? "Figured we'd let you sleep in, looked like you could do with it. But, new day, new problems. We gotta figure out what we do next. Too deep now to back out."

Tom yawned and rubbed his eyes.

"So, I figure we got two options here," Bob continued. "We go back to the city, finish what we started, or we leave. We get in the truck and drive, we just go."

"Go where?" Tom asked.

"Don't matter much, just away. No chance Chester will forget what we done to him, what we done to his people. Too deep in it now. I went up to see Adam this morning, Chester's been around, and he's not best happy. Wants them to watch the road, but now it's for you."

"What makes him think we'd enter the city that way?"

"Adam isn't the only one watching the routes. There's more like that place all over, they're all on alert. Bit of a legend, you are now. They don't know what you look like, they've made you a ghost, a myth - hunting them down. It's great, forgot all about little old me!"

"I'm none of those things!" Tom didn't know how to process this, how had he been elevated to the position of public enemy number one. Or at least Chester's enemy number one. Same thing these days it seemed.

It wasn't truly a conversation, they all knew what needed to happen before it was said. The premise of options kept them talking half the morning, but they already knew what they would do. What they had to do. They had to go to war.

"This is madness," Kate sighed, exasperated. "He's got an army in there. He's armed them, and he's a fucking psychopath. We've got five people, barely any bullets and no way in."

"That's not totally true," Bob's voice rang over from the other end of the kitchen, he was boiling the kettle again. For Bob, a good cup of tea made everything better.

"I don't reckon all those in that city are best pleased with Chester. Think if we play it right, we could probably get an army of our own. I think Adam and the guys there would join us, if they saw it as another option. If we can prove we have a chance."

The rest of the day was spent planning, ideas being banded around were just as quickly discredited. New ideas made their way forwards, shot down just as soon.

They couldn't agree on how they were going to achieve this. There were too many variables. They didn't know where Chester was, they didn't know if Adam would agree to help them again, or even if he'd just turn them in, maroon them in the street, call for Chester and watch them die.

They had to take the risk; it was the best shot they had.

Tomorrow.

Tomorrow they would enter the city under cover of dark, early in the hours of the morning. They would approach Adam; they would make their case and hope. Hope that things went their way, hope that they could make it through the day.

"We're gonna need more guns." Bob had been unusually quiet during the conversations. Tom turned to see the smile fixed across his face, it wasn't there.

"We've the six rifles we took, but that might not be enough. From what I hear, Chester's armed nearly 30 of them now, those odds, never gonna go our way."

Tom didn't want to do this. He never wanted to go back there, but he knew it might be their only option.

"I thought... When we were at the camp, I wondered if there might be an armoury there?" he looked hopefully at Bob. "I mean, they had the trucks, soldiers were clearly staying there, guards outside, they must have something, right?"

Bob shrugged. "Maybe, I guess they could have had something. But I doubt it'll be much – they locked people inside, waiting for them to die. Would you have put weapons somewhere they could have got their hands on them?"

He hadn't considered that. Bob was right, the

more he thought it through, that would have been a bad decision.

"There must be somewhere. There must be something," he said, more to himself.

"Cleared most of it out when they jumped town," Bob replied absently. "Maybe the barracks, but I'm near certain Chester would already have checked that. As far as I know, he didn't come out with any guns."

Tom sat silently in thought, they needed a way to turn the odds in their favour. It was a big ask, even if they could persuade Adam to help them.

Chester had much more manpower at his disposal. Tom had fired a gun only a handful of times now. He had no doubt Bob could handle one, Chloe too; although she seemed resistant, he still didn't know why. Kate acted hard and cold, but he'd seen the softer side to her, she wasn't comfortable killing.

How many would they have to kill? Tens, hundreds? Tom didn't want to think about it. For every death he'd secretly enjoyed, he wasn't ready for mass murder yet.

No, they needed to find a better solution. A shoot out was sure to end badly, too many dead, too many risks to the people he'd come to care about. If he wanted to keep them all safe, he'd have to do this alone.

The sun set, the evening drew in. One by one, they made their way to bed, to rest for the night, to run the events of the day over in their mind. Sleep surely would elude them all tonight. It was only Tom and Bob left in the darkened sitting room.

"Whiskey?" Bob asked, opening a glass-fronted cabinet. Inside was an assortment of half-empty bottles of brown and clear liquids. He removed two small glasses and poured whiskey from an old bottle; the label faded.

He handed one of the glasses to Tom." Enjoy that, likely the last bottle that'll ever be made, this." He studied the fading label. "Shame."

Tom used to enjoyed a whiskey in the evenings, but the whiskey he brought was whatever was on offer that day, nothing like this. He felt the liquid warming his insides, running through his veins, the sensation reached every inch of his body. It felt good, he felt revitalised.

He knew what he had to do.

"Bob, I'm going, tonight." His focus was hard, he looked directly in the big man's eyes. "There isn't another way, if we try to fight this lot, people will die. People in this house will die. I can't allow that. Chester wants me now, he's after my blood, not theirs."

Bob looked into the emptying glass. "You're right," he said finally. "But you can't go alone. I'll come too, the two of us have a much better chance of sneaking in quietly. Plus, I know the best ways in."

"No," Tom replied firmly. "You need to be here, Bob, you need to look after your home. You need to look after the others, too. They need you. They don't need me. I need to end this; I need to do it tonight."

"Okay then," Bob replied solemnly. Tom never felt the whiskey bottle break over his head, he didn't feel himself fall in a heap to the floor. The next thing he knew, the sun was high in the sky, light bathing his face, his head was splitting with pain.

"Urgh..." He groaned as he tried to sit upright.

He grabbed for his head and felt the bandage that had been wrapped around it. It was wet at the back. He saw blood glistening on his hands.

Bob. The bastard must have hit him. Through the pain throbbing in his head, he smiled to himself. So, they didn't want him to die. That was nice to know.

As he left the bedroom to join the others in the kitchen, he could hear a whispered conversation from the room below. Hush descended around the room as he entered.

Kate walked over to him and raised her hand to his face, lightly touching his cheek. Then she slapped him. The pain returned as it shot through his head, he stumbled backwards.

"How dare you!" she almost screamed. "How dare you?" Quieter the second time, she turned from him and returned to her seat around the long wooden table.

Carole approached him with a glass of water in hand. She opened the palm of her other hand, revealing three small white pills.

"For your head." She didn't seem to be much happier with him. He thought about his own stash of painkillers, he'd treasured them. His prized possessions. Burned away now, with the rest of the life he'd come to know and love.

He felt ashamed, the reaction of those he was starting to call family filled his heart with joy and pride. He felt he'd let them down. He was going to run off into the night, to play hero and probably never return. He hadn't even intended to say goodbye. He should be grateful to Bob.

Bob, where was Bob? He looked enquiringly at Carole, still stood in front of him.

"He's out," she snapped, picking up on his enquiring glance. She offered no more.

Chloe hadn't said anything, she sat at the table, her back to the wall, a large jumper pulled over her arms, covering her hands. He could feel her glare. They didn't talk much, she didn't talk much in general, but in this moment, he knew she hated him for what he'd nearly done. He knew she cared.

The hours dragged out sat in front of the kitchen window, watching the meadow in the distance. It was teeming with life. Tom had made his apologies and promised he would confine his solo plan to the past. He meant it, he hadn't realised how much everyone cared for him, he hadn't realised how much he was loved. He couldn't remember ever being loved, not like the love of his wife, he felt his heart twinge at the memory, that was different.

She had loved him in the traditional sense, but she hadn't needed him. These people needed him, they cared for him. They would stand at the edge of the world with him. That was good, if they weren't going to let him go into this war alone, they might just need to.

The pain in the back of his head had dulled, the pills had worked,

Bob finally returned as the sun started its daily descent behind the mountains in the distance.

"So?" Carole demanded before he'd fully entered through the door.

"Calm down woman," he replied, pushing her aside. "Let's get me boots off first!"

"What did they say?"

Bob turned to Tom. "Sorry about the head. Real shame. Waste of good whiskey..." He grinned. "They're in," he said, still watching Tom.

"In? They're going to do it?" Carole asked from behind him.

"Yep, in! They were quite up for it, really. Didn't take too much to convince them, all of them, I think. A dozen bodies on our side. Better than we looked this morning, the four of us and a sleeping Tom!"

"Did they know anything, anything that could help us?" Carole asked.

"Lots." Bob sat down, looking lovingly at the kettle perched on the side. Carole walked over to it.

"Perfect! So, Adam was thinking about skipping town anyway, things are getting heated. Chester's becoming more...unpredictable. Obsessed with Tom, he's built him up to some Roman warrior or something. Hasn't spoke about me in weeks." He genuinely looked slightly disappointed about this. "Been searching himself, all around the city. I'm worried he'll find us here soon."

It was happening already, Tom was putting them in danger without making a move.

"Have to do this soon. Gave me a thought though. If he's out lookin', maybe we go back to the ambush plan, could work. But we don't know where he's going, no one does, seems to be random. Think it's best we stick to the idea from this morning."

"What idea?" Tom interrupted.

Kate answered him. "We thought the best chance would be you getting caught." She shrugged.

Maybe they didn't need him after all?

Kate informed him of their plan. Tom was going to get caught at the outpost. Adam would find him and report back to Chester. Bob had joined in to describe the finer details.

Adam hated Chester, he always had. Chester was the only protection he could find. He had been charming at first, when Adam and the small group of survivors he'd been with came across one of the large fires, burning throughout the city. He'd given them food, shelter, and the promise of safety.

He was building a new society; he'd proudly announced. It had gone well for a few days. Chester had made sure they had a bed in a nearby hotel.

The sheets were clean, breakfast was provided every morning. It hadn't taken long before one of the group he'd arrived with went missing, no one seemed to know where he'd gone. Probably run off, Chester had assured him, after months living wild, couldn't take to civilised life again.

It was later that Adam had found out the man who disappeared, had in reality been murdered. He'd left his room late at night. Adam never knew why. A smoke, maybe just to stretch his legs, it didn't matter.

The men Chester had left on the hotel door, to guard them, they must have gotten bored, their bloodlust not fulfilled by playing babysitter. They had beaten him to death, it was never clear why. Adam had heard the same men bragging about it weeks later. He'd already been moved to the factory by this time. Slowly he'd learned of what Chester was capable of, although often by others hands.

He'd thought about leaving many times, but deep down he knew if he did, everyone at the factory would be punished. They likely wouldn't survive the day once his escape was known. He'd heard reports, stories, of other cities in the country, still ravaged by the virus. People were dropping dead in the streets. He was told there was nowhere safe left to go, this was it, all that would be left of humanity was right here, in this burning, hate-filled place.

Tom shuddered, he thought back to where his journey had started. The dingy flat, the dead littering the ground. He had seen the bodies wash up on the shoreline, freshly deceased.

It could be true, the virus could still be burning its way through the population. What if the world was still dying around them? Piece by piece turning dark, desolate, dead.

Adam communicated with Chester by a military issue radio, a fancy walkie-talky, Bob eloquently described. Adam would call him, tell him that Tom had passed alone on the road out front, heading for the city.

Chester would surely race to their location, and once there, well, they hadn't figured that far ahead yet.

"What about guns?" Tom asked. "Arming the others?"

"Aren't none," Bob replied. "There were, but sounds like Chester's just about got all of them. Since you showed up, he's been taking whatever he can find, mainly from the dead. Don't think he's got too many bullets though, the armoury was empty. Government took anything of use with them. We've got a couple of spares, the ones I got from the camp, but not enough to go around. Figure we get Adam and whoever he trusts with rifles, have them cover us from the windows."

"This seems flawed." Tom didn't like the idea of being bait. "And if more of them turn up than you planned? Or if he doesn't come at all? Then what?"

"Well... we'll cross that bridge when we come to it – better than you wandering into the lion's den alone."

The sun had set; another day passed them by with little action. Tom didn't like the plan, but he wanted to get it over with, whatever might happen. Like the day, he wanted it to pass.

CHAPTER TWENTY-TWO

They hadn't turned up. Chester was furious. He wanted the show-down, he wanted to face the man causing fear in his subordinates. He'd made the fire, ensured it would burn high and long into the night.

No one had turned up. Light flirted on the horizon.

Fine, he'd do it himself. He slammed the truck door as he sat inside, the engine roared to life, the tyres squealed as he set off down the road.

He didn't know where he was headed, but he felt lucky. He'd found the other two, he would find Tom too.

He'd make him watch whatever he did to Kate, he wanted him to suffer. He knew this obsession was haunting him, he didn't care. It had to end his way, it was the only way.

He left the city behind him. He'd had it searched, they weren't there. They had to be nearby, near enough that they could continue to strike at him. But where?

He'd been searching for that inbred farmer for months and he'd found nothing. He'd ripped the nearby villages apart, there was nothing left. Could they have a vehicle? Could they be further out than he'd thought?

Maybe they hadn't seen his fire, maybe they didn't know he was hunting them.

Where had he thought he'd seen something, a man entering a house? That village, where he found the girl. He'd put that to the back of his mind, that trip had been a good one. But he was sure he'd seen someone, a man, that's why he was in that house. Maybe he just had the wrong house, he'd only glimpsed movement, and it was from some distance away.

What if he was still there? What if there were more of them? He'd driven off alone, the rifle resting on the passenger seat his only companion. He didn't want anyone to see him being consumed by this. That would make him seem weak. He couldn't have that.

He wasn't weak; he took this God damn city by himself, a man in a house by the coast wasn't going to get the better of him. He didn't care if there was more of them, he'd kill them all. With purpose hard in his eyes, he sped off towards the idyllic village nestled next to the sea.

Chester had no real idea what he was looking for, he just knew he needed to do something. Heading back to the sleepy road where he thought he glimpsed a man, he parked his truck in the same place he had months earlier.

Nothing stirred, no curtains twitched, there was no sign of life. He left the truck running in the road, he liked the ignition to stay on, he could escape quickly if he needed to, or give chase faster.

He looked at the small cottage he'd entered that day. The red door still ajar from when he kicked it open, dragging the girl out by her hair. Nothing had entered that house since, the mildew stained the walls, the paper peeling from the damp. He noticed the house next door, similar in every way, that door stood ajar too. He hadn't been in there, he didn't remember it being open when he was last here, he would have gone inside if he had.

The house was unassuming, it had been ransacked, someone had searched it, not recently. He carefully pushed the open door aside, he peered his head into the empty rooms within. The bathroom was trashed, a mirror lay shattered on the floor. The bath was full of stagnant water, grey and murky.

The gloom nearly concealed it, he only noticed its dull material as he turned to leave. In the corner of the room, he saw a pile of filthy clothes, torn and stained, a satchel rested on top. He kicked the bag to the centre of the room, it slid across broken glass as it came to a rest in the small stream of sunlight floating in from the window. Opening it, he inspected the contents within.

There wasn't much, a mask, he threw that to one side, a box of matches. Nothing exciting. At the bottom of the bag, screwed up and nearly lost in the lining, he pulled a golden necklace. It didn't appear to be real gold, some fake gold-plated keepsake no doubt. A locket attached to the front, it was inscribed 'Dear Julia, I love you. xx'. He tossed it aside in rage.

This had been a dead end. He'd found nothing, the meagre possessions of a man he didn't care about in the corner of a ruined bathroom in a village that would soon be unrecognisable. He threw the bag across the room.

He had been sure he'd find Tom here, he'd find something to lead him to him, at the very least. He'd chased down a ghost and came away empty-handed. He kicked at the shards of broken mirror on the floor, they scattered like ash, reflecting gleams of light as they shot around the room. He stormed out of the dilapidated house and drove to the coast.

The beach nearby was beautiful, the sand backed onto trees, he sat in their shadow watching the waves. The crows cawed, the bodies on the beach were decomposed beyond recognition, they still pecked at the bone, ripping the remaining sinew free and loudly vocalising at their achievements.

Chester had now spent most of the day away from the city. He'd left the others at the hospital, he didn't like that place, so many went through the glass doors, so few left. He could feel his mind leaving him. The monster he'd become was winning now. He knew he was falling further into the abyss, he just showed it in different ways to most.

The despair grew deeper and then manifested as rage on his return to the city. He stood in front of the dead bodies of the few people he trusted. Shot in the back of the head, executed. This was professional.

The bodies of the others lay further up the street, these were shot in the back multiple times. He studied the wounds, more than one gun. More than one person.

Who was he facing, what was he facing? Had the army chosen to oust him, pull him from this throne of power, claim back their city, take what was his, what he'd worked so hard for? No, he must be rational. He knew it was Tom. It was too professional for the army. Bullet holes would have littered every surface if it was, these men wouldn't have stepped outside simply on orders. It had to be something else, trickery, a trap – his enemy was more dangerous than he'd realised.

He retrieved the walkie from the truck, someone had had to have seen them.

"Report," he hissed into the mouthpiece. "Everybody, what the fuck have you seen today?" He was greeted with static from the radio.

"REPORT!" he bellowed.

"Negative," the first reply, the broken voice shrouded by static.

"Nothing's been seen all day."

The second repeated the same message, the third, then the fourth. He didn't have enough lookouts; they had got into the heart of the city without being seen. They had circumvented every trap he'd laid out; they had foiled his every plan.

He screamed as loud as he could, his voice howled deep into the night sky. He thrashed his closed fists down onto the roof of the truck. Everything was falling apart, he needed to end this, he needed to win.

There wasn't many left in the city he truly trusted. Most of those he had were slaughtered by Tom and his mystery assassins.

He imagined them again, a well-versed unit, working together with surgical precision, the silenced pistols dropping his men before they knew they were there. He pictured automatic rifles slung around their back, the bulletproof vests resting atop bulging muscles.

But then what about Kate? The boy had told him she was with Tom, there was only the two of them, three, if you include the girl. She was soft though, not a problem. It couldn't have been those three. It just couldn't.

He rubbed his temples; this was getting the better of him. He was imagining things, who knew what was real and what was in his mind now. He felt reality slip further out of reach. He needed to focus. He needed to round up the others, those he trusted. Perhaps some of those he didn't, there wouldn't be much choice otherwise.

He'd been busy these past few months. His original group of junkie wasters had expanded, once he stopped them killing anything that moved, he'd grown his group exponentially.

People wanted to feel safe; he'd learnt how to make them feel just that. He requisitioned the hotels around town, he made sure all new faces had a clean bed for the first few nights. He made sure they felt comfortable. Soon, he would need to move them on. He needed hands, he needed people to work the fields, they would need to grow food, the rations they were ransacking from the city would run dry soon. He needed eyes to watch the roads, fingers to shoot the guns.

He had a growing collection of rifles now. He'd managed to pull over 20 from the dead soldiers outside of the city. They were all loaded, there was spare ammunition, the supplies they died with too, it wouldn't last forever.

He must try to get more next time he saw the grey-haired lady from the government. Assuming she isn't dead by now, a long time had passed since their last meeting. He would have to be careful with who he gave them to, he feared one of them pointing at his own back, he'd never know the shooter, only the pain of the bullet ripping through him.

He slapped his face. The paranoia was growing, gnawing at him, he needed to snap out of it. He sat in the black truck. Where now? He needed to regroup. He'd set up his base of operations in the financial district.

He had admired the sleek and modern style whist he ordered the two dead men to be cleaned off the road. The glass buildings didn't do much for cover, but he didn't need to hide any longer. The expensive décor and furnishing suited him; he liked the ambiance, the finer things in life, what was left of them.

He was done hiding in the dark, this was perfect. He'd moved a large part of his group into the surrounding buildings, but not directly into the lobby of the one he wanted. They would only infect it with their filth.

He walked through the lobby doors, head held high, fake smile on his face.

"Boys!" he shouted with a grin. "Miss me?"

"Boss, good to see you." One of the few left Chester could rely on.

"Jay, good to see you too." He leaned in closer to whisper into his ear. "There's a situation at the hospital, they're all dead, I want it cleaned up."

Jay winked. "Consider it done."

As he left, Chester watched him walk to two men stood in the street outside, the voices muted, they soon headed off towards the hospital. Jay returned to the lobby.

"Sorted. Any luck with those bastards?" he asked.

He shook his head. "Like a fucking ghost. You

get anything?"

"Nothing decent," Jay replied. "I went to the outposts, no one has seen a thing. I don't know if there's many left out there. There's nothing moving out there, Boss. Shame about Matty and the others by the hospital. Do we know what happened?"

Jay had been one of the first to join Chester, he didn't take drugs, that enticement hadn't worked. He liked the culture, though, the violence. Chester often wondered if Jay could be clinically classed as psychotic at times, but then again, in this world, who couldn't? More than once, he'd grappled with getting rid of him. He was concerned he was more trouble than he was worth, but he'd proved himself to be loyal. Loyalty was getting harder to find.

"No, I wasn't there. I came back, and they were all dead - executed."

"We thinking it's Tom?"

"I think it's likely."

"So, what now? How many has he killed? I can't even count."

"Ten, ten fine souls murdered by this man." He rubbed his temples again. Ten of his best, dead. At least, nine of his best and one peculiar chap who couldn't take a hint.

"Why don't you get some rest, Boss. Been a while since you've slept?"

"Yeah, I think you might be right, Jay. Wake me if you hear anything."

Jay nodded. Chester was glad he hadn't killed

him.

He followed the stairs to the room he'd prepared upstairs. He'd had one of the luxury beds from the nearby hotels brought in. The room used to be an office, large windows overlooked the streets below.

It felt like his head had barely touched the pillow before the knocking on the glass window woke him.

"Jay, what the fuck?"

He saw the sunlight from the window. "What is it?"

"You're going to want to take this Boss," he handed over the walkie. "It's Adam, from the factory."

"Chester?" Static interrupted the voice. "Chester, it's Adam. We've got him. We've got Tom."

CHAPTER TWENTY-THREE

They had risen before the sun, all of them sat around the kitchen table, waiting for the time to leave, waiting for their reckoning.

They were going to walk, the vehicles risked giving them away. It should take an hour or so from here to get to the textile factory to meet up with Adam.

Bob had the spare rifles wrapped around his neck. Even with his large frame, the sight was comical, the guns bounced off each other as he walked. He laughed when Tom offered to help carry them, he was quite happy, he didn't need the help. *Jolly as always*, Tom thought. How has he lasted this long?

They trekked out into the morning mist, the chill of the night quickly evaporating. Bob led the way; he'd made this journey many times. Tom followed behind. Kate and Chloe walked next to each other, both looking at the floor as they stumbled forwards. Chloe had begrudgingly accepted a rifle, she held it close to her chest. Carole followed up at the rear, she was unusually quiet this morning.

Bob even spoke less during the trip, although he still delighted in reminiscing about all the things he'd done at places they passed.

"There," he half-whispered, pointing to a bush on the path. "That's where I found a young woman and her baby, many months back now. She'd nothin', no food, barely enough clothes to keep her warm. Took her home, Carole kept her warm and fed, she was doing alright. Then one night, she just ups and leaves! Can you believe it, just walks out the door and never looked back. Poor girl, I reckon she's gone now, think she tried to walk to that bloody camp, her and the kid."

Tom shook his head, he still struggled to believe people flocked willingly to the camps. Any hope of salvation and people followed like a moth to flame.

The stories continued. Anything to pass the time, to calm the sinking feeling in his stomach that grew with every step closer Tom took. He glanced behind him, the three women walked in silence, each wearing an expression he couldn't read. He supposed it was fear, or maybe determination. It was hard to distinguish those these days, they so often went hand in hand.

The city loomed high above them; Tom took in its splendour for possibly the last time. The city that had given him Kate, he was grateful for that. It had also taken so much, Rose, Matt... It had made him a killer; it unleashed the bloodlust inside of him; it was about to do it one last time.

"We're here." Bob held up a giant hand. "Quiet now, just in case."

He edged forwards, peering around the corner, the factory loomed in front of them. The road was clear.

"Good," Bob said cheerily. "Fancied time for a cuppa before we get this movin'!"

Bob knocked on the steel loading dock door, it slowly lifted up, the sound of the metal chain rasping on the cog as it ascended.

"Adam," Bob greeted him. "We still good for this?"

"Yeah, Bob. We're good."

"He been?"

"Not personally, seen some of them though, heard him checking in on the walkie."

"Not found nothin' then?"

"That's right, he's real unhappy Bob. Worse than when he was after you."

"That's a shame, quite liked being the centre of attention."

Adam laughed. "Come on, let's get you lot inside."

The interior of the factory was in stark contrast to the one they had made their home, before Chester destroyed it. The main floor was full of tables, industrial sewing machines located on each one.

Vats stood unused at the far end; scaffolding towers had been erected to the high windows, guards stood lookout on each one.

Tom could imagine the factory floor bustling with life, workers going about their day, before jobs were a thing of the past. Most of the workers were probably long dead by now. The virus had spread through the poor areas of town with wild speed. Entire neighbourhoods were wiped out overnight, those spared succumbed shortly after, to the infection or hunger, or at the hands of others.

Tom realised the truth. Chester hadn't brought brutality here, he simply nurtured it.

Bob was in discussion with Adam out of earshot, Tom assumed they were discussing the best distribution of guns. Adam trusted everyone he lived with here, but Tom wondered how difficult it would have been for Chester to insert one of his trusted into the fold. He eyed those around him suspiciously.

They appeared a normal group, just regular people, going about their regular jobs. They were clean, that struck Tom first. Their clothes were not stained and ripped, like so many he'd seen. A man and a woman talked in the corner near them, they were an unassuming couple, the kind he might have walked past in the street without looking twice.

There was none of the macho jousting, the whooping, laughter, sexism he'd seen with the others. The people here spoke in hushed voices.

They were mostly middle-aged, a few younger. The ones not fit to fight, judged unworthy to continue the carnage further in the city. Tom wondered if the other outposts were staffed the same, would they also be just scared people looking for somewhere to call home, someone to call a friend?

He doubted anyone in this factory would have killed before, would they even have fired a rifle before? Or like Tom, would they be cast into the unfamiliar roles which would define their new lives?

Tom was nervous about fighting alongside these people. He didn't know them, Bob had told him they hated Chester, but would they do what needed to be done? Chester had housed them, given them purpose, offered them safety. Tom was offering an end to that. Tom offered only insecurity, a future into the unknown, why would they follow that? He couldn't help but doubt the plan, like he'd doubted every one they had come up with so far.

It was too late now, they had to continue, this was the only way to end it.

Adam was procrastinating, Tom sensed he was nervous. He wanted to show them what he'd built here. Adam and the others had been placed here by Chester several months before.

It was lifeless and empty then. He'd tried to make it as bearable as possible. There was no heating in the building. The vats at the end of the hall extended up to the large chimneys poking from the roof. They had learned to use these to provide warmth, the wood burning inside. It was okay if you slept by them, Adam had informed him. There was an open grass area out the side door, the dirt had been freshly dug, they had planted vegetables, hoping to harvest the small offering later in the year. The water was supplied from rainwater, large barrels collected below the guttering, storing the precious liquid until it was needed.

Like the factory Tom had stayed in, this one had staff facilities, a shower room, kitchen and canteen. It also had a large break room, the plush purple carpet now dusty, depressed from the thousands of boots that had walked over it. There were sofas pushed against the wall, pictures hung up of distant lighthouses, mountains in pastel, the sunset painted in oil.

He could see why they would stay here, other than because they were told to. They were making a home here, but it would never be free, they would forever be under the boot of Chester.

"You decided?" Bob asked as he turned to Adam. "Who's with us?"

"Yeah, Bob, I got them," Adam's tones dropped, he was trying to put this off. "We got three guys here who know how to shoot a rifle, that's it. The rest are likely to do more damage than good."

"We sure about them?"

"These folks, yeah, I'm sure."

"What about the others?"

"We won't do it here. I'll call Chester from

further up the road, tell him I followed Tom, caught him out in the open. If it goes wrong... well, then these guys are going to have a problem, hopefully they'll have enough time to get out. Maybe they can argue they never knew, I don't know. Let's just make sure it doesn't go wrong."

"You can still back out, Adam," Bob said softly. "Won't no one think bad of you if you do."

"No. You're right, we need to do this. We got a good thing going on here, but it could be ripped from us at any moment. On the whim of a madman, we could be dead."

Bob nodded. "Good man." He handed over four of the rifles from his shoulder.

"Not me, big man. Can't have Chester show up with a rifle on my back, he'd shoot me dead before he asked where it came from."

"Smart, knew there was a reason I liked you."

"You ready?"

"Yeah"

"Let's do this." He turned to face Tom. "And you, all good?"

"Yes," Tom replied confidently, he didn't feel it.

Adam raised the walkie from his side, let out a deep breath and pressed the button on the side.

"Chester?" he called into the static. "Chester, it's Adam. We've got him. We've got Tom."

The voice on the other end of the walkie caused chills down Tom's spine, a voice of pure venom, the delight of Tom being within his grasp clear to hear through the static. This was the voice of his nemesis, the nemesis he'd never asked for.

"You've got him, are you sure?"

"Yeah, I'm sure, found him walking the road, heading into town – we followed him for a short while, made sure he was alone, stopped him on the crossroads, we've got him here now."

"Keep him, I'll be there soon."

Adam turned the radio off, and looked to the others. "Let's go."

They solemnly walked the road to the junction further up; the light breeze stroked his face. Adam walked step in step, the machete pointed at Tom's back in pantomime fashion. He could see the sweat beading on his brow. This could be it, Tom could be walking to his end, the funeral march of birdsong ringing in his ears.

The day felt peaceful, calmer. The warming air soothed his skin. He took one last glance behind him, Kate stood further down the road. The sunlight formed a glow around her, she looked heavenly.

Tom smiled, he'd like to keep the image, in case it ended up being one of his last.

He knew what Chester was likely to do to him, he had to hope they could stop him. The cold metal of the handgun pressed into his back, tucked into his belt, his potential salvation. The others had taken positions around the crossroads, hid from view by whatever cover they could find. Adam and another man, Tom hadn't asked his name, flanked him as they walked him into position. They needed it to look realistic, Tom needed to look like a prisoner.

The others Adam had brought from the factory tagged behind, walking nervously, the rifles swinging uncomfortably in their hands.

"You good?" Adam whispered into his ear again.

"Yeah." He heard his voice breaking, the fear threatened to overtake him.

They stood in the centre of the crossroads, displayed like a trophy. A rose blossoming in the garden of weeds.

Tom stood and listened, he heard only the rapid beating of his heart. He couldn't see the others; he was grateful for that. *Please, god, let them be safe*, he thought. The birdsong was deafening, they were mocking him, taunting him in his last moments.

Then they were silent. In the din, the sound slowly becoming louder, the sound of a black truck, the modern-day reaper bearing down on him.

The roar reverberated off the abandoned buildings, growing ever closer. He saw in the distance the gleam of the chrome from the front of the truck, its features becoming clear as it drove ever closer, Tom was nearing his reckoning.

The truck rolled to a halt up the road, the engine idled. The driver's door opened, a boot hit the floor, a leg clad in tight blue jeans, followed by the body of a man. A man who Tom knew was dangerous, he could see why.

**

Chester stood next to the truck, rifle resting on his shoulder. Sunglasses obscuring his face, a cigarette burned between his lips. He finally had him. He studied the man stood before him, Tom. This was the man he'd been after, the man he'd obsessed over. The man threatening to tear down his empire by the roots. He slammed his fist onto the roof of the truck, the others sat inside exited, standing by his side. Two more climbed from the flat back of the truck. He'd brought six others with him; this was all he trusted now.

He walked with purpose, striding down the road with confidence. People were watching, they expected him to take care of the situation, and that's precisely what he would do.

He reached Tom, the man was shorter than him, he wasn't well built, his blond hair and sparkling blue eyes gave him a saint-like appearance, but there was nothing special about him. He looked just liked a usual guy. He briefly imagined him sat at a desk, typing away into a computer screen. Nothing was threatening about this man, but he had a hardness behind his eyes. He never dropped his gaze as his bright blue eyes bored into Chester's soul.

"I thought you'd be taller." A smirk spread across his face. He pulled a small lock knife from his belt and held it close to Tom's face, the blade shining in the sun, he wanted this to be slow, painful.

"Where are the others?" Chester asked, a frown appearing on his face. He'd been so excited at the prospect of finally having Tom in his grasp, the rest hadn't occurred to him. What if this was a trap? He eyed the two men either side of Tom, if it was a trap, were they in on it? Were his men starting to turn against him?

He forced the grin to return to his face.

"Nothing to say?" he teased.

"Get fucked," Tom spat; his gaze held firm.

With a flash of light, a red streak appeared on Tom's cheek where the blade bit into his skin. Tom winced at the pain, he felt the warm blood trickle down his face.

"Where was he?" the question directed to Adam, who stuttered slightly at being directly addressed.

"Erm... the scouts saw him, walking up the road out front. He was alone, no weapons – heading to the city."

"Just walking alone..." Something felt wrong, he scanned the street around him once more. "You searched around, made sure there aren't any more of them?"

"We've had people watching all morning, there was no one else out there." Adams voice cracked as he spoke.

Chester directed his gaze back to Tom, the blue eyes still bored into him.

"Where were you going?" he demanded.

"To you," the man stood in front of him replied simply.

"Why?"

"To kill you." Had he shrugged as he said that? How was he so calm, he must know what he could do, what he would do to him?

Chester felt the blade of his knife as it cut through tissue and flesh, he felt the resistance from the muscle as it pierced the heart. The man to the left of Tom fell in a heap to the ground. Tom had never asked his name.

It happened in an instant, Tom saw the man fall, confusion on his face. Adam had released Tom's arm and was running towards cover at the side of the road, blood glistened on Chester's blade. Without thinking, Tom grabbed for the gun tucked into his belt. He wasn't quick enough, Chester lunged towards him, blade aimed at his chest.

**

Tom tried to jump sideways out of the reach of the blade. With his hand still grappling for the gun, he lost his balance and fell onto the concrete below.

He rolled sideways, further out of reach of the knife in Chesters hand. He saw the others who had arrived in the black truck readying their rifles, they were still too far away to be an immediate threat.

Kate had revealed herself from the hiding place the other end of the crossroads, she had her rifle raised. Tom heard the crack of a shot and saw one of the men fall to his knees, she'd hit her target.

The sound of shots filled the air. He no longer

knew where they were coming from, he felt concrete shards bounce off his face as a bullet hit the ground near his head.

Everything was a blur as he tried to take stock of the situation. Bodies ran in front of his eyes, some fell, he couldn't tell who. Screams and shouts filled the air, the gunfire relentless.

Tom pulled himself to his knees, the world around him becoming clearer. He saw the figure of Chester staggering towards him. His arm swung loosely, as if he had no control of it. He'd been shot. One of them must have aimed for him when he swung the knife. The bullet had gone through the top of his arm, blood seeped down the sleeve of his leather jacket.

Tom reached for the gun, still tucked into his belt. It came free as Chester stood over him, he swung his arm up, trying to aim for a clear shot – Chester's boot slammed into his face, he heard the gun slide across the floor as it flew from his hand. The pain erupted in his nose, the blood blinding him. Through the chaos, he was sure he heard Chester laugh.

Chester dropped to his knees, his arm pressed tightly on Tom's throat, he could feel the warmth from his breath as he spoke.

"Nothing can save you now. This is it; this is where you die."

His eyes danced with lunacy, he knew in this moment Chester wasn't losing it, he was already gone.

"You killed my men," he screamed in Tom's face. "You stole from me!"

Tom felt the first punch land on his damaged nose, it exploded with pain once more.

Chester had released his throat, he held him by the front of the shirt now, pulling back his arm, he punched into the side of Tom's head with every word he spoke.

"I.. win..." The blows were raining into Tom's face. He tried to lift his arm to protect himself, they were firmly stuck under Chester's legs, there was nothing he could do now. He felt his head growing heavy, the repeated blows making him weaker with every hit.

He could faintly hear the sound of gunshots still reverberating in the air around him. They sounded distant, dull, they could have been coming out of the speakers from a television, not feet from his head. He knew this was it, he prepared himself that now he would die. He hoped Kate, Bob, Carole and Chloe were okay, he hoped they were still standing. Maybe he could keep the attention of Chester for long enough for them to escape, or perhaps they'd shoot him from where they stood, drop his lifeless body to rest next to Tom's.

The blows had stopped, he felt the pressure on him ease, his arms were no longer restricted. Blinking the blood out of his eyes, the fog lifted from his beaten mind.

He tried to push himself up on his elbows, his body ached with pain. Through bruised eyes, he saw Chester in front of him, struggling with something on his back. It was Chloe, she was straddling him, screaming, her fingernails scratching down his face.

With a grimace, he dragged himself forwards. The knife that had cut into his cheek lay on the floor, dropped in the melee. He crawled towards it, every inch of movement agony. His arm outstretched, he grabbed for the handle, his fingertips brushed it and pushed it further away.

Chester was still struggling with Chloe; he hadn't noticed Tom moving.

With a final burst of energy, he fought through the throbbing pain and lunged forwards, his hand clasping around the handle of the knife, gripping tightly.

Chester was just feet from him now, he'd managed to wrap his hand around Chloe's dangling leg as she hung to his back. Tom watched as he pulled her free and tossed her into the road like a rag doll.

This was his chance, he lurched forwards and drove the blade of the knife deep into Chester's calf. The larger man howled in pain as he dropped to one knee, he'd been preoccupied, he hadn't cast a glance in Tom's direction.

They now stood on level ground, both men on their knees in the dirt. Tom looked into Chester's eyes, the fire and hatred clear through the pain.

The street behind him was calming, the gunfire slowed. Tom could make out the huge figure of Bob, the handle of his rifle connecting with a man's skull, the man fell to the floor.

That was it he realised. They had won. Chester lunged at him, his fingers grasping around his throat. Tom felt himself fall backwards, the familiar pressure of Chester's weight pinning him back to the ground.

He struggled for breath, his vision started to fade, the world was fading. The last thing Tom heard was the sound of a solitary shot, a crack penetrating the air, echoing off the buildings.

His world went black.

Tom's eyes flickered slowly open, the sun beating down on him. He heard the birdsong in the distance, the buzzing of insects around his head. He tried to swat them away, his arms wouldn't respond. He felt sluggish, his head was swimming. It took a moment to come back to him. He tried to sit up, the dizziness forced him back to his lying position, eyes screwed shut with the effort.

Slowly sound returned, as if someone had suddenly turned the volume up, his focus sharpened.

He heard his name, being shouted by a woman from somewhere nearby. She sounded upset, there was urgency in the voice.

Kate.

His eyes shot open; the blue sky floated in front

of him. He slowly brought his gaze down to the ground. Blood stained the grey concrete; he saw lifeless bodies around him, he strained to see whose, he prayed no one who had accompanied him lay amongst the dead.

"TOM!"

The scream pulled him back to reality. Kate knelt above him, her hands grasped around his battered face. His eyes blinked as he focused, her beautiful face floated above him. She had a deep cut running down her eyebrow, the top of her shirt was ripped, but she seemed okay, he was grateful for that.

"Tom," she said softer, a smile spread over her face. "I thought you were gone." Tears filled her eyes.

Painfully, Tom forced himself to sit up, he looked around, five people stood in a circle around him, all five he left the farmhouse with that morning. The pain melted away, the elation taking hold of him. Chester's body lay slumped in front of him, a bullet wound clear on the back of his head. Chloe had killed him, with one expert shot to the back of the head.

He'd later learn that Chester stood no chance, the others had ambushed them with such surprise, most of them were dead before Tom had a chance to move. There had been a shoot-out from the two hid behind the black truck. Bob had flanked around and ended that, the stock of the rifle had broken their skulls. They had seen Chester strangling Tom, and with no time to act, Chloe had aimed from the ground where she'd been thrown and fired the shot that ended him, that ended the nightmare he'd made the city.

Adam had run. Bob had been wrong about him, as soon as it went wrong, he'd fled, no one knew where to.

"Come on," Kate said kindly. "Let's get out of here."

She helped him to the passenger side of the black truck, he climbed inside and let the soft seats envelop him. He closed his eyes and listened to the world passing him by. The door closed, the engine burst to life, he heard the tyres softly rolling on the road.

He smiled to himself as the breeze from the window blew gently onto his face, whatever came next, they would be ready, together.

The End

ACKNOWLEDGEMENT

Pete. love you. my dude. Rest well.

Printed in Great Britain
by Amazon